Seeking
Paradise

Dear Eve!

Here's my 'Eve'

story. Enjoy!

Love, Deborah

Novels by Deborah Galiley

Polished Arrows

Seeking Paradise

Yohana

Seeking
Paradise

Deborah Galiley

OAKTARA

WATERFORD, VIRGINIA

Seeking Paradise

Published in the U.S. by:
OakTara Publishers
P.O. Box 8
Waterford, VA 20197

Visit OakTara at
www.oaktara.com

Cover design by David LaPlaca/debest design co.
Cover art (*Oleander Tree by Sea of Galilee*) and interior illustrations ©
2009, Gail Ingis Claus, ASID, www.gailingisclaus.com

Author photo © 2009 by Gail Ingis Claus, ASID

Scripture verses are taken from:
The HOLY BIBLE, NEW INTERNATIONAL VERSION®. NIV®.
Copyright © 1973, 1978, 1984 by International Bible Society. Used by
permission of Zondervan. All rights reserved.
The JEWISH NEW TESTAMENT, © 1979, 1989, 1990, 1991 by David
H. Stern, Jewish New Testament Publications. All rights reserved.

ISBN: 978-1-60290-169-8

Seeking Paradise is a work of fiction. References to real people, events,
establishments, organizations, or locales are intended only to provide a
sense of authenticity and are used fictitiously. All other characters,
incidents, and dialogue are drawn from the author's imagination.

This book is dedicated to
the memory of my grandmother
(1899-1985)

RENCIA SPINDELL TEITELBAUM

A woman of noble character who can find?
She is worth far more than rubies.
Proverbs 31:10

PART ONE

Paradise

One

The woman opened her eyes. She was lying on the ground on a bed of soft moss, her head resting on a pillow made from crushed flowers. Enormous stately trees formed a green canopy over her, their interlocking branches swaying gently back and forth in the undulating breeze. Brightly colored birds flitted about, calling shrilly to one another. The gurgle of rushing water came faintly from the distance. Muted sunlight drifted lazily through the foliage, enhancing everything with its golden glow.

At first it all appeared as one riotous blend of color and noise, but soon items differentiated themselves. *That's a tree*, she instinctively knew. *That's a bird.* Slowly she lifted her left arm and brought her hand before her eyes. She noted the taut flesh, the well-formed forearm, the long and supple fingers. She gazed at her fingers for several minutes, bending them back and forth, back and forth.

When she tired of this, she pulled herself up into a sitting position. Something long and shimmery from behind her head uncoiled itself and floated down her back. Startled, the woman grabbed a piece of it, only to realize that her head hurt as she yanked. *Oh,* she thought, intrigued. *This is part of me. It's my...hair.* Fascinated, she rubbed a silky lock between her fingers and examined it. Strands of glittery gold, sparkling silver, burnished bronze, fiery red, glossy ebony, deep-hued and brilliant, melted into one glorious tapestry of dazzling, fluid color. The woman took all of her hair—it was long and heavy—and ran her fingers through it, marveling at the way the color constantly changed as the light touched it.

Next she stood, her lustrous hair swinging down and coming to a halt just above her backside. She tottered on her feet for a few moments, looking with interest at her long, slender legs, before attempting to walk. When she did take her first step, it was with a

1

dizzying lurch, a half-stumble from which she gracefully regained her balance. The second step was easier, and by the third step she was walking with the natural ease of one who had long done this without having to think first.

For several hours, the woman wandered through the forest glade. Everything fascinated her. She stopped repeatedly to touch and smell things. The rough bark of a tree, the velvety petal of a flower, the smooth hardness of a stone: all these things enchanted her. Upon hearing a rushing sound, she headed in that direction, slipping through a tangle of trees into a clearing. A murmuring river, running and swirling over rocks and sand beds, met her curious gaze.

Kneeling down at the bank, she cupped some of the water, letting it run through her fingers and onto her legs. The sensation pleased her. Next she brought the cupped water up to her mouth and tentatively stuck her tongue in it. *Ahh.* The dry sensation in her mouth eased. Again she cupped some of the sparkling water and, with her tongue, lapped some into her mouth, instinctively swallowing it. The delicious feeling of the water trickling down her throat, quenching the thirst she did not even realize she had, pleased her. She laughed.

It was the first time the woman had heard her own voice. She laughed again, tilting her head to the side and listening closely. The tinkling, cheery sound floated back to her ears, echoing across the surface of the river. A small animal, attracted by the sound, bounded out of the denseness of the forest and ran to her, rubbing itself against her legs. The woman reached down and stroked its furry back. It chattered loudly at her. It was a tiny thing, black in color, with a long white stripe that started between its black, beady eyes and went down its back, ending abruptly on its long, bushy tail. Quite quickly it tired of the woman and scampered back from whence it came.

The woman continued on her walk. Now that her thirst was satisfied, she began to be conscious of a gnawing, hollow feeling in her belly. She found her gaze drawn to the fruit that hung heavy on the trees all around. There were all different types of fruit, but it was the red globes that most intrigued her. She pulled one off its branch and held it in her hands, contemplating it. Then she took a bite.

Ugh! The tough outer skin was not meant for eating. The woman made a face and spit her mouthful out on the forest floor. It was then that she heard it:

Laughter. Deep, resonant laughter. She jerked her head up and peered between the trees, trying to discover where the sound came from. In the distance, a flash of gold caught her eye.

"Who's there?" she called out boldly, knowing no part of fear.

The gold flashed again, closer, and the sound of footsteps caused the woman to tilt her head to the side as she listened.

When the figure who belonged to the footsteps came into view, the woman eagerly ran forward. "Abba!" she proclaimed reverently, the familiar word for *father* rolling off the tip of her tongue.

"My beloved daughter," he replied, gazing at her with great delight. He looked like the woman in that he had two arms and two legs, a head and a torso. Unlike her, however, his body seemed made of a fiery gold. Snow-white hair framed his face and a beard of the same color rested against his chest. Peace and security emanated from him, and the air about him thickened with glory.

Taking hold of the woman's hands, he gently drew her to him. It was obvious he was very pleased with her. Joy flowed from him in abundant waves. Pleasure radiated out at every breath. The air around him pulsated with the joy of his presence.

"Who am I?" asked the woman. "What is this place to which I have awakened?"

"Ah," he said, his voice so resonant and rich that the very earth rumbled at the sound. "You are the helper I have made for the man."

"The man?" questioned the woman. Her eyes, rich brown with flecks of gold, green, gray, and blue, widened. "Who is 'the man'?"

"Come and see." Holding the woman's hand, he led her away from the pomegranate tree and further into the forest. Soon enough, they came to a raised wooden platform heaped with the same sort of moss on which the woman had so recently found herself. A man lay sleeping there. His hair, cut short around his face, was black as ebony. High cheekbones, bearded chin, long straight nose, and sculpted lips made a very pleasing picture. Though he was motionless, a sense of barely contained power still managed to spark from his brown, muscular frame. A thin, red line running from his left breastbone almost to his waist was the only thing that marred his handsomeness.

"What is that?" asked the woman, pointing to the red line.

"That is the place from where I took the rib when I fashioned you."

"I came from the man's rib?" Wonderment caused the woman to blink. Tenderly, she placed her forefinger on the red line and traced its passage. Her touch, light as it was, succeeded in awakening the man.

He opened his eyes and saw both the Lord and the woman. Pure astonishment passed over his features before he rose from his bed and knelt before the Lord.

"My Lord God Adonai," he exclaimed. "Is this the helper you promised me?"

"Yes, my son," answered Adonai, affectionately placing his hand on the man's shoulder. "This is the woman that I made from your rib while you were sleeping."

The man stood and looked at the woman, who looked back at him. He was probably a good six inches taller than she. He extended his hand and touched the side of her face. It was smooth, and soft, not hairy like his own. Her hair entranced him, and he stroked one of the long, bright locks. When he gazed at her full round breasts, her firm, supple navel, and down at her long, shapely legs, the man felt a stirring of desire within himself that shocked him by its ferocity.

She, in turn, was thrilled with the man. Everything about him pleased her. His broad shoulders, muscular chest, narrow waist, powerful legs. She reached up and touched his curly black hair. When she looked into his brown eyes, so like her own, yet shaped differently, she laughed with delight. The man laughed as well.

"You are pleased, my son?" asked Adonai, smiling contentedly, much as an artist would who had just put the finishing stroke on a particularly brilliant work.

"Very, very pleased, my Lord," answered the man, beaming.

"Come, children, I will give you my blessing." Both the man and the woman knelt in front of him, and he placed his right hand on the head of the man and his left hand on the head of the woman. His melodious voice, pleasing to the ear yet somehow so pronounced as to be heard throughout the earth, nay, throughout the centuries, flowed

4

through and among them. "Be fruitful and increase in number," he admonished them. "Fill the earth and subdue it. Rule over the fish of the sea and the birds of the air and over every living creature that moves on the ground." He bid them rise, and they stood, wonder further lighting up their already glowing faces.

"This is The Garden I have given you for your home," continued Adonai, as he gestured with sweeping arm toward the forest and river and plains and far-off mountains. "You can see that all around you are trees that are pleasing to the eye and good for food. I give you every seed-bearing plant on the face of the whole earth and every tree that has fruit with seed in it. They will be yours for food. And to all the beasts of the earth and all the birds of the air and all the creatures that move on the ground—everything that has the breath of life in it—I give every green plant for food."

The Lord God turned to the man. "Adam," he said, "you're to take the woman and show her the length and breadth of The Garden. Show her the different types of fruit and vegetables and the manner in which they are eaten. Let her know that it's the seeds of the pomegranate that are edible, but that she can bite directly into the peel of an apple.

"Point out the animals, and the birds, and the things that crawl on the ground. Go over the names and share with her all that you've learned. She is your partner—your helper—and she must know all that you know.

"But don't forget to caution her not to eat from the tree in the middle of The Garden—the tree of the knowledge of good and evil. Don't forget to warn her that if you eat of it, you will surely die."

Adam nodded gravely. "Yes, my Lord. I will do all that you command."

The woman spoke up. "The man is called Adam? Not 'the man'?"

"Yes." The Lord God smiled. "The man is called Adam."

"What of me?" pursued the woman. "What shall I be called?"

The Lord God turned to the man. "I have already brought you all the livestock, the beasts of the field, and the birds of the air, and you have named them. What do you think? What should the woman's name be?"

Adam thought about the blessing the Lord God had just uttered in which he commanded them to be fruitful and increase on the earth. Then he looked again upon the woman whom he had been given as his helper. "Eve," he said decisively, "because she will become mother to all the living."

"Eve it is," agreed the Lord God, pleased by the man's choice.

After the Lord God took his leave, Adam and Eve strolled through The Garden. Proudly, the man pointed out the stunning vistas of mountains in the distance with their many-hued shades of purples and blues fading against the backdrop of the sky. Vast stretches of green with trees of every size and variety heralded the way. Birds flew from tree to tree and Adam would cry, "Look! there's a red-winged blackbird, or, Look! That's a parrot!" Likewise, when a herd of zebra thundered past, or a soft-eyed doe approached to nuzzle Eve's hand, he would tell her their names. The grass beneath their feet was blanketed with flowers of every color and description while the soft, warm air caressed their naked bodies. Hand in hand, they walked for miles alongside the river, its cool, clear murmuring rising and falling.

"I will show you the hot springs where I bathe," Adam told her.

"Bathe?" asked the woman quizzically. "What's that?"

"When you get dirty, or sweaty, and want to get clean," explained the man. "Or sometimes, just to relax, it's nice to soak in hot water."

"Oh," said Eve. This was a lot of new information to process. She had yet to be alive for a full day and already she had learned so much.

"My stomach is making noise," she told Adam.

"That means you're hungry." He laughed. "Here's an orange tree. We'll have some of these." As he was talking, he reached up and pulled two golden ovals off the dark green tree. With his fingernail, he pierced the soft rind and ripped it off in segments, dropping it to the ground. When the fruit was peeled, he split it in half and took a bite, gesturing to the woman to do the same. She did, and her eyes lit up.

"This is marvelous," she said, as the sweet, tangy juice awakened her taste buds. Companionably, they sat against the trunk of the tree and ate their fruit. When Adam finished, he wiped his mouth with a leaf and dropped it on the ground beside him. The woman copied him.

"I like to eat oranges with almonds," Adam told her. "It's a short walk to the almond tree." He got up, holding out his hand, and helped the woman up. She didn't need any help but touching her soft hand filled him with delight.

Together, they wandered over to the almond tree. Adam plucked several hard objects off the thin, dark branches. Taking a stone that had been left propped against the base of the tree, he smashed the objects, Then he peeled away the shell and pulled out a teardrop-shaped brown nut.

"Try it," he told Eve.

She popped one in her mouth and chewed. *Mmm*, the flavor was delicious. "These are wonderful," she said, mouth full.

Adam watched, transfixed, as she chewed. Her curvy lips, the tip of her pink tongue, her dazzling white teeth, all entranced him. He felt that stirring of desire again, and he put his forefinger under her chin and leaned close. Eve stopped chewing and studied him intently. Instinctively, Adam pressed his lips to hers, kissing her. "You are so beautiful," he murmured, gathering her in his arms while sinking down to the soft earth with her. "So incredibly beautiful." His kisses grew more and more passionate.

Eve yielded to his embrace, and they explored each other's bodies, heady with passion. "I am so happy with the man the Lord has given me," said Eve, cheeks flushed, eyes bright.

"And I," said Adam. "Never did I imagine that the helper the Lord gave me would be so incredible." They stopped talking, intent on this new discovery of pleasure and fulfillment as they consummated their relationship.

Later, much later, Eve lay nestled in Adam's arms under a velvety black sky. The light from the full moon and countless numbers of stars cast a shadowy sheen. Adam could just see Eve's features and sighed with contentment. He had not realized to what extent he had longed for a mate until this day. But the Lord God knew. *Ah, what an awesome*

God he is, thought Adam gratefully. Throwing back his head, tightening his grip on the woman, he blessed the name of the Lord, thanking him for the gift of the woman, proclaiming over her, "This is now bone of my bones and flesh of my flesh; she shall be called 'woman,' for she was taken out of man."

Two

The days passed in rapid succession: days of paradise and wonder. Quickly, very quickly, Eve grew to know her way around The Garden.

"This place is called Eden," Adam told her. "The river starts here and waters the land before separating into four headwaters south of The Barden."

"South of The Garden?" Eve asked, puzzled. "What lies outside The Garden?"

"The whole earth," Adam patiently explained. "The Lord God has created a vast globe with many deep waters and huge areas of dry land. It is a wild and rugged place, spectacular in beauty and daunting in its restlessness. It would take us years, were we to attempt to walk around it."

"Really?" asked the woman, intrigued. "In what ways is it different from Eden?"

"I'm not really sure," admitted the man. "I know from what Adonai has said that there is nowhere as wonderful as right here. I know we can spend all eternity here and not lack for anything."

"But Adonai implored us to be fruitful and fill the earth," said the woman. "Will our children live in Eden, or will they go off and inhabit other places?"

"Well," said Adam, "since we're to fill the earth, then I suppose our children will eventually leave and find other places to settle."

"Our children," sighed the woman, caressing her belly absently. "When do you suppose that will start to happen?"

"Anytime, I expect," answered her husband as he reached for her in love.

The man and the woman found that their days had a certain rhythm. Adonai put them in The Garden to work it and take care of it:

though the fruit grew free for the picking, it did not pick itself. Eve learned to weave baskets together from the rushes that grew on the river's edge, and she and Adam filled them day after day. They picked grapes from the spreading vines and set them out on mats in the sun so they shriveled into raisins; likewise, they dried figs, banana slices (cut with a sharp stone), apricots, and pineapple. Almonds, pistachios, walnuts, cashews, hazelnuts, and pecans were poured into baskets and kept in their shells until they were needed.

Adam kept the tree branches cut back so the trees would yield more fruit. He also directed the animals, leading the livestock to the grassy places on a rotation basis so they could eat but not overgraze.

The animals particularly fascinated Eve. She insisted on being introduced to each and every one she encountered and came up with names for them beyond the generic species name Adam had already designated. They loved her too; it was unusual to see Eve and not also see a menagerie of birds, dogs, horses, deer, badgers, squirrels, sheep, or a thousand potential others.

Adam had discovered after naming the animals that he could communicate with them. He needed to concentrate, then was able to discern what their particular mooing, baaing, barking, meowing, neighing, chirping, and tweeting meant. They could understand him as well, as long as he kept things simple. Of course, as the complexity of the animal increased, so did its ability to understand. Horses were fit companions, whereas squirrels only wanted to chatter about their next meal, scampering off, bored, should more be said.

Before the Lord God created Eve, Adam had taken to riding one horse in particular. It was a big, chestnut brown stallion that fairly danced with energy. The horse (called *horse*, by Adam), pawed the ground, snorting furiously, while Adam effortlessly rode him by wrapping his legs against its sides. Together they would gallop throughout the whole of The Garden of Eden, checking on all the plants of the field and the living things that dwelled there. It took a full week to make a complete circle, so vast was the land allotted by Adonai for The Garden.

"You can't just call him *horse*," said Eve one day as she stroked the horse's head with one hand and fed him a big, red apple with the other.

"Why not?"

"Because it's dull. It's like calling you *man* or calling me *woman*."

"What's wrong with calling you *woman?*" protested Adam lazily. He was lying on his back in the sun with his fingers interlocked under his neck and studying Eve through half-opened lids. *What a gorgeous woman!* he thought, for possibly the thousandth time, as he watched the light reflect the golds, reds, and coppers in her hair.

"My name is Eve, and you're the one who named me," she reminded him, giving the horse a final pat on the head and then turning to face Adam, hands on her hips. "You didn't name me *woman*. What do you want to call this *horse?*"

Just then the horse gave a shrill neigh, shaking his mane and baring his teeth. Both Adam and Eve cocked their heads and listened intently.

"I believe he's saying...Rahm," said Adam, raising himself up on one elbow.

"I think so too," agreed Eve. "Is that true, Rahm? Is that your name?"

"*Neighhh!*" whinnied the horse, stamping his hoof affirmatively.

Soon enough Eve found a horse suited to her temperament: a magnificent, snowy-white mare named Yafah, who could be alternately gentle or tempestuous. Eve loved riding Yafah at full-speed, arms gripping the horse's neck, legs clenched, hair streaming behind her. When Yafah slowed down to a walk (usually at the bank of the river so she could drink), Eve would half-fall in her dismount, laughing from the exhilaration of the ride.

Before Eve was created, Adam had slept in various parts of The Garden, depending on where he was when nighttime fell. Eve, however, didn't like that lifestyle.

"I want to have one spot that we call home," she announced. "I don't like being so scattered."

Adam smiled at her fondly. "You're like the birds in the trees. You want to build a nest."

Eve thought about that for a moment. "Yes, that's right. Foxes have holes, and birds of the air have nests, but we have no place to lay our heads."

"All right," said Adam, "let's find the perfect place."

The next day, as soon as it was light, Adam swung himself onto Rahm while Eve nimbly hopped onto Yafah, and they started riding north along the west side of the river. Great flowering trees, their roots firmly planted in the rich, moist, black earth, formed a canopy, arching high above their heads. Birds called shrilly to one another from the lofty branches. Close by, on the surface on the river, fish jumped in semicircles, their scales glittering in the sunlight. Flowers grew in profusion, perfuming the warm, sweet air.

"Another glorious day," stated Eve, breathing deeply.

"And to think we have all of eternity to enjoy it," added her husband as he nosed Rahm closer to Yafah.

"If only..." A troubled frown passed over Eve's face.

"If only what?" prompted Adam.

"If only we had those children the Lord God told us about."

"Let's ask him," suggested Adam. "Later today, when we meet with him."

"Yes, of course," agreed the woman, satisfied with this obvious solution.

All that day, Adam and Eve pointed out to one another potential places where they could live. It had to be near the river and the hot springs, said Adam, so they could easily have access to water for drinking and bathing. Yes, said Eve, but also in a copse of trees. Big trees, she added, with sheltering branches. Not too far from the date trees, said Adam. Or the almonds, countered Eve.

By late afternoon, they had scouted out three possibilities. Adam glanced at the position of the sun in the clear sky (there were no clouds until the Great Flood). "Let's stop now," he announced. "It's time to go and meet with Adonai."

Every day, at about this time, the man and his wife would go and meet with the Lord God in a specific part of The Garden, not far from where Eve had first awakened. If they were too far away, then the Lord knew where to find them. Such was the case today.

It was the best part of the day, the hour they looked forward to with great anticipation. In the presence of their Creator, both the man and the woman realized and were reminded of their true purpose in life: to worship him.

Now they saw him approach from the fields beyond the river. He strode forward, in the greatness of his strength. Joyfully, like little children, Adam and Eve ran toward him, calling him both *Adonai* and *Abba* interchangeably. Hand in hand, they ran, blessed with one another, happy with life, thrilled with their God.

The Lord God swooped down on them and gathered them up in his arms. Laughing, joyful at being together, they clung to him tightly, dancing with him in a close circle. With great abandon, they sang and danced in their worship of him.

"Tell me, my children," said the Lord, after a while, "what did you do today?" Often he asked that question.

"We went looking for a place to live!" exclaimed Eve, holding contentedly onto the Lord's arm.

"Did you find one?"

"We're not sure," said Adam. "We saw three that looked good, but we're going to continue searching tomorrow. Do you think that's a good idea?"

"Take your time," counseled the Lord. "There's no rush."

They fell silent then, the man and the woman calmed and revitalized in the presence of the Lord God.

After a while, the woman spoke. "Adonai?"

"Yes, my daughter?"

"Remember when you told us to be fruitful, and increase on the earth?"

"Yes."

"When will that happen?" The woman's voice had a shy, hesitant quality to it, in sharp contrast to her normal, confident tones.

"Is this something you desire?"

"Oh, yes!" she said eagerly. "It sounds wonderful!"

"How about you, Adam?" asked the Lord, turning to the man. "What say you?"

Adam furrowed his brow. "It sounds good, but I'm so happy now that I have Eve I don't see how it could get any better."

The Lord laughed. "Your love for one another delights me. Indeed, I say to you that the day will come when you will have children, but now your bodies are newly made. They need time to mature and develop on the inside."

"Then what happens?" asked Eve, extremely interested.

"Then," said the Lord God, "during the times when you lie together, the seed from the man will cause a new human to grow in you, after the fashion of all living things."

"How big will this new human be?" pursued Eve.

The Lord God held his hands one-and-a-half feet apart. "About like so."

"Oh!" said Eve, staring intently at his hands. "That looks quite...big."

"The babies will seem much smaller when they are first born," Adonai assured her. "They will be curled into a ball-like shape."

Eve nodded but didn't say anything further on the subject. She cuddled next to the Lord, leaning contentedly against his side and listening drowsily while her husband talked over the daily affairs of The Garden. Adam told the Lord the plans he had for harvesting food, shepherding the livestock, managing the daily work of the vast geographical area they were in charge of. The Lord listened closely, and when the man finished speaking, he praised certain ideas while pointing out flaws in others. Adam took everything Adonai said with the utmost seriousness.

All too soon the Lord stood up. "I will take my leave now, children," he told them, ignoring their protests. He kissed each of them on the top of their head and blessed them. "I look forward to seeing your new home, once you decide where it is."

Adam and Eve stood as well, their arms around each other's waists, and bid the Lord farewell for the night. They watched his retreating back, the gold of his body shining intensely in the fading light of evening. When he could be seen no more, Adam put his other arm around Eve and drew her closely to himself. Thus they stayed for quite some time as the noises of the nighttime forest descended around their ears.

It took over a week, but Adam and Eve found the perfect spot for their home. Tucked away in a small grove of oak trees, near both the river and a stream, with spectacular views of the mountains in the distance, rested a cozy alcove. Adam set up a bed using long, supple sheets of bark, pine needles, moss, and stones. With a stone needle, he and Eve sewed together fig and palm leaves for a blanket. The days were so mild that they were entirely comfortable naked, but the nights had just the beginning of a chill, mostly toward dawn.

Although no rain fell from the sky, Adam and Eve devised a way to protect themselves at night from the dew the Lord God sent in order to dampen the earth. Stones and pieces of wood seemed to work well as bed platforms, and containers. Leaves, large and small, had all sorts of wonderful uses. Eve became quite handy with a needle and some thread formed from the flax plant. There was no end to discovering the many, many functions possible from the thousands and thousands of creations—plant, animal, and inert—that the Lord God had placed on the earth.

Daily, Adam taught Eve the names of all living creatures, birds, and fish, as they came across them. She grew familiar with lions (so velvety), elephants (not as easy to ride as a horse but a nice change of pace), hippos (just enormous), frogs (cute), falcons (swift), peacocks (gorgeous), camels (haughty), sheep (adorable), pigs (so fat), ibex (breathtakingly fleet-footed), wolves (really loud at night), bears (tremendously strong), mice (talkative), rabbits (sweet), porcupines (sharp), sparrows (friendly), ravens (brooding), lizards (shiny), bees (very industrious—love that honey), and on and on and on.

Once, while out walking, a long, slithery creature with four short legs scampered across their path.

"Oh, what's that?" asked Eve, for she had never seen it before.

"That's a snake," said Adam. He tried to get its attention, but it quickly slid into the underbrush.

"I would have liked to have met him," said Eve, peering in the direction the snake went.

"He's not very friendly," said Adam. "That's actually the first time I've seen him since I named him."

"Oh." Eve paused. "Maybe we should ask Adonai about him."

"That's a good idea," agreed Adam.

But they forgot.

Three

Months passed. In later years Eden would be referred to as "Paradise." Adam and Eve had no point of comparison, but they were still aware that life was wonderful, precious, scintillating, fabulous. Every day dawned clear and bright, with adventure, excitement, new discoveries. Their love for one another grew and grew until they thought they would burst from the headiness of it all. Every so often, Eve would get a longing for children, but when she mentioned it to Adam, he didn't seem perturbed.

"In the right time," he told her every time she asked. "The Lord God will bring forth new humans in the right time."

His answer always satisfied Eve, but eventually the longing returned.

One beautiful day in late summer, when Adam was pruning several of the trees, Eve took a walk through a sheltered woodland path. She hadn't gone very far when she came upon a black and green creature perched on a rock at the side of the path.

"Oh," she exclaimed. "You're the snake, aren't you?"

The creature stared at her, its sharp, beady eyes unblinking.

Intrigued, Eve took a step closer. She held out her hand, palm up. "Come to me," she coaxed. "Don't be shy." (Eve had yet to meet anything with a heartbeat that didn't warm to her immediately.) She determined to show Adam that the snake was nicer than he thought.

You're very beautiful close up.

With a start, Eve realized the snake had just spoken to her. None of the other animals ever commented on her looks. How strange. "Thank you," she said, absently tucking a long, burnished curl behind her ear.

Do you like The Garden?

Again, an odd question. Eve cocked her head to the side, fascinated by this inquisitive creature. "Yes. I think it is absolutely marvelous."

It's missing something.

"And what would that be?"

The sounds of children running and playing among the trees.

The mention of children pierced Eve's heart. She experienced again that sharp stab of longing, that desire to be a mother. *After all,* she asked herself, *am I not named Eve? Mother of all the living?*

"My husband says the Lord God will bring forth children when the time is right, and not before," she dutifully told the snake.

Perhaps the Lord God wants you to do your part as well, suggested the serpent, his eyes narrowing into black slits.

"What do you mean?" asked Eve, puzzled. The snake, however, didn't respond but abruptly turned and ran down the rock and into the forest.

Perplexed, Eve stood there for a few minutes, staring after it. She felt strange—rather moody—and not at all like her usual cheerful self. She had fully accepted all that her husband told her and now the words of the serpent caused a gnawing doubt in her heart. *Perhaps Adam is wrong,* she thought. *Perhaps there* is *something we're supposed to do in order to have children. I wonder what it would be?*

Later that day, during Adam and Eve's time with the Lord God, Adonai noted Eve's pensive mood. "What's wrong, my daughter?" The Lord was sitting on the grass, leaning his back against a date palm.

Eve came and flung herself on the grass at his feet. "I had a conversation with one of the animals today, and it disturbed me."

"Tell me about it."

"It was odd. This creature spoke in a manner quite different from anything else. He knew of my longing to have children, and he suggested that I should be doing more than I am. He made me—" Eve stole a glance at her husband, who was listening intently—"he made me wonder if Adam was entirely right in what he's told me."

"Who was this creature?" demanded Adam, half-rising from his sitting position as he spoke.

Adonai motioned him back down. Eve hesitated when she saw Adam's reaction to what she had said.

"It's all right, my daughter," Adonai assured her. "You can answer. Who was the creature?"

18

"It was the snake," said the woman.

The snake! Adam's mouth tightened. "That's the strangest creature in the whole Garden! Why didn't you tell me you had seen it?"

"I didn't have time!" Eve defended herself. "It was just before we came here. Besides," she added, "I needed to think about it first."

The Lord God stepped into the conversation. To the woman, he said, "It was good for you to tell me about this. Come to me with anything you don't understand; I am always here for you." To the man, he said, "Your wife is your helper, but she is not you. Allow her to mull something over if that is what she needs. Be careful not to build any walls in your relationship."

Slowly, Adam nodded. He still wasn't smiling. "Adonai, can she tell me what she thought I might be wrong about?"

The Lord God put his hand on Eve's. "Go ahead," he counseled her.

Eve took a deep breath. She faced her husband. "You told me we would have children when the time was right. Well, the serpent suggested there's something we need to do also. He intimated that we weren't quite doing our part."

"The serpent said all this?" asked Adam incredulously. *"The serpent!"*

"I thought it odd too," said Eve, her lovely oval face troubled. "It is rare for any of the animals—particularly the smaller ones—to entertain such lofty thoughts."

"Did the snake say what he thought you needed to do?" prodded the Lord God.

"No," said Eve. "He ran off."

The Lord looked at Eve, and his never-ending love for her shone in his eyes like the sun in all its brilliance. "Do you think he was right? What else could—should—you be doing?"

"I don't rightly know," she answered. "Is there anything?"

"Don't you think I would tell you?" asked the Lord. "Don't you think I would make it clear to you?"

The woman lifted her gold-speckled eyes to her Lord. Her heart felt full and her throat swelled so she could not swallow. "Oh, yes, my Lord," she said in a hoarse, choked voice. "I know you would not leave me ignorant."

"That is true," said the Lord God. "I have told you all that you need to know, and I am here every day, should you desire anything." He spoke then to both the man and the woman: "Beware of the snake! Know that he cannot harm you as long as you stay obedient to me. I have given you wisdom. Use it!"

The man and his wife assured the Lord that they would; thus, the matter settled, the conversation turned to other issues.

Although Adam and Eve were as yet the only humans on earth, they were by no means alone. Aside from their daily time with Adonai, aside from their continuous contact with all the animals, was the flurry of activity that came from the angels.

Angels—those tall, awesome beings named for their identity as God's messengers—were invariably around. Some angels tended to be friendlier while others...not as. None of the angels had God's comforting, fatherly presence, but at the same time, none were as potentially terrifying, either. Before the creation of Eve, Adam had formed close relationships with two in particular: Gabriel and Michael.

The first time Eve met Gabriel, she squeezed Adam's hand so hard that, hours later, he could still see the red imprint. She wasn't afraid, but she was very, very awestruck. If Eve measured around five foot, eight inches, then Gabriel must have been close to ten feet tall. He glowed, and the brightness of his white robes could be seen on the darkest of nights. A sharp, golden sword hung from a sheath at his side. The sword must have been at least as long as Eve. A noble sternness characterized his brow, and he rarely smiled. Angels apparently lacked some of the warmer, more cuddly, human qualities.

"Gabriel," said Adam, pleasure lighting up his face at the sight of his friend, "I want to introduce you to my wife, Eve."

The angel bent down and studied Eve's face; his extremely clear, sapphire-blue eyes looked into hers. Eve felt as if he were reading her soul, past, present, and future. A vague sense of unease came upon her but quickly left.

"Yes, the Lord God has spoken of the woman whom he created," said Gabriel, smiling gravely. "All in heaven have followed your birth with great interest."

"Oh," said Eve, graciously, queenly, inclining her head (though she still had a grip on Adam's hand). *All of heaven? Oh, my!* "Will you stay and eat with us, Gabriel?"

"Yes," he said, "I would be honored."

The man, his wife, and the angel sat under the shade of a spreading oak, the coolness and constant breezes delicious in contrast to the hot, noonday sun. Eve brought a large basket, woven from papyrus reeds, filled to the brim with pomegranates, and they split open the luscious fruit, eating the seeds and dropping the unwanted scarlet rinds. Eve loved the way the pulp-encased seeds went *squish!* in her mouth. For quite a long time, they sat, content, speaking of many things, until Eve asked a certain question:

"Why do you wear a sword? What is it for?"

Gabriel's face, serious to begin with, grew sterner still. "Ah," he said, flinging down yet another pomegranate rind. "That is the result of the Great War in heaven."

Both Adam and Eve leaned forward, startled. *The Great War? What Great War?*

"What Great War?" asked Adam.

"The Lord God hasn't told you about it?"

No. They both shook their heads, interested.

Gabriel looked pensive for a moment before slowly nodding. "All right, I can tell you."

Intrigued, Adam and Eve settled themselves comfortably on the lush grass, across from their friend the angel. Adam leaned against the sturdy trunk of the oak while Eve stretched out next to him, hands behind her head, eyes closed, listening to the angel's deep, resonant voice.

"A long time ago," Gabriel began, "when first Adonai crafted this great planet, a conflict arose in heaven. One of the angels—Lucifer, his name was then—was the most beautiful and accomplished among us.

His voice, when raised in worship, emerged purer and clearer than any other angelic voice in heaven. Clothed in gold and adorned with precious stones—rubies, topaz, emeralds, chrysolite, onyx, jasper, sapphires, turquoise, and beryl—he was considered our ruler apart from God. The Lord God anointed him a guardian cherub and placed him in Eden.

"But his beauty and magnificence made him proud. He thought himself God's equal, perhaps even his superior." Gabriel shuddered in recollection. "In his heart, he thought, *I will ascend to heaven, I will raise my throne above the stars of God. I will sit enthroned on the mount of assembly, on the utmost heights of the sacred mountain. I will ascend above the tops of the clouds; I will make myself like the Most High.*"

"This happened *here?*" asked Adam, amazed.

Eve opened her eyes and roused herself to a sitting position, thoroughly alert.

Gabriel nodded. "It was before you were formed. I am the one whom the Lord God chose to replace him as the guardian cherub." He bowed his head humbly.

"What did Adonai do?" breathed Eve, shocked that any created being would dare defy her beloved Lord.

"Before he did anything, Lucifer gathered about himself one of every three angels—all who would align themselves with him—and attacked God and the rest of us. The war that followed was fierce." Modestly, Gabriel fingered the hilt of his sword before looking at them, his sapphire eyes suddenly ablaze with passion. "But the side of the Lord God won—as it always has and as it always will."

"What did Adonai do to Lucifer afterwards?" asked Adam.

"He drove him in disgrace from the Mount of God, expelling him from heaven. God threw him down to—" Gabriel paused—"earth."

"Earth!" exclaimed Adam and Eve simultaneously. "Is he here?"

"I don't know where he is," answered Gabriel. "He's not what he was, that's true enough." Then, observing their concerned expressions, he added, "As long as you obey the Lord God, nothing can harm you."

That being said, the three friends, as if by mutual agreement, stood up, brushed the stray pomegranate seeds to the ground, and took a stroll on the banks of the river.

One starry night, when Adam and Eve were walking hand-in-hand through The Garden, they came to one of the many streams that ran throughout the land.

"Listen to that," said Adam, as the musical gurgling, bubbling, and rushing reached their ears. "It sounds like the waters themselves are praising God. If only we could worship like that!"

"Why can we not?" asked his wife, her face tilted toward his, a smile upon her lips.

"Why not indeed!" exclaimed the man.

The next day he rose early and made some string from fiber and wound it tightly around a piece of wood, then gave it a *twang!* Experimentally, he tried to recreate the sounds of the water.

"Not quite," said Eve, "but why don't we not worry about how the water sounds and do something different?"

"You know, you're right," agreed Adam, fingering his new creation and looking inordinately pleased.

Adam and Eve became thoroughly occupied with the creation of music over the next few weeks. They invented drums, tambourines, harps, lyres. They wrote songs of praise and worship and sang along with the instruments. Wanting to use their songs in front of Adonai, they practiced, memorizing all they created.

"It would be nice to be able to refer to something and not have to memorize it," sighed Eve one day as she struggled with a particularly complex arrangement, not sure if she remembered it exactly as they had first composed it.

Adam looked up from his harp and stared at his wife. "Say that again," he commanded.

"It would be nice not to have to memorize everything," restated Eve, perplexed.

"That's it!" shouted Adam, jumping up. "That's what we've been missing!" He grabbed the startled Eve and swung her around and around until, dizzy and laughing, she begged him to stop.

"Whatever are you so excited about?"

"Look," said Adam, slowly and carefully, futilely attempting to curb some of his enthusiasm but not really succeeding. "If we are able to make marks, or signs, of some kind and store them on something, then we could come back to it later and remember it exactly."

Eve's eyes widened. "That's brilliant! But what could we use to do it?"

"Hmm." Adam turned in a circle, his eyes scanning the trees all around them. He raised his finger in the air, grinned, and ran over to the banyan tree. He and Eve had often used the long, smooth, easily detachable bark of this tree for building projects. Now he carefully cut a medium-sized piece with his stone knife and brought it to her.

"If we take something like this—flat and smooth—then we only need something that will make marks on it. What do you think?"

For several minutes, they were both quiet, thinking about what would work. Suddenly Eve spotted the peacock innocently wandering about. "I'll be right back," she told Adam. Springing into action, she gracefully walked over to the peacock and had a short conversation with him. He squawked, shaking his head, Eve said a few more words, then he stood submissively, head bowed. Eve yanked three multi-colored tail feathers out of the proud bird, stopping afterward to shower him with praise before bounding back to Adam.

"I can't believe you talked him into that," marveled Adam.

Eve grinned. "Now all we need is some sort of substance we can dip these into."

"How about blueberry juice?" suggested Adam. "You know how much that stuff stains."

"Let's give it a try."

24

Adam and Eve hiked over to the east side of The Garden where a vast profusion of berry bushes grew. Blackberries, raspberries, strawberries, and blueberries provided a continual feast for the birds of the air, many of the animals, and the man and woman as well. They collected a large basket of blueberries, eating many in the process. Then they ground the berries, dipped the peacock feather into the resultant goo, and spread it onto the flat piece of bark. Eve chuckled with delight as lines and circles emerged on the bark. Adam whistled between his teeth. "I can't wait to show Adonai!" he said.

"He'll be proud of us," beamed Eve.

"What kind of marks should we use?" asked Adam.

"I don't know," said Eve. "But I think we did enough for one day. Want to go in the hot springs?" She put her arms around the man and molded her body to his.

Adam looked at her, and his face reflected his intense love. "You are a fabulous helper," he told her, right before he kissed her. "Let's wait on the hot springs. I have a better idea."

Over the next several weeks, Adam and Eve learned to make little pictures with their blueberry ink. Thrilled, they showed Adonai, and he praised them for their ingenuity.

"You know," he said, "if you put the pictures together, you can tell stories with your writing." He sat back and watched their expressions.

"Stories?" said Adam thoughtfully. "You mean, tell about the things that happen in our daily life?"

"So we can go back and remember certain things?" added Eve.

"And so your children after you can learn about me, about the angels, about early life in The Garden," said the Lord God.

"Children," repeated Eve. Lately it seemed that she and Adam made a wonderful new discovery every day, so she hadn't thought about children in a while. Now longing spread in her body, causing a pleasurable glow. "Will we have children soon, then?"

"Not yet," answered her Lord, taking her hand. "Don't fret, dear daughter. Just continue to be obedient to my word, and all will happen in its proper time."

Silently, Eve nodded. When Adonai was with her, she had the strength for anything.

As the weeks progressed, Adam and Eve put together a whole series of pictures that they used in different arrangements to form words. Their first picture was of the ox, so they called it an *aleph*, the word for *ox*. The second picture they made in the shape of their house and called it *bet*, the name for *house*. The third picture, *gamal*, was of a camel; the fourth, *dalet*, was of a door, and on and on. Altogether they came up with twenty-two pictures and variations on five of those.

In addition, Adam devised a series of notations that represented the varied sounds made by their musical instruments. Different from the pictures, these symbols represented distinctions between beats and levels of pitch. When he had worked it all out, he taught it to Eve, who quickly learned the system. Next, he and Eve wrote down all the songs they had composed for the Lord God: thirty to date.

"What song should we use for worship when we meet with Adonai today?" Eve asked her husband.

They were sitting at a carved wooden table in their home, eating breakfast. Big slices of luscious pale-green melon, the smallest, reddest strawberries, and sweet, chewy figs was the meal of choice this particular morning. One of the lambs lay under the table, *baaing* softly. Every so often, Adam absentmindedly reached down to pet its head. He had an irrigation project planned for a grove of banana trees that needed more water. Working out the engineering in his head made him preoccupied and he didn't hear Eve.

Playfully, aware she was being ignored, she put a berry between her teeth and slid over to kiss her husband.

Startled, suddenly very aware of her, he ate his half of the berry and pulled her down onto his lap. "Sorry, *dodi*, I was thinking," he said by way of apology.

Eve snuggled against his bare chest. "You're always thinking."

"Yes." He ran one hand through his hair while holding her with the other. "There's so much to do—and enormous amounts of things to learn. I know Adonai is watching, cheering us on, waiting to see if we can discover the treasure hidden in the field." He tightened his grip on Eve, and his voice grew husky, passionate. "I love him so much, Eve. He's such an amazing God, and he's been so wonderful to us. All I want to do is please him."

"Oh, but you do please him, Adam! I can tell by the way he looks at you. He's inordinately pleased with you. Didn't he say after he made you—us—that not only was it good but it was 'very good'?"

"He did say that. I know I don't have to earn his approval, Eve. I know I had it before I uttered my first word. But that doesn't mean I don't want to bless him day and night."

Eve traced the contours of Adam's face lightly with her forefinger. "You're an extraordinary man," she said softly. "It's an honor to be on this adventure with you."

"And with you," he replied, looking deep into her eyes. Then, "What did you say to me before we had this conversation?"

"Oh," she laughed. "It was about our time with Adonai today. What song shall we use for worship?"

"How about the one we wrote last week—'Sphere'? You know," he started singing, "love is the sphere within, the force that holds the globe together, the circle completes as we love each other...."

Eve clapped her hands together. "Oh, I love that song! While you're out today, I'm going to work on a dance for it."

"Excellent." Adam kissed her again, lifting her off his lap as he stood. "I'll see you later, beautiful." Leaving their snug home, he went outside and whistled for Rahm, who trotted right over.

Later that morning, after Eve had tidied up and written a new worship dance, she took a stroll through The Garden with several of the animals. As always, she stopped to gaze at the view of the distant mountains.

"Isn't that just breathtaking?" Her eyes drank in the visual feast of mauves, golds, greens, blues, stretching across fields, up pastures, through fruit orchards, and racing ever higher into the hazy blue mountains. "I'd like to immerse myself in that beauty!"

The ibex at her side shook his great curved horns and bellowed loudly.

"What?" asked Eve, turning around. "You think I should create another view? How?"

The ibex, however, had no more to say. Instead he nuzzled her hand, almost toppling her as he pushed close.

"Oh, you little sweetie!" laughed Eve, as she stroked his soft nose. She continued her walk, pondering the concept of creating another view. *How would I do that?* she wondered. About an hour later, it hit her. Of course! It was just like writing, only this time the pictures would be for the sake of pictures. She would draw the view on a piece of bark with multi-colored inks and be able to enter into the view.

At the appointed time that day, Adam and Eve met with the Lord God. The man sang his latest worship song, accompanying himself on the harp while his wife danced with abandon, her gestures mirroring the words of the song. When they had finished, the Lord God blessed them, receiving their act of worship with great pleasure. Eve then slipped off and retrieved her picture from where she had hidden it behind a tree. Neither Adonai nor Adam had yet seen it.

"What do you think?" she asked shyly, holding the large, rectangular-shaped piece of bark in front of her, at an angle so they could both see it.

"What a clever idea!" stated Adam. "You used the word pictures to make picture-pictures."

"Very good, my child," said Adonai, taking the picture from Eve and examining it closely. He looked up at her sharply. "You like to create, don't you?"

"Oh yes!" said the woman, happiness radiating from her face in a soft, rosy glow. "It's because *you* create, dear Lord, and I desire more than all else to be like you."

"Come here." The Lord God opened his arms wide and the woman he created melted into them. She sighed softly, a sigh of utter contentment.

PART TWO

The Fall

Four

I am very old now, older than any who walk this tragic earth, except for the man. I have wearied of life for a long time, and all I desire now is to be with my God. I have begged him to take me home and he in turn has encouraged me to have patience. But now I begin to have a glimmer of hope that my days are indeed numbered. Perhaps, perhaps, this long, grinding existence will soon end, and I shall once more be at peace.

Yesterday, I saw my face reflected back at me for the first time in many moons. *Who is that woman?* I thought, startled. My skin, once as translucent as a rose petal in first blush, was leathery and lined with countless wrinkles. My lustrous hair, renowned throughout the world for its dazzling variety of colors, hung limp and gray. My body, with its fairness of form that once caused my husband to seek me out daily, had long since lost its taut, full lushness. Wizened and frail, I looked as old as the grave. It's been many, many years since last we lay together as man and wife. Though older than me, my husband has other wives to whom he has turned for his needs.

For more years than there are grains of sand on the seashore, I have bemoaned and regretted my foolish action. All of mankind has been plunged into a world of sin because of me. It is an unbearably heavy burden. Were it not for my Lord and his forgiveness, I would have long since taken my own life.

Even now, in these last days on earth, after hundreds of years, I still clearly remember everything about The Garden. In my dreams, I smell the tantalizing scents of the fruits and the flowers, feel the sun warm on my back. I remember my husband's arms around me when he loved me with all the fullness of his being, before...before.

Oh, curse the day I fell prey to that wicked serpent, HaSatan himself! The angels warned me, the Lord Most High warned me, yet I did not heed them. I tripped through my days like a babe, unthinking, unwitting. Woe to me that I didn't speak more to my Lord about my desire to suckle an infant, that I let that desire rule me until it wiped all wisdom from my young mind.

I had forgotten about the snake after my first encounter with it. Little did I realize that it had by no means forgotten me but rather lurked about, waiting for an opportune time to accost me again. Soon enough, it seized its chance.

My husband had been spending a lot of time with the angel Michael as he had enlisted the angel's help with an aqueduct project. Adam always got very excited when he had a new challenge: throwing himself into it heart and mind. At first I was happy and listened attentively when he came home and told me every last detail and the thought processes that had taken him there. Soon, however, I grew somewhat weary of all this talk of water, and irrigation, and plants. I worked harder at my painting, I took long walks with my many animal friends, I delighted in our daily time at the end of the day with Adonai, I spoke with the never-ending parade of angels who routinely came to visit, I loved my husband. I didn't want to disappoint Adonai by admitting that I had grown restless so I hid it even from myself. Now I realize that I had never fooled Adonai; he was simply waiting for me to confide in him so he could turn and help me. He had given me freewill, so was not inclined to force me into a confidence I did not freely share.

With this submerged restlessness returned my desire for a baby. I saw how the animals gave birth and tenderly suckled their young. The mothers allowed me to hold their newborns but hovered nearby, anxious to retrieve the infants. Sheep, cattle, goats, dogs, cats, plus many more, all began to give birth. The Garden and, quite likely, the earth beyond, reproduced according to its kind. All except me.

It was in this unsettled frame of mind that I awoke that fateful day. Adam left early to meet with Michael, and I slowly straightened up after our breakfast. Not focused on what to do with myself, I sauntered down the woodland trail and headed toward the middle of The Garden.

Now the Lord God had told Adam not to eat from the fruit of the tree of the knowledge of good and evil, and Adam had carefully instructed me in that. I do admit that I had curiously examined it from a safe distance, afraid even to touch the red globes that hung so securely from the leaf-covered branches. I felt that if I were even to brush up against the tree, something terrible would happen.

As I walked toward the tree, the snake ran in front of me.

Hello, it said.

"Hello," I said back, surprised to see him. "I haven't seen you in a while. Where have you been?"

Oh, he replied vaguely, *I've been roaming through The Garden and going back and forth in it.*

"Our paths must not have crossed," I said.

Yes, he answered.

We looked at each other for a moment, then I started to turn back in the direction from whence I had come.

Wait! said the snake.

"What is it?" I asked him.

Look at this beautiful tree, he said. *Look at this luscious fruit.*

"What about it? That's the tree the Lord God told us not to touch."

Oh? Did God really say, "You must not eat from any tree in The Garden"?

I laughed then. I thought the snake a foolish creature. "Of course he didn't say that!" I exclaimed, shaking my long, burnished hair back from my face. "We eat fruit from the trees in The Garden all the time. But God did say, 'You must not eat fruit from the tree that is in the middle of The Garden, and you must not touch it, or you will die.'"

You will not surely die. For God knows that when you eat of it, your eyes will be opened, and you will be like God, knowing good and evil. The serpent stared at me, its long forked tongue slipping back and forth out of its mouth.

Besides, added the serpent, cunningly, *God knows that when you eat of this fruit, you will conceive a child. You will not die, but you will be changed. That is what God really meant.*

Could that be true? Could the Lord God just have been keeping us from this tree until it was the right time for us to bear children? I thought about this, shifting my weight from one foot to the other while the snake watched me, not moving except for that slithering forked tongue....

Oh, the vast ability of the human heart to deceive itself! If I had only stayed obedient to what my Lord had told me! If only, if only.

Touch it, urged the snake. *You will not die.*

Suddenly determined, I reached up and gently poked the side of one of the low-hanging pieces of fruit. Its flesh felt firm and juicy, yielding slightly to my touch. I waited, but nothing happened. My heart and resolve hardened. *Surely, God wants me to eat of this fruit and acquire the wisdom to conceive children. After all, isn't he the one who told us to be fruitful and multiply?* I was sorely tempted to pluck the fruit from the branch but hesitated. I needed my husband with me. I couldn't do this alone. I withdrew my hand and turned to look for the snake, but he had disappeared.

Trembling, ignoring the inner warnings of my heart, I quickly walked back home. Adam was arriving from the other direction. When I saw him, I ran and threw myself into his arms, hugging him fiercely.

"Hey, what's this?" he asked sweetly, a little perplexed.

"I have the most wonderful news," I told him.

"What?" he asked innocently.

"I know how to conceive a child!"

"So do I."

"That's not what I meant! I know why it's been taking so long and what we're supposed to do."

"Really?" said Adam as he walked with me into our home. "Let's eat something."

I set out some fruit and nuts before him and watched him as he ate. "Come," I coaxed. "As soon as you finish eating, I want to show you something."

"Why don't you just tell me and we'll stay in," said my husband. "We can work on conceiving children." He winked at me and put his hand on my leg.

"Oh, stop it." I pushed his hand away. "I'm serious. I need to show this to you."

"All right, fine." Adam stood up and held out his hand. "Come on, then. Let's get this over with."

I led him out into the hot midday sun and then through the woodland path toward the center of The Garden. When we approached the tree of the knowledge of good and evil, Adam balked.

"What are you doing, Eve?"

"I'm going to eat a piece of fruit," I told him, my voice quavering slightly. "Look! If I touch it, nothing happens."

"Stop that, Eve!" Face ashen, Adam grabbed my hand and pulled it away from the tree. "You know what Adonai said! Why are you touching it?"

I didn't mention the snake. I felt like I had to convince Adam or my desires (which were righteous desires) would never happen. Now I see how deceived I was, but at the time I was driven by pure desire, tempted by it. And I know that I was dragged away and enticed. After desire has conceived, it gives birth to sin; and sin, when it is full-grown, gives birth to death. Death lurked in that Garden, mocking me, and I was too pitiful and blind to see it!

I did something I had never done before. I pouted. I accused Adam of not loving me. I told him that if he really loved me, he would do this simple thing for me and eat the fruit so we could have children. In a way I was detached from this scene, watching it. At any point, I could have exercised self-control and stopped my behavior, but I chose against it.

In the same way, Adam didn't have to listen to me. He could have run from the tree and pulled me with him. He could have called on the Name of Adonai, he could have...but he didn't. He loved me so much that it led to his downfall. Never before had I emotionally manipulated him like this. He wavered in his obedience to Adonai as a result of his loyalty to me. He fell.

I saw the point at which he became persuadable. Quick as a flash, I pulled the red globe off the branch and sank my teeth into it. *Mmm*, it was delicious! The air about me swirled faintly, then became clearer. I felt like my eyes focused in a new way.

"Go ahead," I told Adam, holding out my half-eaten fruit. "Try it. I'm sure the Lord God wants us to be more knowledgeable, like him. You know how pleased he is whenever we discover new things."

Adam stared at me, and a deep sadness filled his eyes. "All right, Eve," he said in a new voice, a voice that struck fear into my heart. Whatever happens to you, I'll share. Such is my love for you."

With those words, Adam accepted the fruit from my hand and bit into it. O cursed day! We looked at each other and our sin was exposed and naked. We determined that it was our naked bodies that were causing us shame, so we returned to our home and made coverings. I took fig leaves and sewed them together, and we covered our most vulnerable parts.

It didn't help. Our nakedness went far deeper than our skin: it pierced our hearts and souls.

Later that day, when it came to our usual time to meet with the Lord God, we both felt so dreadful and ashamed at our disobedience that we neglected to go to the appointed place. We heard him then, his deep, purposeful footsteps, pounding the earth with the glory of his presence. He strode through The Garden, searching for us.

Instinctively, without communicating, both Adam and I hid among the trees. Crouching and miserable, we dared to think that an apple tree could cover our sin!

"Where are you?" called Adonai as he walked in The Garden in the cool of the day. "Present yourselves to me!"

We dared not defy a direct command. White and terrified, Adam had more courage than me. He answered first: "I heard you in The Garden, and I was afraid because I was naked; so I hid."

Adonai's voice thundered across the treetops. "Who told you that you were naked? Have you eaten from the tree that I commanded you not to eat from?"

Emerging from his hiding place, Adam crept over to the Lord God and flung himself down at the ground at the Lord's feet. "The woman you put here with me—" he choked—"she gave me some fruit from the tree, and I ate it."

O, how I died inside when I heard those words! My husband—the man who fit me perfectly—despised me! I could hear in his voice how his love for me had changed, and I knew it was my fault, my fault! Dejected, sorrowful, no longer caring about myself, I crawled out from behind my tree and presented myself to the Lord God. I couldn't bear to look at his face, so I buried my face in the ground near his feet.

"What is this you have done?" Ah, my Lord's voice. It wasn't angry, but it was very, very sad. I would have preferred fierce hot anger to this crushing disappointment.

Blinded by salty tears, I cried out, "The serpent deceived me, and I ate!"

The Lord God sighed, and in his sigh the earth shuddered. "You are each responsible for your own sin."

I looked up then and saw that The Garden was filled with angels. They stood solemnly, swords at their sides, surrounding the Lord, the God of Hosts. The serpent, that deceiver, stood before him, as did Adam and myself. The Lord passed judgment on us, first to the serpent.

"Because you have done this," he said to the sullen creature, "Cursed are you above all livestock and all the wild animals! You will crawl on your belly, and you will eat dust all the days of your life. And I will put enmity between you and the woman, and between your offspring and hers; he will crush your head, and you will strike his heel."

I lifted my woebegone face at this, hope stirring slightly in my breast. Was the Lord God making a pathway back for us? Would I bear children after all, and would my children reclaim what was lost? These thoughts were swept away, however, in the shock of seeing the snake's legs vanish from beneath him! Snarling, hissing, and spitting, he slithered away, but not before an angel forcibly ejected him from The Garden. *Good, he's gone,* I thought.

I realized then that all the hosts of heaven were looking at me. I stood before my Lord, feeling ashamed and ludicrous in my fig-leaf outfit. The Lord God spoke to me: "I will greatly increase your pains in childbearing; with pain you will give birth to children. Your desire will be for your husband, and he will rule over you." Tears pricked at my eyelids, and I knelt down on the ground. It was no more than I deserved.

Slowly I became aware of something else happening. I raised my head and saw my beloved, humble and contrite, standing before his Lord. Sorrowfully, the Lord was saying, "Because you listened to your wife and ate from the tree about which I commanded you, 'You must not eat of it,' cursed is the ground because of you; through painful toil you will eat of it all the days of your life. It will produce thorns and thistles for you, and you will eat the plants of the field. By the sweat of your brow you will eat your food until you return to the ground, since from it you were taken; for dust you are and to dust you will return."

Then the Lord God took two of the sheep and one of the cows and slit their throats with a knife. I screamed when I saw their lifeblood streaming out of their dead carcasses. *My friends, my friends, this is all my fault!*

"The life is in the blood," said the Lord God. "It is an atonement for sin."

Next he stripped the skin from the dead animals and formed it into leather. He made garments for Adam and myself, clothing us as tenderly as a mother would clothe her young child. How I yearned to throw my arms around his neck as he tied the dress about me, but I felt constrained. Never before had I hesitated to show my love and affection to Adonai. This new wall that sin brought about, it is too awful.

The Angel of the Lord came down from heaven, and Adonai spoke with him. These two powerful beings glowed so bright I couldn't look at them—my eyes were dazzled—but I heard Adonai's voice. He said, "The man has now become like one of us, knowing good and evil. He must not be allowed to reach out his hand and take also from the tree of life and eat, and live forever."

I started to say that we had learned our lesson, that the tree was safe from us, when Gabriel scooped me up in his arms.

"What is it?" I asked him, frightened by his grim expression. "Where are you taking me?"

He didn't answer. It was then I saw that Michael had likewise grasped Adam. Both angels walked east with us, away from the center of The Garden.

My heart beat so hard I thought it would burst in my chest. Never before had I experienced fear, and the overwhelming, dark breathlessness of it wiped all reason from my mind. I am ashamed to admit that I started shouting and crying.

"Hush!" warned Adam from his tight perch on Michael's shoulder. "Hush. Whatever happens to us is only as we deserve!"

His words quieted me, if for no other reason than to give me a command I could hang on to, much as a drowning man grasps at a floating log.

When the angels reached the farthest point east in The Garden, they put us down. Stretching in front of us, wrapping around the perimeter of The Garden as far as the eye could see was an enormous hedge composed of brambles and thorns. Pushing apart a space with their mighty hands, they forced us out and then followed, closing up the gap. Adam and I sat, confused and disoriented, on the bare ground, and looked with pleading eyes to our friends.

Gone were the days of comfortable companionship. Gabriel and Michael unsheathed their swords and held them high in the air. Fire sprang from the blades and glowed in the darkening sky. Cowering, Adam and I backed away, stunned and fearful.

"Go!" commanded Gabriel, his face emotionless as he wielded his sword. "Your disobedience has lost you the privilege of dwelling in God's paradise! This way is barred to you forever." So saying, he flung his flaming sword into the air and it hung, suspended, flashing back and forth.

That night, and the weeks and months following, were so awful it pains me even now to recall them. That first night we slept on rocky ground. I cried without cease while Adam sat melancholy and lethargic. When the sun rose on our sorry heads the next morning, we blanched at what we saw.

Instead of our beautiful Garden, filled with trees and fruit for the picking, was a plateau dotted with stones, scrubby bushes, and the occasional tree. We were hard-pressed to find any shade and grew hotter than we ever had before as the sun rose in the relentlessly blue sky.

"How will we eat or drink?" I whispered, my voice hoarse from crying.

Adam, his hand shielding his eyes, scanned the horizon. "There," he said, pointing, his first word to me since we had been driven out of

The Garden. "I can see a blue line where it would make sense for our river to be."

Our river! At least he was still grouping himself with me, I thought grimly.

"Come on, Eve." Adam stood up and extended his hand to me. "Let's head over there and see if we can get some water. There's nothing for us here."

I took his hand and let him pull me to my feet, pathetically grateful he was willing to touch me. "Adam, I'm so sorry about everything! How can I make it up to you...?"

"Shh." Adam frowned, shook his head, and put his finger on my lips. "Not now. I can't discuss it now. Let's concentrate on surviving."

"All right." Relieved to be doing something—anything—I followed him as we walked to the river.

It took longer to reach the river than I would have thought. Distances were deceiving outside The Garden. By the time we got to the riverbank, my feet—accustomed to lush grass, crushed flowers, and pine needles—were cut and bleeding from the thousands of sharp stones scattered everywhere. I didn't care, though. All I could think about was my tremendous thirst. Shedding my new clothes, I rushed down the slope and waded into the water, plunging my face right into it and lapping furiously. The river looked a lot muddier and browner than it had in The Garden, but the water was cold and drinkable.

Next I washed, attempting to scrub sin away. I felt cleaner on the outside, though not on the inside.

Emerging from the water, my long hair dripping copiously, I threw myself on the bank and dried off in the sun. Adam, newly clean as well, lay beside me. Reaching out, he clasped my hand and briefly kissed it. That small act of love took my breath away.

"O, Adam, my love!" Tears, stilled for the past hour, started to flow again.

"Don't," cautioned Adam, distraught at my distress. "There's no time. Believe it or not, we don't have long until it's dark again. We need to build a shelter before then." He stood up, pulling me with him. "Let's go."

We walked for miles that day, following the river as it wound northeast, further and further from The Garden. We spoke little. Eventually, we came to a sheltered spot overlooking a particularly green and fertile valley. It was no paradise, but it looked a lot better than anything else we had seen that day.

"Here," Adam announced, looking intently in all directions. "I don't know if we'll be here for very long, but at least we can start."

With our bare hands, we dug clay from the riverbank, mixed it with dried grasses, baked it in the hot sun, and formed bricks for a house. Foraging in the nearby valley, we ate wild berries, greens, and whatever we could find.

Within the week, a mother goat and her two young kids showed up, and we helped ourselves to some of her milk. I spoke to her—as I always did with the animals—but she merely cocked her head to one side and looked at me with uncomprehending brown eyes. Concerned, I listened for her voice and realized that the sounds she made had no significance for me now. Our ability to communicate with animals had died with our innocence. That was a very, very hard blow.

"What did you expect?" asked Adam when I lamented to him. "Eve, the reverberations to our sin are beyond calculating."

The next day, a brood of chickens wandered into our shelter and we were able to add eggs to our meager diet. I knew then that the Lord God, though we hadn't yet seen him, was still caring for us and providing for our needs.

"We need to clear the field and plant seed so we'll have food," said Adam.

"Where will we get the seed?"

He scratched his head. "I don't know. Let's pray and ask Adonai to provide it."

After we prayed, Adam said, "You know, let's walk around and see what's growing by itself, and harvest the seeds from that."

We found wheat, lentils, millet, barley, greens. Adam and I worked from the time the sun rose in the morning until it grew too dark to see. We painstakingly cleared the fields of stones, turning up the soil with tools that Adam fashioned from wood and stone. My hands grew hard, the fingernails torn and split. *Did I really just wander about amusing myself, picking my food off trees?* I thought to myself in amazement at the end of yet another brutally difficult day. The worst part of our banishment was the lack of contact with the Lord God. No longer did we have daily access to him, no longer was our relationship with him carefree and innocent.

Oh, he forgave us. His mercy and lovingkindness know no bounds. But there had been an irrevocable shift: a wall had gone up.

I could see it in Adam's eyes. He bore the day-to-day hardships stoically, but each evening, when the sun came down toward the horizon, and we would have met with the Lord God, he grew pensive. It was then that my mouth grew dry, my palms sweaty, and I thought my heart would burst from anguish.

We learned to pray and to hear Adonai's voice in our heads. Every so often, he would come and physically manifest himself, and those times were joyous indeed. I vividly remember the first time.

About a month after leaving The Garden (*only a month? It felt like a lifetime!*), Adam and I were barely subsisting. We had built a crude shelter, foraged for food, and were working on planting crops. Hot and weary, we straggled home late one afternoon after hours of backbreaking work. Both of us had lost weight, and we were weak from our meager diet. When we were yet a long way off from our hut, Adam noticed a flash of gold in the distance. "Look!" he exclaimed, pointing excitedly. "Is it? It's the Lord!"

The Lord? I jerked my head up and stared. Yes, it was he! Without another word to each other, we started running toward him. When he saw that we had seen him, he ran toward us. As soon as we met, Adam and I were suddenly overcome by guilt and shame. We stopped just short of his embrace—the embrace we had been longing so desperately for—and hung our heads.

The Lord God had compassion on us and threw his arms around us and kissed us. "My children, you are forgiven."

Adam said to him, "Father, I have sinned against heaven and against you. I am no longer worthy to be called your son."

"You're still my son, and my daughter," he answered. "I have not removed my love from you."

I wanted to ask him if that meant we could return to The Garden, but restraint held my tongue.

"I see you have been clearing the fields," said the Lord God approvingly. "Come! I will show you how to do some things that will help you."

He held each of us by the hand and led us to our home. Strength and vitality flowed into me from his secure, warm grasp, and I felt alive again. When we arrived, he took several sheaves of wheat, threshed the berries, and, using two stones, showed us how to pound them into flour. Next he added water, kneaded the mixture into a dough, ripped it into six equal pieces, and then, with the palms of his hands, flattened each ball until it was very thin. Building a fire, he baked the dough over the fire, flipping it with a stick when brown spots appeared on the underside.

Adam and I watched, wide-eyed. The tantalizing aroma made our mouths water.

"What is it?" asked Adam.

"It's bread," said the Lord God. "Try it." He pulled the first cooked bread off the stone and handed it to Adam, who took a bite and gave some to me. Then he sat back and watched with pleasure as we hungrily chewed.

Mmm, it was delicious. I had never eaten soft, warm food before. How wonderful! Ravenously, we polished off that first bread and waited eagerly for more.

"You'll come up with many different ways to make bread," said Adonai. "This is the basic recipe. If you have bread, you'll live."

"We need you so we can live," I said reverently, kneeling down and kissing the holy ground at his feet.

"Ah," said the Lord, "I am the bread of life. He who comes to me will never go hungry and he who believes in me will never be thirsty. You would do well never to forget that!"

After baking the rest of the bread, he gathered us to him and spoke tenderly. "I will not come down from heaven every day like I did in The Garden." He ignored the stricken looks on our faces and continued. "I will always hear you when you call to me. You now know the difference between good and evil: you know what sin is. It is up to you to master it." He left us then, and the earth turned colder, duller.

Five

A year went by. We learned many things, and our life went from one of merely survival to one where patches of color, gladness, and hope more liberally sprinkled our days. Our first harvest burst forth, and with joy we gathered in the fruitfulness of the land. That night my husband came to lie with me, and it seemed that a taste of our love from our former life in The Garden was recaptured.

The weeks that followed brought strange and new physical sensations for me. I grew weak and dizzy, and couldn't keep my food down. Adam became concerned, calling out to Adonai. The Lord God's answer revealed itself in our mutual realization that I was with child. How thrilling!

As my belly grew big with the coming child, I often pondered the curse that Adonai had uttered against the serpent. I remembered how he said that there would be enmity between our offspring, and that my seed would crush his head. It seemed to me that my child would be the messiah who would rebuke the curse of sin and restore paradise on earth. I kept this to myself, however, and didn't share it with Adam.

One balmy night in early summer when I was so huge I could barely walk, I was awakened in the night by severe stomach cramps. When they came so fast and furious that I could no longer be silent but cried aloud in pain, Adam awoke as well.

"What is it?" he asked sleepily, reaching out his hand to stroke my shoulder.

Another sharp pain hit, and I screamed loudly. Adam bolted out of bed, suddenly wide awake. "Eve, what is it? Are you okay?"

"I think it's the baby," I gasped, in between contractions. "This must be the pain of childbearing."

"What should I do?"

"I don't know! I've never done this before!" I laughed weakly until another contraction turned my laughter into a cry.

All that night and into the early morning, Adam held me and prayed for me as I struggled with one ripping, agonizing contraction after another. When at last I thought I could do no more, I realized there was an intense pressure between my legs that hadn't been there before. "Look, Adam, look! What is it?"

By the soft light of the new day, my husband peered closely in the area I had mentioned. "I think it's the baby! I can see a small patch of dark hair. Push it out, Eve. Go on, and push!"

With all my strength, I squeezed and pushed as hard as I could. After ten minutes, Adam said, "Keep going, that's it, don't stop!"

Another hard push, and then exquisite relief as the pressure was suddenly released. I closed my eyes and through my exhaustion heard my husband exalt, "It's a little boy! Oh, Eve, we have a son!"

A son! What a blessed miracle! Before I could comment, though, another sharp pain jolted me and I felt something slither out between my legs. "Adam, Adam, what is it?" I panicked.

"Oh," he said, perplexed. "It looks like something that helped the baby to grow. Don't worry. I'm sure all this is what's supposed to happen." Then he said, "It looks like the baby is still attached to you by a cord. I'm going to cut it."

Cut it? "Is that a good idea?" I faltered.

"Relax," said my husband, excitement stretching his voice to a higher octave. Unseen by me, he took his knife and cut the cord an inch from the baby.

"Let me know when it's done," I demanded nervously.

"It's already done," he told me.

I pushed myself up into a sitting position. "Let me see him," I urged.

"Wait," said Adam. "He's all slimy." He took some braided grasses and wiped the baby, which set off a series of tiny cries: *waa waa waa.* Next he handed me a tiny human: red, squalling, black-haired, and shaking tiny fists. Enchanted, I put him to my breast like I had seen the animals do, and he acted like a newborn lamb, nuzzling and suckling. Overwhelmed, I saw this baby as the Lord God's method for the deliverance of mankind from sin, and I exclaimed, "I have brought forth a man: Yahveh."

Adam frowned. "Do you think he's the messiah?"

I shook off his pessimism impatiently. "Of course. Don't you?"

"I don't know, Eve. Let's rejoice in the birth of our son and let Adonai work out the rest."

The baby enchanted me. He was so small and sweet. I showered him with love and affection, kissing him constantly.

"Don't smother him!" laughed Adam. "Take a lesson from the cattle. They let their babies breathe."

"We're not animals," I quickly retorted, hugging the (now) sleeping baby to my breast, his little face constantly changing expression, even in repose.

"He needs a name," stated Adam. "We can't just call him *baby*."

"You're right," I agreed. "What should it be?"

"If he were Yafah, or Rahm, he could tell us himself what his name is."

"Yes," I said, somewhat sadly. We both fell silent. The loss of our favorite horses—not seen since we left The Garden—weighed heavily on both of us. I sighed.

"His name needs to define who he is," said Adam. He studied the baby's face. "I see power and resolve."

"You do?" I looked carefully at the baby's face as well. It was on the tip of my tongue to suggest calling him "Messiah," as I strongly believed that's who I was holding in my arms, but I refrained as I knew it would only irritate Adam. I wasn't so sure I saw what Adam did, but I tried to be conciliatory as much as possible since I had gotten us into this mess. So I merely looked up and asked, "What kind of name connotes power?"

"How about a weapon?" asked Adam thoughtfully.

"Like a knife, or a...?"

"Or a blade!" he finished triumphantly. "I've got the perfect name: Cain."

Cain. I looked back down at the baby, who was now smiling in his sleep as if pleased with our choice. "That's a wonderful choice, Adam. Our Cain will be a powerful man of God." *And will be used as a blade to smite the head of the serpent,* I thought to myself.

48

The weeks went by and I failed to regain all my strength. At first, we weren't very worried, since I had lost a lot of blood during childbirth and had experienced much trauma. After a while, though, Adam grew concerned.

"I'm going to ask Adonai what we should do, *motek*. I want to see you well."

I nodded. Having only been used to perfect health, even during pregnancy, it frustrated me to be this way.

When we did see the Lord God, his answer shocked us.

"She needs meat," he told Adam.

Meat? Flesh? Our mouths dropped open. *How?*

"Remember when I sacrificed the livestock for your clothes?" Painfully, we both nodded. Yes, how well we remembered. "Do you recall the smell?"

"Yes," said Adam. "It was somewhat," he paused, "pleasing."

"A fragrant aroma," said Adonai, touching the tips of his fingers together. "Today I give you new instruction as to what you may eat. In the past, you have only had what grows from trees or green plants that spring up from the earth. Now you may eat certain birds, fish, and animals: those that are clean."

"Which ones are considered clean, Adonai?" asked Adam, intrigued.

"For animals, only those that have a split hoof and chew the cud, like sheep, goats, cows, deer."

"How about pigs?" I asked.

"They have the split hoof, but don't chew the cud."

"Camels?" asked Adam.

"The opposite. Though it chews the cud, it does not have a split hoof and so is ceremonially unclean for you."

"Rabbits?" I asked, though as soon as the word was out of my mouth, I realized they had paws.

"No." The Lord God smiled. "It does chew the cud, but doesn't have a split hoof."

"I knew that," I muttered.

The Lord laughed. "Now as to the creatures living in the water of the seas and the streams, you may eat any that have fins and scales. But all creatures in the seas or streams that do not have fins and scales you are to detest."

Adam and I looked at each other. This seemed very straight-forward.

"Now with birds," continued Adonai. "You are to detest and not eat: the eagle, the vulture, any kind of kite, or raven, or owl, the osprey, the story, any kind of heron, the hoopoe, and the bat. All other birds will be considered clean for you to eat."

"What about insects?" asked Adam.

"Ah," said the Lord God. "Good question. You are allowed to eat any kind of locust, katydid, cricket, or grasshopper. All other winged creatures that have four legs you are to detest."

"Why can we eat some and not others?" I asked.

Adam answered me. "Because the insects we can eat have jointed legs for hopping on the ground. At least, that's the only difference I can think of."

"Very good, my son," affirmed Adonai. "That's precisely the reason."

"My Lord?" said Adam.

"Yes?"

"How do we kill the animals for food?"

The Lord's face grew solemn. "With a very sharp knife across the throat. You must be careful lest you hesitate and cause the animal pain. Should you do that, the meat will be considered *treif,* or torn."

"All that blood, and distress..." My voice trailed off.

Sadly, the Lord looked at me. "Yes, my daughter. The wages of sin is death. The blood of the innocent animal covers sin. Every time you kill an animal for food, you will be reminded of your sin." His face was compassionate and loving, but stern. "Since the life of the animal is in the blood, *never, never, never* eat blood. Do you both understand me?"

"Yes, my Lord," said Adam.

"Yes," I whispered.

"Good. You also need to sacrifice the fat to me," said the Lord God. "Don't eat it, but burn it in the fire: along with the kidneys and the covering of the liver."

We shook our heads in agreement. So much new information was extremely wearying. The Lord God knew we had absorbed all we could. He held us, breathing new energy into our tired frames. Blessing both of us and little Cain (did he shake his head as he stared into the baby's eyes? I blinked and wasn't sure), he bid us farewell and disappeared from sight.

"What do you think we should do?" I asked Adam later that night after the baby fell asleep. Cain lay sleeping on one side of me and Adam lay on the other. Carefully, so as not to disturb the baby, I rolled over and pressed my body against my husband's, kissing his shoulder.

"Oh, this is nice," he said, turning to meet me. Running his hand through my hair, he let it drop through his fingers, fanning onto my back.

"What should we do?" I persisted after a while.

"About what?" asked Adam drowsily, touching my milk-engorged breasts.

I purred, enjoying his hands on me. It took me awhile to respond. When I did, I was out of breath. "Should we really kill one of the animals?"

"Sacrifice, not kill. Yes, the Lord told us to."

"But who?" I cried, agitation replacing my formerly relaxed mood as I contemplated the untimely death of one of my many furry friends.

Adam lay on his back, hands clasped under his head, and thought. "Probably something small," he finally said. "Like one of the lambs, or the kids."

"What?" I exclaimed too loudly, for the baby began to stir. I lowered my voice. "That would be a horrible thing to do to the sheep or the goats! It would be like someone killing our baby." I shuddered.

"Eve," patiently said Adam, in his I've-been-on-earth-longer-than-you voice, "Adonai put us in charge of the animals. As much as we love them, they're *not* our equals. Get used to it." That was the last thing he said to me that night. Rolling over, he promptly went to sleep.

The next day, Adam went through the flocks and pulled a lamb who had just been weaned from its mother. Using his sharpest knife, he slit its throat in one quick, fluid motion, as Adonai had instructed. Building a fire, he sacrificed the fat and inner portions, then cut the rest of the flesh and roasted it.

Meanwhile, I stayed a fair distance away, restraining myself from stopping him but still highly reluctant to be part of this awful killing.

"Don't get proud," Adam told me. "The blood covers your sin too."

"I know," I replied. "I'll get better at this, really I will."

Only we're not there yet, I thought grimly, appalled at all the blood, mess, and anguish that went into feeding ourselves in contrast to blithely picking a piece of fruit off a tree and tossing the peel. For the thousandth time, I thought, *If only.*

When Adam came to me, holding out a strip of charred flesh, I sought to look away in revulsion, but my body betrayed me. The tantalizing odor caused my saliva to flow. Reluctantly, I accepted the meat and tentatively took a bite. The hot, chewy moistness startled me with its pungent earthiness. Forgetting about the mother sheep losing her baby, I took a second bite, and a third. Soon I finished all that Adam had given me.

"It's good, isn't it?" he said, eyes bright, chewing his second? third? piece.

Before I could answer, Baby Cain yelled, awakened by the new smell in the air.

After several days of eating the flesh of sheep, I *did* feel stronger, more alert. "This stuff works," I admitted to Adam.

"Yes," he agreed. "I've been feeling a lot better also." He looked up in the sky and eyed some low-flying birds. "You know, I think that next time I'll catch some of those quail!"

Life went on. The Garden became more of a distant memory, though never forgotten. One year after giving birth to Cain, I had another son. This one we named Abel. By now I knew what to expect with pregnancy, nursing, and infants, so it was less stressful. Also, Abel was an easier baby than Cain: calmer, happier. Threatened and upset by the appearance of Abel, Cain grew querulous and demanding, crying and pulling at my leg whenever I held the new baby. In retrospect I should have given him a sharp slap and stopped him, but I was convinced that he was the Messiah, so I gave in to his whims and caprices. I have had many years to repent of my foolishness.

With the help of the Lord God, Adam and I struggled along, living our lives as best we could. I gave birth to a new child on average once every eighteen months. I spent decades either pregnant or nursing. Some years I had twins, twice even triplets. As I told Adam on more than one occasion, I certainly earned my name.

As the children grew older, they helped with the many tasks necessary for feeding and clothing ourselves. From the time they were five, the boys helped Adam while the girls helped me. Cain worked in the fields: he loved the smell of fresh, black dirt. Abel was drawn to the animals, acting as chief shepherd for our many flocks.

We introduced the children to the Lord God. Every time a baby was born, we built an altar, sacrificed an animal, and dedicated the baby to Adonai. Often at night we sat around a fire and told tales of life in The Garden. Abel's eyes shone brightly and he asked many detailed questions while Cain would just get moody. "Why did you have to eat that fruit?" he said, scowling, soon after his twelfth birthday.

I was so surprised that I began to cry.

Adam stopped talking and stared at his oldest son, then jumped up and grabbed him by the arm. "Don't you ever talk to your mother like that!" he warned, his voice low.

Cain shook himself loose and ran off into the darkness.

"Oh, Adam," I said. "Should you go after him?"

"He'll find his way back; don't worry," said my husband, staring pensively into the fire.

"But what if he gets hurt? The lions aren't friendly anymore (we had learned the hard way that the wild beasts were no longer our friends. A few frantic leaps into trees to narrowly escape sharp fangs had taught us quickly), and he's, well, uh, he's the messiah..." My voice trailed off because this was a sore subject with us.

"Stop it, Eve!" shouted Adam, suddenly furious. "Stop treating him like the messiah. You've ruined him!" He quickly rose and walked off.

Several of the children whimpered and cried at their father's harsh tones.

As for me, I went hot and cold at Adam's words. My heart beat violently, and I was too shocked to cry. Morosely, I stared into the flickering flames of the fire, momentarily ignoring my ever-growing brood of babies. For the first time in a long while, Adam slept somewhere else that night. It was the beginning of a wedge between us.

The children grew. By the time Cain reached twenty years of age and Abel nineteen, we had eighteen children. Besides the boys, there were two sets of twins (all girls), one set of triplets (boys), five other girls, and four more boys. It became glaringly obvious that the only way to find wives for our sons was to marry them off to their sisters. Cain chose our oldest daughter, Ana, while Abel took her twin, Naamah.

Ana was such a gentle spirit that I was concerned lest Cain overwhelm her with his intense personality. She looked so pale and troubled after the wedding night that I took her aside when no one was looking.

"Are you all right? Are you hurt?"

Her eyes filled with tears, and it took her a few moments before she could trust herself to speak. "I'm fine, Ema. It just wasn't the way you described. I guess I was a little shocked."

"Shocked? What do you mean, shocked? What happened?"

Ana shook her head. "It was more painful than I thought it would be. I think Cain needs to think of me more as a wife now and not like a sister."

I reached out to embrace my daughter when Cain suddenly appeared. His eyes narrowed dangerously when he saw me. "Ema! What are you doing with Ana?"

Hastily, I drew back. "Just talking, son. She's my little girl, after all."

Cain threw his arm around Ana and drew her close. "*Was* your little girl. She's a married woman now." They walked away, but not before I heard Cain tell Ana, "Let's go back to our tent and pick up where we left off this morning."

Helplessly, I stared after them.

Later on, when Adam came in from the fields, I drew him aside and shared my concerns about Cain's treatment of Ana.

"Are you so surprised, then?" my husband asked, eyebrows raised.

"What is that supposed to mean?" I countered.

Adam scratched his beard. "Just that he's always been a difficult, surly kid and you're the only one around here who hasn't seemed to notice."

"Well," I said, my voice cracking from emotion, "if it's so obvious that he's horrible, why didn't *you*, as his father, take control of the situation and fix him?"

"Who could get near him, with you protecting him like he was god incarnate?"

"Adam, that is so unfair!" I burst into tears.

Adam sighed, pulling me against his chest, absently playing with a lock of my long, multicolored hair. "Look, Eve, it's out of our hands now. He's grown up and married. Just pray for him."

I lifted a tear-streaked face to Adam. "Oh, I do pray for him," I said fervently. "I do!"

Abel and Naamah were a pair of lovebirds right from the start. Only a year apart in age, they had always been close friends, and marriage was a natural extension of that relationship. I tried to talk to Naamah after her wedding night in case she had any questions for me, but she merely blew me a kiss and cooed, "I don't think I need to talk to you, Ema. Everything is really wonderfully well."

Oh, okay. I should have been relieved that, unlike her twin, Naamah was content, but instead I felt suddenly unnecessary, cast aside. It was hard to watch my children turn into adults after so many years under my protection.

Both couples built their own homes but continued to work as they had. Cain rigged up a harness for oxen and plowed bigger and bigger swatches of land. Abel experienced a tremendous deal of satisfaction as he saw the flocks of sheep and goats continually expand. Quite regularly, Abel would take a choice lamb or kid and sacrifice it to the Lord God in thankfulness for God's hand of blessing on his life.

The two sisters, once very close, grew apart. "I can't understand it!" Naamah complained to me one day. We were at the river, doing wash, and it was a rare moment without anyone else around. "Ana acts weird around Abel and me. She keeps alluding to comments that she thinks Abel made which I *know* are entirely untrue."

"Do you tell her there's no way Abel said these things—whatever they are?"

Naamah nodded. "But she'll get all mysterious and say, 'Oh, but Cain told me....'" She plunged a shirt angrily into the muddy river water. "Really, Ema, it's upsetting."

"Well, what kind of things does she claim Abel says?"

Naamah looked embarrassed. "Oh," she said, blowing at a lock of hair that fell across her face. "You know, stuff."

Now I was really interested. "I don't know, Naamah. What do you mean by 'stuff'?"

"Like nasty sexual remarks about some of the girls. And you," she added, so softly I could barely hear her.

About me! "What about me?"

Naamah laid her hand on my arm. "I'm not even going to say the words, Ema, because they're too disgusting. I think that Cain is putting Ana up to this vicious *slander* of my husband. I'm furious with Cain!" She stomped her foot and glowered.

"Are you the only one Ana has talked to?"

Naamah shook her head. "She's been busy. I'm surprised neither you nor Abba have noticed anything before now."

Hmm. Now that Naamah mentions it, the older children had been acting somewhat strange lately. As my days were so full with babies, cooking, cleaning, laundry, sewing, etc., I hadn't bothered to interrogate them. Now I wished I had paid more attention.

"Are you sure?" I asked Naamah. "Are you absolutely certain the source of these lies is Cain?"

Naamah stared at me, her face reddening. "I can't believe you!" she exploded. "Abba is right! You just don't see how—" she fumbled for a word—"*evil* the wonderful Cain really is. You don't care about the rest of us. Just *him!*"

"Oh, Naamah, that's not true. I'm listening to you very carefully! I'm...." But it was too late. My daughter held her hands over her ears and ran off, leaving her laundry lying in a heap on the riverbank.

After she left, I stood there for a while, my ears ringing from her shrill accusation. If truth be told, I felt maligned and vastly underappreciated. I dropped my laundry down as well and took a furious walk in the opposite direction from home.

Twenty minutes later, I found myself on the edge of the wheat field. *Oh-oh.* There was Cain in the distance, behind the plowing oxen. My first instinct was to slip away before he noticed me, but then I thought, *Absolutely not!* Squaring my shoulders, I pushed forward to overtake him.

"Hello, son!" I called out a little too heartily.

Surprised, Cain looked up from the wooden yoke that joined him to the oxen. Sweat and dirt mingled on his young face and he looked weary. "Ema! What brings you out here? Is Ana all right?"

"Ana's just fine," I hastily assured him. By now he had stopped completely and the oxen pawed restlessly at the rich black earth, their muscles quivering under sleek brown hides.

"Then what do you want?"

He was so intense, combative. Why was he always so argumentative? His tone hardened my resolve.

"What I want," I said, hand on my hip, "is for you to explain to me why Ana is slandering Abel."

"Slandering Abel?" Innocently, his eyebrows shot up. "What did she say to you about Abel?"

"Well, not her exactly," I admitted. "Someone else came to me complaining about comments that defame your brother's character."

"So you didn't actually *hear* Ana say anything? How do you know she really did then?"

I looked at Cain, confused. He always had the ability to make me doubt myself. It was happening again, and I shook it off. I had to get to the bottom of this. "Look here, son," I said. "I want you to be straight with me. Are you saying anything about Abel?"

"What would I say, Ema?" Dramatically, Cain raised his hands in the air. "I love my brother, and I'm very concerned for him. Sometimes he says things that are shocking." Slowly, he turned his eyes from me. "It's best that you don't know what they are."

This was getting me nowhere. "You better not be causing trouble, Cain," I warned him, shaking my finger.

"Oh, I'm not Ema," he said sweetly, but his eyes were mocking.

Though Adonai's visits were less and less frequent, still, our children all knew him. Adam and I spoke of him every night, and we taught them how to pray and worship. We stressed the need to honor the Lord with sacrifice and offerings. "Whatever you put your hand to," said Adam, "Do with diligence as to the Lord. Present your first fruits to the Lord God because it is to him that we owe our very breath."

That same year, during the harvest season, Cain made an offering to the Lord of some of the new wheat, barley, olive oil, and grapes. He had Ana arrange the items very prettily on a stone altar. He even had his wife bake two loaves of bread from the wheat. He seemed very pleased with the arrangement until Adam took a closer look. Apparently, the wheat and barley were second gleanings, the olive oil dark, and the grapes stunted.

"What's this?" demanded Adam. "Why are you giving the Lord God second-best?"

"I am not," protested Cain angrily. "Look at the bread! It's beautiful."

"I'm not denying your wife's ability to bake," answered Adam. "But you're not giving Adonai the best." Cain, however, refused to listen.

Abel, on the other hand, took the choicest, most unblemished, fattest kids and lambs he could find and offered them up as a burnt offering to the Lord. He burned the fat portions in the fire, their fragrant aroma wafting up to heaven.

Adam checked on his second son and approved of Abel's offering. "God will be pleased," he told Abel.

Abel smiled, but his eyes were dark. It had been a tough few months. The rumors that had circulated about him, though most of us didn't believe them, nevertheless hung over him like a dark shadow. Both he and Naamah had lost their natural cheerfulness and were weighed down. Cain insisted that he had nothing to do with the talk.

As the animals were still on the altar, I saw three men in the distance. "It's the Lord!" I said excitedly, before racing off to get Adam.

Indeed, it was the Lord. When he approached our dwellings, Adam and I ran forward and flung ourselves in the grass at his feet. One by one, each of the children came forward and bowed down as well, some more enthusiastically than others.

After the Lord God greeted us, he specifically called for Abel. Tentatively, my son drew near, his head down, his countenance humble.

"Look up, Abel," I heard the Lord say. "I have seen your sorrow and forgiven your sin." He breathed in deeply the aromatic fragrance of the burning flesh on the altar. "I am well pleased with you." He kissed Abel, as a father would kiss his son.

When Abel lifted his head, his face, no longer burdened, positively glowed. "O Lord, you have given me hope! The arrogant mock me without restraint, but I do not turn from your law. In the night I remember your name, and I will keep your law."

They walked together then and spoke more, but I did not hear any of it. After the Lord dismissed Abel, he called for Cain. Smirking, Cain accompanied him to the altar where his offering lay, shriveled now in the hot sun.

"What is this, my son?" asked Adonai, waving his hand at the remains of bread, oil, grains, and grapes. "Is this your offering for me?"

Boldly, Cain glared at the Lord. "Yes," he stoutly affirmed.

"It is not acceptable." The Lord folded his arms against his chest and stood very tall, staring down at Cain until Cain looked down.

This was not what Cain expected to hear. He had seen the Lord's loving response toward Abel, and it filled him with wrath and indignation. His face grew red, and the cords of his neck bulged. He clenched and unclenched his fists but did not dare look at the Lord.

"Come, come, my son," said the Lord to Cain. "Why are you angry? Why is your face downcast? If you do what is right, will you not be accepted?" He looked meaningfully at Cain, who still refused to meet his eyes. "But," said the Lord, "if you do not do what is right, sin is crouching at your door; it desires to have you, but you must master it. Do not hate my instruction or cast my words behind you. Don't use your mouth for evil or harness your tongue to deceit. You have spoken continually against your brother and slandered your own mother's son. These things you have done and I kept silent; you thought I was altogether like you. But I am not."

He spoke other words to Cain as well, but Cain's back remained rigid, his head down.

Life improved after the Lord's visit. Abel and Naamah regained their youthful high spirits, and the pall of slander lifted from our homes. Cain seemed to soften as well, and sought out Abel with gestures of friendliness. My second son, bless his kind heart, took Cain's repentance at face value and was relieved at the apparent change of heart. Naamah, however, wasn't entirely convinced of Cain's motives.

60

"Watch him," she warned her husband. "I still don't trust him."

"Should I not love my own brother?" he rejoined.

One fateful day, Cain ran after Abel as the latter was leading his flock of sheep back home after a few days spent at a new grazing pasture. "Wait!" called Cain. Abel stayed where he was until Cain reached him.

"Yes, my brother? How can I help you?" graciously asked Abel.

"I would like your help," said Cain. "Will you come with me into the lentil fields now and give me your opinion on some new ideas I have as to crop rotation?"

Abel hesitated. He scratched his head. "I don't know," he said slowly. "The sheep..."

"The sheep will be fine," cut in Cain. "It'll only take a few minutes."

"*B'seder,*" agreed Abel, following Cain after a quick backward glance at his sheep, contentedly milling about.

When the boys—men!—were in the far corner of the lentil field, hidden under the leafy branches of an oak tree, Cain picked up a hefty-sized rock.

"What's the rock for?" asked Abel, still without suspicion.

"It's to kill you with, you miserable suck-up," taunted Cain, advancing menacingly.

"What are you talking about?" Alarmed, Abel stepped farther away from Cain.

"You know exactly what I'm talking about. Everyone thinks you're so wonderful and I'm so awful. Even the Lord prefers you. Well, he can have you! I'm sending you back."

"That's not true, Cain! Ema has always treated you as the special child. Your position as firstborn is unchallenged." In deliberate and measured tones, Abel spoke to his brother, attempting to calm him down. Cain would have none of it.

"Ema doesn't know what she believes," snarled Cain, still gripping the rock.

Suddenly, he rushed forward, attacking Abel by smashing the rock down on the top of his head. Blood spurted out, running down the sides of Abel's face and into his beard, where it dripped onto his chest and back.

Shocked and dazed, Abel reached up and felt his wounded head, staring with stunned surprise at the blood that now covered his hand. "Cain," he said hoarsely. "Don't do this! Don't..."

Crash! Again and again, Cain battered the rock against Abel's head until Abel slumped to the ground, motionless, his lifeblood seeping into the dirt.

Breathing hard, Cain looked this way and that. Then, seeing no one, he pulled Abel by the armpits and dragged him into the underbrush. He covered him up as best as he could and then went to the river and washed.

That night, sitting around the fire after the evening meal, Naamah grew increasingly uneasy. "I wonder where Abel is?" she announced to whomever would listen. "He should have been home by now."

"Don't worry. He's probably giving the sheep an opportunity to eat the wild flowers for an extra day," I said. "You know how he indulges them."

"Maybe," she said, unconvinced.

Just then Ana drew near the fire. "Mind if I join you?" she asked.

"Of course not, honey." I smiled.

"Hello, Ana," said Naamah.

"Hello, Naamah."

The twins studied each other. "Why aren't you with Cain?" Naamah asked.

Ana pushed a pebble into the dirt with her toe. "He's really moody tonight," she allowed. "I thought it best to leave him alone."

"Do you know if he's seen Abel?"

"I have no idea."

"Will you ask him?"

"Uh...I'd rather not," said Ana. "Not when he's like this."

Naamah swung around and looked at me. "How about you, Ema? Will you ask him?"

"Maybe we should wait until morning..."

"Ask who what?" said a deep reassuring voice from out of the darkness.

"Abba!" shouted Naamah joyously.

"Adam!" I said, relieved he was back from his after-dinner chores.

"Shalom, Abba," allowed Ana.

Several of the younger children poked their heads up from various evening activities when they heard their father's voice such that when Adam reached us, the flickering light of the fire revealed five kids— four boys and one girl—hanging off him at various junctures.

Naamah jumped up and pushed three of her brothers off her father so she could slip her arms around his waist. "Ask Cain if he's seen Abel. Please, Abba, please!"

Adam gazed down at the sweet face of his daughter. "Why, *beeti*? What's wrong?"

"Maybe nothing. It's just that Abel never came home, and I'm worried."

Thoughtfully, Adam wriggled his shoulders and dislodged two more children off his back. "*B'seder.* I'll be right back."

It didn't take long before he returned. "Cain hasn't seen him," he announced, his voice a little strained. He sat beside me, his shoulder touching mine. I reached out and rubbed the tense muscles knotted at the base of his neck. Together we watched as the fire died down, its glowing embers shrinking against the black night sky.

Five days passed, slow, fretful, excruciating days with no sign of Abel. Naamah grew more and more distraught, wavering between hope and fear. By the third day, we called on the Lord, asking for his help. On the fifth day, he showed up.

"Adonai!" Naamah saw him first, as she spent most of every day gazing off into the distance, scanning the horizon for her husband. Quick as a gazelle, she flew to him, and he held her tightly. When he let her go, she slumped to the ground, stricken.

Before any of the rest of us could approach him, the Lord God strode off to Cain's tent, where he and Ana were eating their midday meal.

Surprised, Ana bowed to the ground at the sight of the Lord God, but Cain merely rose from his chair. "My Lord," he said, eying the Lord warily.

Then the Lord said to Cain, "Where is your brother Abel?"

Fear caused Cain to tremble, but he stoutly replied, "I don't know. Am I my brother's keeper?"

The Lord said, "What have you done? Listen! Your brother's blood cries out to me from the ground! Now you are under a curse and driven from the ground, which opened its mouth to receive your brother's blood from your hand. When you work the ground, it will no longer yield its crops for you. You will be a restless wanderer on the earth."

From her place on the ground, Ana moaned as news of her husband's crime and sentence reached her despondent ears. Cain sobbed as well, his face crumbling into tears of self-pity.

"My punishment is more than I can bear!" he exclaimed, throwing himself at the Lord's feet. "Please don't let it happen. Please! Today you are driving me from the land, and I will be hidden from your presence. I will be a restless wanderer on the earth, and whoever finds me will kill me."

The Lord God looked at Cain, and compassion aroused within him—compassion for this son of man who had given himself over to grievous sin. "Not so," he said, lightly touching Cain's shoulder. "Not so. If anyone kills you he will suffer vengeance seven times over." Then the Lord pressed his finger into the middle of Cain's forehead, leaving a discernible, round indentation.

By now, everyone had seen the Lord's appearance and was gathered around Naamah. It was abundantly clear that something horrible had happened to Abel and that Cain was responsible. It was without surprise when Adonai led a chastened Cain and a wailing Ana to the middle of the camp.

"A terrible thing has occurred," the Lord God informed us, his eyes resting on each of us, in turn. "Tell them, Cain."

Head bowed, all sullenness gone, Cain whispered something.

"What?" shouted Jared, my ten-year-old. "I can't hear him!"

"Speak louder, Cain," ordered the Lord.

Cain lifted his head, and it was with shock that I saw his red eyes and puffy face and that strange mark on his brow. "I said, I killed Abel."

Killed? Like the animals? No human had ever died...we weren't even sure if it would really happen. Maybe the Messiah would return first. But not now....

"*Aaaaahhhh!*" I heard a horrible scream, then realized it was coming out of my mouth. My screams mingled with those of Ana's and several of the other girls.

Naamah was strangely quiet, but suddenly she threw herself at Cain and beat at him with her fists, crying, "You murderer, you murderer!" again and again. Cain just stood there, meekly allowing the barrage. Adam pried her away, and she fell against her father's neck, sobbing uncontrollably.

When the cacophony died down, the Lord God explained to us his punishment for Cain, pointing out the mark on his forehead.

"When will he leave?" asked Adam quietly, his eyes shrouded with a pain too deep for me to bear.

"Immediately," answered the Lord God.

"Will Ana go with him?" further asked Adam.

The Lord God turned to Ana, hunched on the ground, her face streaked with tears, her hair wildly askew about her face. "Will you? It's your choice."

Ana looked around at the circle of faces, some weeping, some stony, some perplexed. Then she looked over at Cain, at his hungry, pleading eyes, at his crushed spirit.

"I'll go with him," she whispered.

Cain heaved a visible sigh of relief as he realized that he was not to go off into the wilderness alone.

"It's a good decision," affirmed the Lord. "Now go and pack your things. I will be waiting to take you from this place."

How can I describe what those next weeks and months were like? The last embers of hope that we would be redeemed from our fallen state of sin were thoroughly crushed from my spirit. I had been so sure that Cain was the redeemer who would vanquish the serpent, and then, if not Cain, definitely Abel! Now Abel was no more and Cain as good as dead. I grieved for many, many days.

Even worse than the grief—were that possible—was my estrangement from Adam. He avoided me, sleeping in a separate dwelling. When I tried to speak to him, he stood, frowning, arms folded against his chest, his normally pleasant features hard and unyielding. I began to understand more fully those words uttered by Adonai when we left The Garden: "Your desire will be for your husband and he will rule over you." I desired him all right, but he wanted no part of me. As dreary day replaced dreary day, my shoulders slumped and my eyes grew dull. I cried out to the Lord God at night, alone in my bed. I threw myself down on the ground, repenting of all my wickedness and pleading for a return of my husband's love, before returning to the bed I shared with my newest baby but not my husband.

About six months after Cain and Ana left, Adam sought me out. I was washing clothes down at the river, and my stomach contracted when his shadow fell across my path.

"How long have you been standing there?" I exclaimed, looking up from my crouching position, hugging a wet shirt to my chest.

Adam knelt beside me. "Eve," he said, his voice kinder than in many moons.

Immediately, tears pricked at my eyelids. "Don't," I said, shaking my head, afraid of what he might say. No more rejection, please!

But Adam didn't reject me. Instead he cupped my face in his strong, calloused hand and looked into my eyes. "I'm sorry," he said hoarsely. "I'm sorry I've refused to forgive you. I love you."

"Oh, Adam!" The tears ran freely, and he held me while I cried.

Six

The years after that fell into a pleasant routine. Adam moved back into my dwelling and lay with me. I gave birth to boy twins that next year, and to a girl the year after that. The rays of the sun were tempered by the waters above the sky, so we aged slowly, imperceptibly. As our older children reached marrying age, they paired off. Soon we discovered the joys of being grandparents.

Naamah grieved for over a year, then married her younger brother, Joab. She gave birth to a strong, handsome, black-haired son, and found solace after Abel's death. She seemed like one of the girls again, happy and laughing as she went about her daily chores. Every so often, though, she and I would catch each other's gaze and the pain would rush back into her eyes.

We heard from the Lord God that Cain and Ana had a baby, whom they named Enoch. Far to the east of us, in the land of Nod, Cain threw his restless energies into building a city, which he named for his firstborn son. I longed to see the baby, but Adam said no. "Leave them alone," he warned. "Don't interfere with the Lord's discipline."

I continued to have babies, but now they were spaced four years apart, soon five, then six. When I had given birth to 39 children, I ceased to become pregnant. Initially, I was relieved, but after six years when Jared, my youngest, grew staggeringly independent, I wasn't so sure. I found that I missed nuzzling a sweet nursing infant, missed the feel of tiny arms and legs wrapped lovingly around me in adoration and dependence.

"Do you think the Lord God will bless us with another child?" I asked Adam. We were snuggling in bed at the end of a long day.

"Do you want another?" he responded, stroking my arm. "I'm enjoying having our bed all to ourselves."

"You named me 'Eve,'" I said. "Do you think there are more 'living'

I'm to be mother of, or are we through?"

"I'm not sure," said Adam. "Why would we need another?"

"Well," I said, my voice squeaking from nervousness as I delved into a topic that still caused Adam to flare with annoyance, if not downright anger. "You know how I thought that maybe Cain was the promised messiah, or if not Cain, Abel?"

"Uh," came the expected response.

I rushed on. "I don't really see which of our sons would fit that description, do you? None of them seems to have the heart to worship Adonai that Abel had."

Were it not for the warmth of Adam's body, so near mine, and the barely discernible sounds of his breathing, I would be hard-pressed to know he was present in the inky blackness of our bed, he was so still.

"Adam?"

"Look, Eve," he said, his voice irritated. "Don't pull me into this messiah stuff anymore, all right? Take this to the Lord God and wait on him for an answer." He turned on his side and, presumably, went to sleep.

I did what Adam suggested. I prayed and asked the Lord God if I was done having children. *Prayer and patience* were the words that came back to me, again and again.

Sixty years passed. I had all but forgotten about ever giving birth again. By now, our children had married and given birth, and *those* babies had grown up, married, and given birth, and *those* babies had grown up, married, and given birth, and *those* babies had grown up, married and given birth, such that the fabric of my life was rich and vibrant with the generations. In approximately 115 years, Adam and I had succeeded in populating the earth with thousands of people! Even Cain, banished to the east, had grown and multiplied.

I was now 120 years old, but still looked lovely. No longer young, true, but not old either. Adam, at 130, had some gray in his hair, and a few lines around the corners of his eyes, but from a distance he could have been a man of forty. I found him as intensely attractive as the first time I saw him. I hoped he felt the same about me. I wasn't always sure.

Our visitations from Adonai dwindled to almost never. I spoke to him via prayer, and often felt a strong sense of his presence, but the days when I jumped into his arms, or walked hand-in-hand with him were a distant, bittersweet memory. Thus, it came as a shock one early summer morning while I was berry picking to find the Lord God waiting for me.

"My Lord!" I whispered, dropping my basket, blackberries scattering in all directions. I fell at his feet, with my face to the ground.

The Lord God walked over to me and placed his hand on my head. The glory and warmth of his presence enveloped me like a golden fog. I closed my eyes, dizzy with happiness.

"You and Adam will bring forth a male child by this time next year," he told me. "It is he through whom the messianic line will flow."

I don't know how long I lay there, but eventually I realized that the quality of the air had returned to normal. Light was only light again, and not filtered gold. The buzzing of bees intruded on my consciousness. The glory of the Lord had departed.

Distracted for the rest of the day, I was basically useless at my tasks. It was too soon to speak of my encounter with the Lord, so I kept silent. It wasn't until late that evening that I even remembered the words he had spoken to me. I had been lying in bed, almost asleep, but now my eyes snapped open and my brain went into a fit of feverish activity. *Adam! I must tell Adam.*

Arising from bed, I felt for my robe and slipped it on in the dark, tying it firmly around my waist. Then I crept noiselessly to Adam's baked-mud brick shelter, which was next door to mine. Adam had developed a tendency to snore after he turned 100, so often chose to sleep alone. I told him it wasn't necessary but he insisted. I missed cuddling with him but it *was* quieter. Ah, well.

"Adam?" I whispered loudly, before pushing my way through the door. "Are you awake?" The only response was a long, shuddering snore. Unperturbed, I made my way to the bed, careful not to bang my knees into anything. When I got there, I shook him, hard. "Wake up!"

"Huh...what? Who's there!" Groggily, Adam threw himself into a sitting position, fists raised.

"It's me, Adam. It's me!" I hastily assured him.

"Eve? What are you doing here? Is something wrong?"

"No." I lifted the covers and joined him in the bed, throwing my left arm across his chest and draping my left leg over his leg. "Mmm," I cooed. "You're nice and warm."

"And you're cold. Why are you waking me up?" He sounded grumpy.

"I had a fantastic visitation from Adonai this morning."

"What!? You did? How come you didn't say anything?"

"I couldn't say anything yet. You know how it is, when you see him."

Adam didn't respond, but I could tell that he nodded. Yes, he understood what it was like to encounter God, and then to be separated. He knew.

"He spoke to me, and I only just now remembered what he said."

"Yes...?"

"Well," I hesitated, suddenly shy. Even though we had parented 39 children together, it had been 60 years, and our level of intimacy had seriously dropped.

"Well, what did he say?"

"He said we were going to have another child. A son."

I heard Adam's sharp intake of breath. "Eve, you haven't bled in years."

This was true. I no longer had my monthly flow, so necessary for childbearing.

"That's not all he said, Adam. He also said that the messianic line would flow through this child."

"This is amazing." Adam propped himself up on his elbow, thoroughly awake now. "Did he say anything else? Like, how this would happen?"

"Oh, I assume it will happen the usual way." My voice sounded tentative and girlish to my ears.

Adam snorted. "I mean did he say anything about your age?"

My age? I felt offended. "I'm younger than you," I said huffily.

"Neither of us are twenty," said Adam unnecessarily.

"Adam, he made me from one of your ribs! He can do anything!"

There was silence for a long time. Then, "Yes, you're right. Forgive my skepticism." He shifted, stretching his arms and shoulders such that I heard little *pops* from his bones.

70

I had an awful thought. "You believe me, don't you, Adam? You don't think that I'm...?"

"Oh, no, Eve. Of course I believe you! Come here." He held me tight against his chest and prayed aloud. "O Lord God, forgive me for my unbelief! I come before you tonight with the woman you gave me and we offer you praise. We thank you for all your mercies and loving kindness to us these many years we have dwelt on this earth. We thank you for the exciting words you had for Eve today, and ask that they be accomplished according to your great purposes. Protect and bless this baby both as he grows in the womb, and as he grows once he's born. Give us wisdom as parents so that he will fulfill all that you place before him. Amen."

"Amen," I said.

Adam moved back into my dwelling and lay with me regularly for the next few months. In faith, we believed that the pregnancy would come to pass as the Lord had said, despite my advanced age. I didn't have the normal clue of a missed period to alert me to pregnancy, but soon enough the rest of the symptoms manifested. I grew nauseous, my breasts became fuller, my belly rounder. After the nausea passed, I experienced an incredible sense of well-being, such that many of my children and grandchildren noticed and remarked:

"Ema! You seem so different lately. What's changed?"

At four months pregnant, Adam and I shared our news.

"What?" came the shocked responses. "But you're so old!"

Old? What exactly defined "old?" Sure, we were older than everyone else, but Adonai was Ancient of Days beyond reasoning or calculation. In contrast, we had just been created (or born).

When the time came for me to give birth, I was attended by two of my daughters, Tirzah and Tamar. I called for them when the first hard contraction came and twisted deep in my belly with stabbing pain. Though I had been through labor and delivery countless times, it was not something I could do nonchalantly. It remained a very intense, stressful, all-encompassing experience that used every last bit of my strength and mental fortitude. Frequently, I called out to the Lord for help as I struggled to birth the babies. Having helped at hundreds of births in addition to my own, I repented again and again for the curse that my sin in eating the forbidden fruit brought down on the heads of my daughters. What would labor have been like if it went according to God's original plan? We won't know until Messiah comes.

This particular birth was no easier than the others. Fortunately, it was no harder, either. After five hours, the baby's head crowned. "Dark hair!" yelled Tirzah.

Seven intense pushes and the baby's head was forced out, followed by the narrow, slippery body. "Boy!" announced Tamar triumphantly.

Quickly they cut the umbilical cord, cleaned him off, and handed him to me. I lay in bed, holding the sweet little body, and watched as he found my breast for the first time. We fell asleep together, and when I awoke, I was startled to find Adam sitting next to the bed, gazing at us.

"It's a boy," I whispered.

"Yes," he said, "I know."

"He's beautiful, isn't he?" I propped myself up and shifted the baby from his sleeping position on my chest so that we could both see his features more clearly. He really *was* a particularly pleasing child. So sweet, so innocent...*Oh!* Suddenly, I heard the Lord God speak to me. Deep in my spirit, I heard him say that *this* was the child of promise, *this* was the child who would grow to fulfill all that Abel did not.

"What is it?" asked Adam, aware of my every nuance.

"I just heard Adonai speak. This is the child he has granted me in place of Abel, since Cain killed him."

Adam glanced from me to the child and back. "Yes," he said slowly, nodding. "I confirm that."

We stared at the baby some more, entranced by his full little cheeks, dark hair, tiny features, soft body. Mostly though, we both sensed God's strong hand on this child. It was good to be in agreement. I sighed happily.

Adam looked up. "What should we name him?"

Hmm. I thought about my years of pinning false hopes on Cain, and the devastation that came when Abel was no more. I thought about the goodness of the Lord, and how he brings about our deepest desires even after we've caused heartache through our own sin. "How about 'Shet'?" I suggested, "since God has granted us this special child, and put him in our arms."

"Shet," said Adam. He smiled, tenderness causing light to shine from his eyes. "Yes, that's right. Shet it is."

Satisfied and pleased, we clasped hands as we continued to watch our newest baby.

Adam and I experienced a renewing of our love for each other during the three years in which I nursed Shet. He slept with me in my bed and drew great joy from this new baby. For my part, I could feel God's anointing on Shet and was satisfied in my spirit that this was the child of promise. No longer young and starry-eyed, I didn't know if the Messiah was going to come in my lifetime, or in the generation to follow. It was out of my control, and I rested easier once I accepted that.

Shet was an adorable little boy, with silky brown curls, warm brown eyes, olive-toned skin, dimples, and an irrepressible grin. He loved loud noises, and would have stuck his head in the mouth of a lion, had we let him. "No! Stay away!" I scolded when I saw how his little head spun around after hearing a roar in the distance. "They were nice in The Garden, but no longer!" He had a gentleness of spirit, and seemed more like Adam than any of the other children, even Abel.

After Shet was weaned, Adam went back to living in his own dwelling. Shet generally slept in a section of my hut, but he also spent many nights with his father. How I adored that sweet boy!

As Shet grew, Adam and I drifted apart. We still loved each other, and we spent time with each other, but the passionate side of our romance sputtered and dwindled. So it shouldn't have come as a surprise to me when my husband took another wife, but it did. Especially since it was one of my great-granddaughters with whom I had a particularly close bond.

"You're doing what?" I couldn't believe what I was hearing. Adam and I sat across a table from one another, and Maya, my great granddaughter, cowered at Adam's side.

"I'm taking another wife, Eve," remarked Adam calmly. He placed his hand on Maya's arm. "I believe that I'm supposed to keep fathering children. I think Shet is our last child together."

"Have you prayed about this?" I forced myself to speak quietly, but the blood was pounding inside my head so furiously I felt faint.

"Yes."

"And..?"

"And I feel okay about it." Adam tightened his grip on a squirming Maya, who seemed desperate to flee.

"Let go of that poor girl, Adam. It's obvious you've forced her into this."

Adam glared at me. "Look, Eve, you can believe me or not, but Maya has agreed to be my wife so don't cause trouble." He looked down at the frightened girl. "Haven't you, Maya?"

"Yes," she whispered, in such a soft voice that I could barely hear her over the roaring of my own ears.

"What?" I snapped.

Maya looked up, and her rich, brown eyes swam with tears. "I'm sorry, Savta," she said, shame coloring her face bright pink. "I did agree."

I looked at the poor girl, and my heart contracted. "You can change your mind."

"Eve," threatened Adam.

Maya shook her head. "No, I'm not going to change my mind. I'm sorry." She turned her head then, unable to meet my eyes.

Abruptly, I stood up. "All right, Adam. I see how it is." One long lock of multi-colored hair had escaped the tight bun I tied it into these days and hung such that it obstructed my vision. Dully, I stared at it, and not at the two people across from me. The many-hued colors shifted before my eyes as tears threatened to overflow. "I'll talk to you later." I spun on my heel and left.

Dimly, I thought I heard my name called, but I didn't turn around. It was only when I reached my own dwelling, and safely locked myself in, that I was able to release my emotions and cry.

74

I wish I could say that eventually things improved with Adam, but we never regained our closeness. Maya bore him twenty children, and then when she grew old, he took another wife, who bore him eighteen children, and then he took another wife, who bore him twelve children, and still another, who bore him fifteen, and on and on. He continued to father children until he reached the age of 500. I, on the other hand, never knew another man.

While Shet was still growing up, our cluster of mud and straw-baked brick huts grew and expanded. Very often—all too often—young married couples struck off on their own, eager to explore the earth. We heard of new settlements far from us in every direction—north, east, south and west. One of my grandsons who was a shepherd designed a tent made of goat's hair, which was easy to pack on a camel or donkey and take on a journey. Though there were hundreds of families in my bustling village, I still felt lonely and deserted when children left, perhaps never to be encountered again by me.

I'll say this for Adam: he never abandoned me and moved somewhere else. He always acknowledged my status as his first and primary wife, and paid me honor before others. But he no longer lay with me like a man does with his wife. I thought at first it was a temporary thing, but alas it never changed.

This isn't to say that my days were spent mooning like a lovestruck calf, depressed and restless. I had plenty to do! I cooked, I cleaned, I sewed, and I gardened. I made music, I told stories, I taught, I admonished. I helped with childbirth, doctored the ailing, and spent time in prayer with the Lord God. My days were full, and at night I usually dropped swiftly into a dreamless sleep. But I ached deep inside for what I once had and now was lost to me forever. I ached for The Garden.

Sometimes I dreamt of it: Adam and I galloping on our horses across the grass-strewn plains, wind in our hair, laughter carrying our breath away. The clipping of the horses' hooves throwing up clods of mud as we drew nearer to the river, the early-summer smell of new grass and flowering fruit, the murmuring of the river current as it flowed ever southwards drowned my senses in luxury. I would awaken to my dark tent, perhaps the first pale fingers of dawn lacing the sky, remembering my sin, and how that world was no more. My heart would ache until it felt near to bursting from sorrow. Then I would understand Adam better and humbly accept the Lord's admonition, along with his great mercy.

I became a master storyteller. I spoke of The Garden, and the early days just after when almost no one walked the face of the earth. I spoke of the Lord God, and of the great angels. I even told of Cain, and Abel, and what had occurred there. Immensely popular, young children and adults alike continually encouraged me to share at evening campfires, during tasks like laundry or grain-grinding, or simply while walking from here to there.

I spoke most often of the Lord God. I could tell who was more drawn to him by which stories appealed and the questions asked. It was distressing to see how few hearts actually sought out communion with God. Most seemed content to work, sleep, and seek after pleasure. Very few saw the Lord God as the purpose for existence on this lush and fertile land.

My darling Shet was one of the exceptions. Again and again, he questioned me as to what the Lord God looked like, sounded like, seemed like. "How can I see God face-to-face, Ema?" he asked, his young face gazing at me intently.

I taught him the best I could. Though I knew God had forgiven me for listening to the serpent, I still reaped the consequences of that regrettable action. I had not seen a physical manifestation of the Lord since before Shet was born.

Others were interested in my more spiritual stories, but not necessarily because their hearts were drawn to knowing God. A certain group clamored to hear of the angels, but showed no interest in God himself. One girl in particular was Remah.

Twelve years old, already womanly, with long, black hair that rippled like a waterfall and smoldering black eyes, Remah was quite beautiful. Always, though, something about her repelled me. She didn't seem...*clean*. From the time she was a young child, she seemed overtly sexual, more so than any of the others. I did my best to gently correct her, and spoke to her mother about my concerns, but the behavioral changes remained short-lived. Now Remah was approaching an age where she would soon marry and be beyond my influence.

One day, when I was relaxing beneath a terebinth tree, quietly praying and watching the sun slowly sink below the horizon, Remah suddenly appeared, breathless and flushed pink.

"Oh, hello, Savta!" she said, startled to see me. Blowing me a kiss, she began walking quickly away.

"Remah!" I called, my tone sharp and imperial.

Reluctantly, she slowed down and turned her head toward me. "Yes?"

"Where have you been?"

"Uh, nowhere special, Savta."

I didn't believe that. "Come and sit next to me, sweetheart."

She shook her head. "I'm hungry. I'm gonna get something to eat."

"No. Come here now," I commanded.

Sighing dramatically, Remah forced her way over to me and flopped down on the ground. "What?" she asked, not meeting my eyes.

"You've been up to something, and I want you to tell me what."

For several moments there was silence. I heard the birds calling shrilly to one another from the trees, and the crickets as they got ready for the evening. I also heard the soft sounds of Remah's breath. "It's nothing, really." She hesitated. "It's just that I, well, I met someone."

"You met someone? Who?"

Now that Remah had been forced to confide in me, she became eager to talk. "One of your angels, Savta! One of the angels you told me about from The Garden!"

One of the angels? My heart leaped at the thought of seeing one of my dear friends again. Trying to keep my voice steady, I said, "Who? Michael? Gabriel?"

"No, no," she said, waving her hand. "A different one. His name is Abaddon."

"Abaddon? I've never heard of an Abaddon! Describe him to me."

Remah clapped her hands together and her dark eyes shone. "Oh, he's the most beautiful man I've ever seen! He's tall, and muscular. His hair is as black as mine, and he wears it long and tied back. His features are perfect. His voice is deep and powerful. He's the most manly man I've ever seen. And he loves me!" she finished triumphantly.

"He loves you? He's said intimate words?"

Remah bent her head such that her hair fell in one long silky curtain over her shoulder. "Don't tell Ema! She won't understand."

"Remah," I said, trying to keep my voice light so as not to frighten the girl into silence, "tell Savta. Did you lie with him?"

"Don't tell Ema," she said again, her voice low.

"How many times?" I asked, my heart beating furiously, my stomach hollow.

"I don't know. A lot."

"Oh, Remah!" I clasped the girl to my bosom and held her tight, tears seeping out of the corners of my eyes. This was my fault! Another consequence of the fall from grace! Remah, however, didn't seem nearly as upset as me. After suffering my embrace for several moments, she squirmed and pulled away.

"Really, Savta, it's not that bad," she protested. "Abaddon loves me, and I love him. It's a beautiful thing."

"Honey, I've never heard of this Abaddon before. Don't do things in secret. Let him come into the community and meet us."

Remah hesitated. "I'll try, Savta. He doesn't seem to want to do that." She started to leave, so I stood up and grasped her hand.

"One week," I said firmly. "He has one week to show himself to us before I tell your parents!"

Remah glared at me, our bonding time clearly over. "I'll see what I can do," she said, pulling her hand away and running off without a backward glance.

Sighing, I went back to my hut and knelt on my knees before my bed, asking Adonai what to do about this situation. As I prayed, I saw mists of swirling darkness, and I grew afraid. I knew I needed to confide in Adam what I had learned this evening.

Adam stared at me, surprise widening his eyes. "Surely you misunderstood the child! No angel would have sexual relations with a human."

Vehemently, I shook my head. "I did not misunderstand her. What really frightens me is the secrecy and bizarre behavior of this Abaddon. What do you think is going on?"

"I don't know, Eve. I've never heard of anything like this. I'll gather together several of the men and we'll see if we can track him down. Sound good?"

"Yes, only..." I laid my hand on his arm.

"Only what?"

"Be careful."

We weren't able to find Abaddon. Additionally, whenever Adam or I prayed to the Lord God about him, we both felt a tremendous sense of danger. Before the week expired, not only Remah's parents but the whole community knew about Abaddon. Remah was furious with me.

"I can't believe you told everyone, Savta!" she exploded. "You didn't even wait to see if he would come here like you said!"

I tried to reason with her. "I'm sorry, *beeti*. This is really for your own good. You've gotten involved in something much too powerful for you. It's not safe." I tried to stroke her beautiful hair, but she angrily whirled around, eluding my touch, and escaped to her own hut.

Of course, the inevitable happened. Remah was found to be with child. The poor girl grew bigger and bigger until she was so huge I thought surely she would burst. When the labor pains came upon her, I went to help. With my vast experience of midwifery, I still was unprepared for the violence and sheer terror of that particular childbirth. The screams, blood, clawing pain, agony, wrenched my gut. When the horrible time of labor finally, mercifully, ended, the young mother was unconscious but still alive. I held in my arms the most unusual baby I had ever seen—a boy the size of a two-month old and not a newborn. The level of alertness and the look of cunning intelligence in his eyes was downright chilling. It occurred to me that we should put him to death.

Adam agreed. "This child is evil," he pronounced. Others disagreed. Leaving the baby in the arms of his exhausted mother, with Almah, Remah's aunt, to watch them, Adam and I called a council meeting involving Remah's parents and several of the leaders of the community. We argued and debated for hours. Finally, we decided that it would ultimately be best to destroy the child. Wrenched with emotion, we returned to Remah's hut. When we entered the dark, cramped space, we found...an empty bed and a snoring caregiver.

"Almah! Almah! Wake up!" I shook the sleeping woman, hard.

"Huh? Huh?" Drowsily, she opened her eyes, bewilderedly focusing on my face. "Savta?" she mumbled.

"Almah's been drugged!" I announced angrily. Meanwhile, a search went out for Remah and her baby. Two weeks the men searched for them but found nothing. It was as if they had vanished into thin air.

I wish I could say that this was the only incident, but alas it was not. Several young girls were pulled into sexual encounters with dark angels over the years. All of them gave birth to unusual children. All of them disappeared from the community, never to be seen again.

Eighteen years after the incident with Remah, we heard tales of a young warrior hero in the east. Descendants of Cain reported encounters with a man seven feet tall, empowered with superhuman strength. This man was said to be fantastically good-looking, but without any sense of good or morality. He had arisen from the desert wilderness, his dark ringlets pulled back from his face and tied with a piece of rawhide. He laughed at conventional weapons and carried a spear like a weaver's shaft. Women swooned while men blanched. He had quickly taken control of an entire city and was proceeding to build an empire.

Remah's baby, thought I, upon hearing this tale. The spawn of a woman and a dark angel. I shuddered, appalled at the growing tide of evil in this fallen world.

As the years passed, stories of other similar men arose. They were the super heroes, men of renown: the stuff of legends.

(Many, many years later, an extremely old woman was discovered living alone in a cave. Her knotted gray hair hung down below her waist, her face was deeply lined and puckered, her teeth were missing, her hands were gnarled. She existed in a state of abject fear and when faced by her surprised discoverers, she screamed wildly and attempted to flee. They tried to assure her that they meant no harm, but her mind was too far gone to comprehend the truth of their statements. A heart attack overtook the poor woman who, as she lay dying, beseeched Adonai to "have mercy on poor Remah.")

As the demon seed was scattered throughout the earth, and as the products of these unions (always male) went on to impregnate women, humankind grew more and more corrupt. Beginning with my original sin, and proceeding to Cain's murder of Abel, each successive generation grew worse. Once the dark angels found a path to us, the wickedness multiplied exponentially. Sexual sin and violence fiercely competed for the sheer number of wicked acts. Babies were treated with greater and greater contempt, until finally someone hit on the horrifying idea of passing the occasional one through the fire so as to bring greater favor from "the gods." The only God I know of is the one true God, and he despises such things. I can only surmise that the gods these poor deluded souls sacrificed to were demons straight from the pit of hell.

To some extent, we prospered. Cities were built, farming methods advanced, herds of cattle enlarged. Dyes were discovered, and articles of clothing grew much more elaborate. When I think back to my attempt to cover myself and Adam by stitching fig leaves together, I have to laugh (or cry). Now we had all manner and colors of robes, dresses, cloaks, undergarments, sandals, headpieces, jewelry, makeup. Food quality had improved, and most years there was an overabundance of harvest such that we were able to keep some aside for the following year. Famines were few and far between. The Lord God was exceedingly gracious.

Adam and I never went much further than one hundred miles from the boundaries of The Garden, but such was not the case with many of our descendants, who traveled far and wide in all directions. We heard tales of journeys to exceedingly distant lands, where the climate and type of wild animals changed greatly from what we knew in our area.

Learning expanded. The writing, painting, and music that Adam and I had created in The Garden went far beyond our wildest dreams. Others took these ideas and progressed with them in ways that astounded us. Cain's great-great-great-great grandson, Yuval, invented the harp and the flute. I take great joy in the haunting melodic notes of the flute. And the harp! So many incredible worship songs have been written on the strings of that anointed instrument. Yuval's brother, Tuval-Cain, proved to be quite talented at forging all sorts of new and useful tools out of bronze and iron. And on and on.

Some days I saw such promise in my children that I wept with relief at the possibilities. Other days, the new levels of debauchery, sullenness, blasphemy, and complete disinterest in God drove me to distraction. Disease and pestilence came upon the earth, and each successive generation, though we lived long, weakened in health. Bugs invaded our living quarters, bore into our mattresses, danced on our heads. Rats and mice sniffed at our garbage and competed with us for the stored grain from our harvests. Wild animals threatened our very lives if we encountered them unarmed.

I sought the Lord as to my role in this life and he told me to tell of his righteousness, of his salvation all day long. "Proclaim my mighty acts and declare my marvelous deeds," he said. "Declare my power to the next generation and my might to all who are to come!"

"Yes," I responded. "Though I am old and gray, and my troubles are many and bitter, you will yet restore my life. From the depths of the earth you will again bring me up. You will increase my honor and comfort me once again."

So this is what I do, day in and day out. I speak of him to all who listen, grateful that each day brings new opportunities to encourage one of my children to love him. But I long—O how I long!—for that day when he will close my eyes one final time and I will open them in Paradise. And this time, I will stay with him forever.

THOSE WERE THE LAST WORDS EVE WROTE.

When she died, a huge fire was made in her honor, and the first man, Adam, wept. Thousands of her descendants gathered to pay homage, and for seven days they sat on the ground and shared about how she had touched their lives. She was buried in a cave hewn into the side of a hill, overlooking a fertile valley.

Adam outlived Eve by another hundred years. He died fifty-six years before the birth of Lamech, the father of Noah. He was buried in the cave alongside his first wife, Eve. Seven hundred and twenty-six years after Adam's death, the wickedness and evil on the earth had reached such a putrid state that the Lord God punctured the waters above the sky and sent a *mabul*, a Great Flood, which wiped out everything—man, animal, bird, reptile—except for Noah, his wife, his three sons and their wives, and two of every living thing (seven if they were "clean").

Always, the great enemy of man, that fallen angel now known as HaSatan, tried to destroy the messianic line and so escape the curse of destruction that the Lord God had uttered in The Garden. As Adam's line went through Shet, then Noah, it proceeded to Abraham, then King David until reaching Yeshua the Messiah. The wrath of Pharaoh, the diabolical plot of Haman, the scourge of Antiochus Ephiphanes—all were attempts to wipe out the Jewish people before Messiah's birth.

When the enemy failed, he still sought to devour the Jewish people so as to thwart the Second Coming of Yeshua. Scripture clearly teaches that there must be a distinct Jewish people to say *Baruch haba b'shem Adonai* (blessed is He who comes in the name of Adonai) before Messiah returns. The turning of the Church from its Jewish roots at the Council of Nicea in 325 AD, the Spanish Inquisition in 1492, the Russian and Polish pogroms in the nineteenth century, the murder of the six million in the Shoah (Holocaust), are but a few examples of the raging anti-Semitism the enemy has used to incite the world against the Jews.

More than anything, the enemy seeks to keep the Jewish people from a knowledge of their Jewish Messiah. Yet through the millennia, through the centuries, a remnant of Adam's sons and Eve's daughters have acknowledged His Name. And so the story continues, at another time in history when the Jewish people had little hope, but the Great Plan was still at work....

PART THREE

Berlin
1938

Seven

The woman sank onto the cold stone steps of the British Embassy, sobbing quietly. She was not the type of person who normally gave in to despair. Indeed, hadn't it been she who kept up the spirits of all those around her? Hadn't she been brave when they dragged her husband back across the border to dreary Poland? Hadn't she managed to convince her frightened children that all would be well? And wasn't it she who, all this horrible autumn, had relentlessly pushed terrified friends and family to take action and not let themselves be overcome by fear?

Months—even years—of wrangling with authorities had succeeded in obtaining visas from the British for herself and her three children. These precious pieces of paper represented life to her. All she had to do was to bring her husband's passport, and they would issue a visa for him, as well. So they said.

She got her husband to mail his passport from his mother's house in Poland. What risk should it get lost or stolen in the mails! But it hadn't, and the woman now carried it safely zipped into the secret lining of her purse. She had left the children in Leipzig and had come to Berlin only to find that the place was a madhouse, teeming with frantic, desperate Jews who suddenly knew that to stay in Germany meant destruction.

It still seemed incredible to the woman that it had come to this. Five years previously, when Hitler first came to power, she and her husband had soberly discussed the implications.

"He means what he says, Lena," declared Saul, her husband. "But it will be useless to immigrate to any European country. You'll see. He will fight them all."

"But where shall we go?" asked Lena, intensity thickening her voice.

"To either the United States or Palestine," he responded.

Then had begun the long process of applying for visas. The British only let a trickle of Jews through the gates of Palestine. That turned into a closed door. America should have been easier. Lena had one brother living with his family in New York and the wife and son of another brother in Chicago. The relatives sent affidavits to her and then she was assigned a quota number but would be unable to get a visa until her number came up.

That same year, 1933, the Lena's aged mother, who lived with them, became desperately ill. In stark contrast to years past, every doctor Lena phoned refused to come to the apartment. They expressed fear at visiting a Jewish home. Finally, she was forced to take her mother a long distance to an understaffed, underfunded Jewish hospital, where the mother died of pneumonia. The mother's last words to Lena, her frail gray head resting wearily on the white pillow, voice hoarse and thick from infected lungs, were, "If there is a God, where a mother can pray for her child, I'll do it for you."

So they waited, biding their time. Last summer Lena and Saul, growing desperate, hatched a plan. Lena left with the children and went on a summer vacation trip to Czechoslovakia, where she had a cousin. The three children had a marvelous time, frolicking in the cold, clear waters of a small mountain river, in a tiny, rustic town. At the end of the summer, the family planned to cross the border to Russia. But Saul never received permission to join his family. The Gestapo held up his exit visa until the family, disappointed, returned from Czechoslovakia. Only then was his visa issued.

The following month, September of 1938, the family attended their neighborhood synagogue, or *shul,* for the yearly Rosh Hashanah service. The rabbi started to blow the shofar, the yearly call to repentance. A strange thing happened, though. When he put his lips to the ram's horn, no sound came out! Puzzled, he squinted at the shofar, peered at it closely, shook his head as if to say, Nu, what's this? and tried again. Still, nothing. The older women in the shul knelt down on the floor after the second useless attempt to blow the shofar. "This is a bad foreboding," they wailed, pulling at their hair. "This is an evil omen." Chills ran up and down Lena's spine. She felt ill. Later, she discovered that not one shofar had sounded in any of the shuls in Leipzig that year.

And then on a Thursday night in October her youngest, Isaac, had gone to bed healthy but during the night got very sick, running a high temperature. Lena and her husband had been up half the night with their son. Finally, exhausted, Saul fell asleep in the early morning while Lena slipped from bed and got the second daughter, Gerta, off to school. Then she went into the kitchen in order to knead the *challah* dough and start the apple strudel, in preparation for Shabbat. Her thoughts centered on her little boy, the hot tea and toast she planned to serve him once he awoke.

The doorbell rang shrilly, interrupting her thoughts. So early in the morning! Who could it be? With great trepidation, Lena noiselessly walked over to the front door.

"*Ja*," she said. "Who is it?"

"Gestapo," came the harsh response. "Open up!"

Trembling, she pulled her robe tightly around herself, then unlatched the door chain. When she pulled open the door, two men stood outside. One smiled slightly, the other scowled. Both wore the traditional black uniforms and glistening black boots of storm troopers, complete with swastikas on their arms.

"What can I do for you kind gentlemen?" asked Lena carefully.

The one man looked down at his shoes, but the other SS man snapped, "Pack up some things. We will be back to take you and your family away!"

"Oh, but *Herr Leutnant*, my little boy is very ill," she cried. "I have been up all night with him. I cannot leave him alone, and I certainly can't take him with us. He is too sick to go anywhere."

The SS man was about to respond when his partner interjected. "It's all right. We'll come back later and send the boy to a hospital and get the rest of you as well."

"But your husband, the Pole, he comes now," said the SS man. "Tell him to get ready." He spun on his heel, and the two men left, heading in the direction of another Jewish family who lived in the apartment building.

Lena closed and chained the door, then leaned against it, breathing hard. Her fists clenched and unclenched, but she refused to give in to panic. After a few moments she forced herself to walk back to her bedroom, where she woke up her husband. "The SS was here," she said quietly. "They are coming back for you, then for all of us."

Saul sat up in bed. He reached out and drew his wife against his chest, holding her tightly. "As God wills," he said, his voice sad.

"As God wills," she repeated.

They clung together for several moments, then burst into action. Lena sent the oldest daughter, fifteen-year-old, Renate, to the family store to tell the employee to bring suitcases. "Don't talk to anyone; try to stay out of sight as much as possible," she warned the girl, who numbly obeyed. Then she checked on Isaac, who slept fitfully, his face pink and feverish, blonde curls tousled on his high forehead. Her husband hurried through his morning *toilette,* then packed a few changes of clothes and some necessary items in a small bag. Lena wiped away a tear when she noticed him slipping a framed picture of herself into the bag, along with his prayer book and *tallit.*

Much too soon the doorbell buzzed again. Saul went into his son's room and tenderly kissed the boy while his wife hurried to answer the insistent summons. Sighing deeply, he grabbed his bag and went to join her. The angry SS man stood there alone, scowling.

"Come on, Jew, we don't have all day," he snapped. "Let's go!"

Saul attempted to reason with the Nazi. He pleaded, trying to convince him that a terrible mistake was being made. "We are about to emigrate to America," he said. "Look, here are affidavits from the United States; they promise us visas...."

But the SS man was not impressed. "Too bad. You're coming with us," he barked.

Lena wanted to kiss her husband again but hesitated to in front of the SS man. She placed her hand on his arm and he looked into her face. The love she saw in his eyes was all she needed. She nodded.

"*Auf wiedersehen*, my love," she murmured.

"*Shalom, l'hitraot,*" he responded in Hebrew.

And then he was gone.

Down in the street, several storm troopers stood guard over dozens of Jewish families. Men, women, and children, faces pale with dread,

90

discussed among themselves what all this could possibly mean. When Lena's husband exited from his apartment building, it seemed to serve as a signal for the whole group to be herded in the direction of the central train station. As he crossed the street, in the grip of the Nazi, he saw his oldest daughter returning from her errand. Her eyes wide with fear, she looked right at him, but he imperceptibly shook his head *no, don't acknowledge me.* She obeyed the silent injunction, but her sensitive face scrunched into a ball of pain. Tearfully, she tore her eyes from her father and hurried away.

Once in the apartment, Lena clasped her sobbing, hysterical daughter to her bosom. "Shh, it's okay, *Liebchen*," she crooned into the crying girl's hair, holding her own emotions in check so as not to frighten the poor girl even more.

All that day Lena hid the children, anticipating the return of the SS. But mercifully they never came back. That afternoon, when Isaac had significantly improved, she took the letter she had from the American Consulate that stated the family intended to immigrate to the US. Then, dressing carefully and applying makeup, she drew into herself all of her courage, took the letter, and proceeded to walk over to Gestapo Headquarters. Damp with perspiration, she climbed up the front steps and pushed open the heavy, glass door.

"What is it?" asked the man behind the front desk.

"Oh, *Herr Leutnant*," said Lena graciously. "My husband was arrested this morning, but we are immigrating to America. I have here the letter from the American Consul. Please release him." Thus saying, she placed the precious document down with hands held steady by an iron inner resolve.

The man, paunchy, bald, fiftyish, stared at the woman from his high position behind the desk. Though Lena was approaching forty, she had kept her youthful beauty and elegant figure. Her wavy jet-black hair and clear blue eyes made a striking combination. Forcing herself to smile, she looked him in the eye.

"All right," he said unexpectedly. "We'll bring him back."

"Thank you, kind sir," murmured Lena gratefully. "I will tell everyone I know how wonderful you have been!"

Quickly, she bid him farewell and hurried home. Breathing deeply, confident that they had just avoided a catastrophe, she re-entered the apartment, hugged her distraught children, and reassured them that their father would be returned to them any moment.

The family sat down to their Friday night Shabbat meal. The glistening mahogany table, graced by tall silver candlesticks and covered by the snowy white linen tablecloth, looked as it did every Friday night. Only the father's place was vacant. Renate sobbed intermittently.

"Hush," cautioned her mother. "All will be well."

Just then the doorbell shrilled yet again. Everyone jumped.

Lena walked over. "*Ja?*" she said.

"Police," came the response.

Expecting news about Saul, she opened the door. Police, not SS, stood outside.

"Where is your husband?" they asked.

"Why, he was arrested by the Gestapo just this morning," she replied. "They have promised me that he will be returned. We are immigrating to America."

The men looked at each other. "We're going to search the apartment," one of them informed her.

"Go ahead," she said, "but he is not here. I wish that he were!"

Silently, methodically, the men went through their spacious apartment, pulling beds away from walls, looking under couches, emptying closets. Lena and her children watched with sick stomachs. Finally, the men finished.

"We need to take you in for questioning," they informed her.

Gerta now joined her sobs to that of her sister. The police, however, were a kinder breed than the Nazis.

"Your mother will be back," they assured the girls.

Their mother grabbed her coat and, with a lingering look at her children, bravely followed the policemen out of the apartment.

They took her back to the Gestapo headquarters. A different man sat behind the front desk. He called for two SS men who took her into a small room. Trembling, she explained slowly and methodically what had happened that morning, and how her husband had been arrested and taken away. "I even came here," she exclaimed. "And one of your fellow officers promised me that he would be returned!"

It took a while, but finally they believed her. Mercifully, they let her go.

Thanking them graciously for their kindness, Lena left Gestapo Headquarters for the second time that day. She walked home through the dark, menacing streets as quickly as possible, praying silently for strength and protection. When she entered her apartment, three grateful and vastly relieved children hugged her so tightly she could scarcely breathe.

"All right, all right," she soothed. "God is good. He will take care of us."

The next day, she hid two acquaintances who were in danger of being arrested. Then she took the return envelope from the American Consulate and nailed it to the apartment door, claiming that Americans lived there.

Over the next few weeks, Lena did all she could to help people. She hid some, encouraged others, gave advice, listened intently, and in-between comforted her own solemn children. She also was able to get in touch with her husband's cousin who lived in England, and explained to him the gravity of their situation; indeed of the situations of all the Jews in Germany. The cousin, a tall, slender dapper man in his mid-forties with a curving, stylish moustache and a full head of dark hair, came to Leipzig and escorted her to the British Embassy in Berlin. There he was able to obtain visas for Lena and her children.

"When you bring your husband's passport, we will issue him a visa as well," she was promised.

Greatly encouraged, Lena thanked her husband's cousin and returned to Leipzig. She wrote to her husband in Poland, asking him to mail her his passport. A few days later, her cleaning lady, a stout, red-cheeked, genial sort, burst into the apartment, panting heavily.

"My dear Anna, what is it?" asked Lena, embracing her warmly (for she treated the cleaning woman as a friend, not as a servant).

"Oh," the other woman wailed. "My son has told me something awful. Just awful!" And she sat heavily on the sofa, blowing her nose into a small square of handkerchief.

(Anna's son was in his early twenties; he had joined the Brown Shirts, an arm of the Nazis. Often, as a young boy, while his mother dusted and swept, he had sat in Lena's spotlessly clean kitchen and happily consumed large pieces of raisin-and-nut strudel that Lena baked.)

"Yes? Tell me," said Lena, apprehensively.

Anna looked up. "Tonight the Nazis plan to burn down all the synagogues in Germany! They want to punish the Jews for the death of the third ambassador in Paris."

(When Saul had been sent back into Poland, he had been run across the border with large, vicious dogs tearing at his heels. He was one of the lucky ones, however. He was able to get to his mother's house. Those who no longer had relatives in Poland were forced to squat between the borders in a no man's land of indescribable squalor and deprivation. One such couple had somehow managed to smuggle word to their son in Paris about their deplorable situation. He, a young man already fragile emotionally, had come apart. Immediately, he went to the German Embassy in Paris, demanding to see the ambassador. When the third-in-charge had come out to help him, the young man pulled a gun and killed him. The Nazis, on the lookout for a volatile situation they could exploit, had eagerly pounced on this one.)

Lena blanched. "This is horrible," she exclaimed. "Are you sure? Tonight?"

Anna nodded. "Quite sure. My son said there are pages and pages all typed up with the names and locations of every synagogue. Different squads of Nazis already know to which ones they are assigned." Her red-rimmed, pale blue eyes filled up with tears as she nervously squeezed her sodden handkerchief. "It's so awful!" she moaned.

Yes, it is, Lena silently agreed. *Especially for the Jews.* Aloud she said, "Thank you for warning me. Please stay and have a cup of coffee before you leave. Then I must go and prepare the children for what may happen."

The cleaning lady accepted the coffee gratefully. Hesitantly she raised her eyes to her employer's white face. "You know how I love you," she said awkwardly. "And you know how I pray fervently for your family, especially your dear husband so far away in Poland."

Lena nodded as a few stray tears fell down her smooth cheeks.

"I will continue to pray to my Jesus for you," Anna continued, concerned lest she offend her friend but determined to have her say. "We will help you however we can."

Lena stoically brushed aside her vague discomfort at the mention of the Gentile god. "Thank you," she responded simply. "That means a great deal."

Later, after the cleaning lady had tearfully and with many embraces taken her departure, Lena called her children to herself. "My darlings," she began, "there may be trouble tonight."

Apprehensively, the children glanced at one another. *Trouble? What kind of trouble? Hasn't there been trouble all along?*

Their mother continued. "We're all going to sleep in our clothes tonight in my big bed. We will trust that God will defend and protect us."

So they did. Isaac thought of it as a big adventure; a treat to be in the parent's massive, mahogany bed under the luxurious white featherbed quilt instead of in his narrow, white metal one. Soon he drifted off to sleep, though his mother and sisters lay awake quite a long time.

Around four in the morning, Isaac awoke to what he thought was daylight. But when he jumped out of bed and pushed back the heavy, velvet curtain, it wasn't daylight that met his startled eyes but huge flames of fire! Everywhere he looked monstrous flames reached up to the heavens, like hands in the blood-red sky.

His cries roused his mother and sisters, who joined him at the window. For a few moments they stood there, watching their world, the old Germany, burn. Then the mother closed the curtains. "Let's not draw attention to ourselves," she said. "We need a plan."

Just then they heard a frantic knocking at their front door. "Open up, open up!" begged a familiar voice. It was one of their male Jewish neighbors from the apartment building.

Lena unlocked the door and the neighbor practically fell in.

"Oh, my dear *Frau* Cohen, it is terrible, simply unbelievable," panted the neighbor wildly. His normally immaculate clothes were disheveled, soot streaks ran down his cheeks, and he reeked of smoke. "These Nazi swine have taken all of our sefer torahs and are burning them in the streets. They are tearing them to shreds and dancing on them. They are grabbing Jews off the streets and out of their homes and sending them to concentration camps. They are looting stores, breaking into houses, and smashing everything we own. It is terrible, terrible." Crying with impotent rage, he proceeded to tell them how the Nazis were taking Jewish doctors out of operating rooms, leaving the patients to die on the table, how Jews were being shot on the street, and how children were being arrested without parents and parents without children.

The woman and her children melted with fear. "What should we do?" she asked him.

He shook his head sadly. "I don't know. If you can find a safer place than this to hide, maybe it will blow over and we can escape this miserable country. I came to warn you. I myself have a contact at the French consulate and I am going to try to seek shelter there. God be with you, my dear *Frau*." And then he was gone.

So Lena took her children, locked the apartment behind them, and headed for the Polish Consulate. Furtively, they slipped through the shadows of the *Johannespark* across from their apartment house. This was a park which, in the past, had afforded them countless afternoons of glorious pleasure but now seemed a dark, menacing snake pit. Any moment they expected the shadowy form of a Nazi to leap at them from the carefully trimmed bushes and drag them off to a concentration camp. All around them were scenes of horror. The sounds of beatings and screams reverberated from every direction. It was as if Dante's *Inferno* had come to life.

Miraculously, they reached the Polish Consulate without incident. But some of the others fortunate enough to have successfully gained entry to the Consulate had not arrived unscathed. Lena and her children walked between rows of battered and bloodied men, past people who had just witnessed the shock and horror of seeing their friends and relatives beaten and shot before their eyes.

They spent a day and a night there, sleeping on the floor, eating the hard, brown bread and soft cheese the Consulate provided. The boy, Isaac, alternated between fear and a sense of adventure. The younger sister, Gerta, sat quietly, looking about with wide, hurt eyes. But Renate, the older sister, wrestled with God, her heart-shaped face pale with intensity. *If you save us,* she whispered fiercely, *I swear that I will live out my days in Palestine.*

After two days, the Polish Consulate deemed the streets quiet enough for people to leave. Filled with dread and apprehension, Jewish men, women, and children cautiously filtered out the doors and past the gates into the brooding streets of Leipzig.

When Lena and her children arrived home, they discovered that every Jewish apartment in their building had been looted and ransacked *except theirs!* Inside, all was just as they had left it. *How is this possible?* she wondered.

She soon found out. Anna's son, at great personal risk, in full Brown Shirt uniform, had taken it upon himself to stand guard at their door for almost a full 24 hours. He had stopped all potential raiders with a curt, "No Jews live here. Get going." He also advised Lena (through his mother) to find another place to live as quickly as possible.

"You see?" she told her children. "Not all Gentiles want to kill us. There's hope." Gerta and Isaac nodded while Renate looked thoughtful.

Lena took the young man's advice. Within the week, she had somehow managed to sell all their furniture (she! A Jew!) and had moved in with some cousins in another part of the city. By the beginning of December, her husband's passport arrived in the mail. Two days later, leaving the children with her cousins, she made the short trip to Berlin to get the visa for her husband. When she got off the train and made her way from the station to the street where the embassies were, she gasped with dismay.

Everywhere, *everywhere,* were enormous, serpentine lines of frantic people running down the steps and through the streets. The din of thousands of voices was deafening. In bewilderment, Lena attempted to find the end of one line that seemed close to the British Embassy.

"Excuse me, *bitte,*" she said to a young woman on the line. "Are you waiting to get into the British Embassy?"

The young woman, dark hair pulled back tightly, circles under her eyes, cloth coat buttoned high at the collar in a futile attempt to repel the winter winds, nodded yes.

"I've been waiting since yesterday," she said in a voice dull with fatigue. "I haven't even been able to use the restroom. This is unbearable!"

Lena's heart filled with compassion for the young woman. "Can I get you anything?" she asked her.

"You can get me out of this horrid country," the young woman cried, stamping her feet out of both cold and anger. Just then, the line inched up and the young woman hurriedly and carefully made sure there was no space between her and the person in front. Then she sat down on her battered valise and closed her eyes.

Shaken, Lena turned and walked in the other direction. *Since yesterday! So many people! No food, water, or restrooms. No promise of getting into the embassy and then who knows? It would not be out of character for the embassy to refuse to issue a visa. After all, how many visas were they willing to give out? It seemed as if all of the Jews left in Germany who hadn't been deported, killed, or sent to concentration camps were all in this one street, looking to escape.*

And how long can I stay here? she thought. *How long can I last? I dare not leave my children in Germany a day longer than necessary. How safe is it to stay here? But my husband, oh my precious husband! If I leave now, I may very likely never see him again!*

The weeks of uncertainty and terror descended then, and she, the strong one, the one who was a rock to all those around her, sank onto the steps and wept.

The soft, cultured voice with its foreign accent roused her. The small, well-dressed man patiently repeated his question while the woman raised her head and stared at him.

"I say, why are you crying?" he asked kindly.

Bewildered, uncertain as to why he would ask since it was patently obvious to her why *anyone* on this panic-driven street would cry, she nevertheless answered quite seriously.

"Because I have traveled from Leipzig to get a visa from the British for my husband. He has been deported to Poland, and if I cannot get a visa for him, then I must leave with my children and never see him again!" Her eyes filled back up with tears as she spoke.

"Come," he said, "allow me to treat you to a cup of coffee. I want to hear more of your story."

Lena hesitated. Under normal circumstances, for her, a married woman, to agree to go somewhere with a man not her husband, a stranger, a *Gentile*, was preposterous! But these were not normal times, nor were they normal circumstances.

"Sir," she said, "I am a Jewess. I am not allowed to enter any public place."

The man smiled tightly. "I ask that you trust me. I give you my assurance that in my presence you have nothing to fear."

So she trusted him. Together they walked away from the mass of desperate humanity. Two blocks later, where no embassies stood, the smell of fear dissipated. She breathed easier. They stopped in front of a café with fancy lettering on its highly polished glass window. A small sign in the bottom right-hand corner read *No Jews Allowed.* The man saw the woman's uncertainty.

"Come," he said, taking her arm. "It's all right." He opened the heavy, brass door and held it so the woman could enter ahead of him. The waiter who greeted them frowned when he saw the woman but dared not say a word to the man. He escorted them to a small table for two in a back corner. Putting menus in front of them, he departed with a slight bow.

"Are you sure it's all right?" she asked fearfully, her gaze on the retreating back of the waiter.

"Trust me," the man assured her. "You are safe with me."

Lena, usually so decisive, found that right now she was incapable of even ordering something to eat. Nervously, she sat and watched the man, who watched her. In sympathetic understanding, he took the menu from her shaking fingers.

"I know this place well," he said. "Let me order."

He snapped his fingers and the waiter rapidly reappeared. "Two coffees and two slices of the whipped cream and strawberry torte."

After the waiter had left, the man smiled kindly at her. "Tell me your whole story," he said. "I want to hear it."

So she told him everything, from the beginning. She told him of how they had tried to leave Germany since 1933 and all that transpired up to the present moment. In the middle of her narrative, their coffee and cake arrived. The man methodically ate while Lena only sipped at her coffee, leaving her cake untouched while the words poured forth from her mouth.

When she described the burning synagogues and the treacherous walk to the Polish Consulate, she stopped and turned her head, fighting to regain control of her emotions.

"Take your time," the man said gently.

She took another sip of the strong coffee. In faltering tones, she finished her story, ending with her arrival at the British Embassy.

After hearing her story, the man reached into his inside coat pocket and withdrew a small pad and a slender, gold pen. He wrote a short note, signing it with a flourish. Then he ripped the piece of paper off the pad and handed it to her.

"There's a certain door located at the side entrance to the Embassy," he said, describing the exact location. "I don't expect you'll find any lines there. I want you to go, ring the bell, and hand this note to the person who opens the door."

Glancing down at the note in her hand, Lena saw that it was written in English, a language she did not know. "What does it say?"

The man waved the question away. "Don't worry," he said. "It's good."

Feeling unreal, as if she were in a dream, she ate her cake, realizing just how hungry she was. When she finished, the man put several bills on the table and stood up.

"You should go to the Embassy now," he said.

Lena stood up as well, and together they left the café. Silently, they walked back in the direction of the British Embassy. When they were still a block away, the man abruptly stopped. "I have another appointment and must leave you now," he said. He removed his stylish felt hat and looked at her closely. "I know that God is with you. I am confident that you and your whole family will be safe."

"You are most kind, sir," Lena replied, smiling at him, not realizing how beautiful she looked now that hope had brightened her eyes. "I will remember this."

The man put his hat back on. "*Auf wiedersehen.*"

"*Auf wiedersehen*," she responded.

After the man had walked away, Lena hurried over to the side entrance he had pointed out. A large sign prominently over the door announced *Not For Public Use. Please Go Around To Front.* She ignored the sign and rang the bell, as she had been instructed. A tired voice with a similar foreign accent to the man came over the intercom.

"Go away. Use the front gate."

"But I have a note," she protested. "Please open the door."

Slowly, the door cracked open an inch and the glowering embassy employee on the other side snatched the note out of Lena's hand, slamming the door shut again. Almost immediately the door reopened, much wider this time.

"How did you come to know the ambassador?" the employee asked, in a much more gracious voice.

The ambassador! God is good, murmured Lena to herself. Aloud she said, "He is a very kind man, is he not?" And she handed the man her husband's passport.

"Very kind," came the prompt response.

Within five minutes the man returned with the highly coveted visa stamped in the passport. Thanking him effusively, Lena carefully secured the passport in its special spot in her purse. She practically flew down the embassy steps on her way to the train station and then back to Leipzig.

Events moved at breakneck speed. Lena mailed her husband his passport with the English visa in it, and the Germans gave him permission to return for 48 hours only. He arrived at the place where the family was staying on a Friday night, just as the Shabbat began. Never had he gotten such a welcome! The tears, hugs, kisses—oh, it was a joyous thing! His wife had already made all the preparations for leaving so they rested on the Sabbath.

On Saturday evening, the family, surrounded by all their luggage, stood on Track 28 of the Leipziger Bahnhof waiting for the train that would take them to Antwerp in Belgium where Lena had a brother. So close to freedom! So close to escape! Lena, Saul, Renate, and Gerta all prayed silently, entreating God to give them victory. Even Isaac knew not to speak, though his eyes were bright with excitement.

Then they heard the warning shriek of the train whistle and soon saw the big, black locomotive huffing slowly into the station. Quickly they boarded, careful not to draw undue attention. When seated, Saul cautiously handed their tickets to the terse conductor.

"Papers?" he barked.

Saul hastily pulled everyone's passports from his pocket and showed the German the British visas. Grunting, the conductor stamped the tickets and moved jerkily down the aisle, keeping his footing as the train lurched forward.

Suddenly Isaac spoke. "Oh, Papa! When we get to Uncle's house, can I...."

"Sshh!" His father frowned, admonishing his son, putting his finger to his lips. The boy shut his mouth, turned, and stared out the window. Soon the darkness and the rhythmic motion of the train lulled him to sleep. The journey to the Belgium border took about five hours.

The rest of the family sat in petrified silence, trying not to jump every time one of the German officials came down the aisle. The last stop before the border was the German city of Dusseldorf. The conductor announced it loudly. Startled by the noise, Isaac woke up and rubbed his eyes.

"Are we there yet?" he asked sleepily.

"Almost," answered Lena, smiling at her son. He smiled back at her, blue eyes clear and guileless. His mother looked at him and her heart caught in her throat. *Oh God, please don't let anything happen! Please,* she prayed, *let us make it out of Germany safely.*

The train rumbled forward once the passengers from Dusseldorf embarked. It was about a half hour until the border. It was the longest thirty minutes the family had ever experienced. At one point, the conductor came down the aisle, looked right at Saul, and opened his mouth but before he could say anything, his attention was diverted by a commotion in another part of the train. He hurried away. Saul wiped his brow.

And then suddenly it was over. The train pulled into the border station, the German officials disembarked, and the Belgium officials took their places. The engine revved up, the doors swung closed, and the train swayed forward, west, to freedom.

The relief from tension was palpable. Lena, Saul, and the two girls burst into tears, making such a racket that the new conductor, the one who didn't despise Jews, the one from Belgium, came to check on them.

"Are you all right?" he asked solicitously.

"Very all right." Saul blew his nose loudly into his linen handkerchief.

The conductor tipped his cap knowingly, moving back down the aisle to attend to other duties.

"So," said Isaac, blue eyes wide, "can I talk now?"

PART FOUR

Long Island
1961
to
California
1989

Eight

Whenever I think about my early childhood, I can smell the scents of early spring. The sun is warm, the air cool, the sky blue, daffodils and tulips push their way out of the rich, black soil. The raspberry bushes at the side of the house have yet to bloom, as do the peach and cherry trees in the backyard, but the promise is there. Waiting, waiting.

It's odd that I should remember it this way because in reality I grew up in the shadow of the Holocaust. My father's family had narrowly avoided death, escaping from Germany through a series of miracles, the latest being a surprise encounter with a kind-hearted ambassador, and from birth, or so it seemed, I was aware of the crushing details of that terrible time. The town I lived in until I was eight was over 50 percent Jewish, yet even at a tender age I knew that the Gentile culture dominated, and that to be Jewish meant that one was different.

One memory stands out, when I was five years old at Christmastime. My father, Isaac, took myself and my two older brothers to a department store. A pot-bellied store employee with a glued-on white beard and a red and white fur-trimmed suit sat in a big chair, inviting children to share their deepest toy longings.

"Can I, please?" I begged my father.

"Okay, Becky," he acquiesced.

I waited in the short line, then climbed eagerly in the big man's lap when it was my turn.

"What do you want for Christmas, little girl?" he boomed.

"I want to be Christian, but my father won't let me," I babbled, grateful for what I perceived to be a sympathetic ear.

Santa looked at me, startled, but not nearly as startled as my father. Unceremoniously, I was hauled out of the ample red lap and marched to the car. I don't remember if there were additional repercussions, and indeed no one in the family has mentioned this in subsequent years, but I've never forgotten it.

It was a very Jewish childhood. My father took the three kids to *shul* (synagogue) every Saturday morning while my mother stayed home, taking advantage of the only time all week when she got the house to herself. All it took was a couple of hours and she was refreshed. By 12:30 pm, we flew back into the house, pulling off our dressy outfits in search of play clothes. My mother, smiling and relaxed, presided over a table laden with bagels, cream cheese, lox, tuna salad, cottage cheese, and, if we were lucky, pastries. Again, when I think back on these things, it's always May. Or June.

At *shul*, I remember sitting quietly next to my father on a hard wooden pew, the Hebrew chants swirling around my head, meticulously braiding the fringes on his *tallit*, then holding them over my finger and pretending they were dolls. I loved the *kiddush* after the service, as well, little cups of grape kosher wine and slices of sponge cake. The old men sometimes drank slivovitz; the heat from the brandy turned their ears red.

It seemed that everyone was named Cohen, like us, or Greenspan, or Shapiro, or Rosenthal. Other than some kids at school, I didn't really know anyone who wasn't Jewish. The teachers at my school, our neighbors, my parents' friends, all were Jewish, weren't they? Yet still I knew that society was not safe, that we were somehow set apart.

My mother's parents were a rarity for that time: Jews from Brooklyn who had been born in America. They had no trace of an accent, drove cars, wore bathing suits and not wool suits to the beach, and seemed, well, very American. Unhappily, my grandmother passed away when I was five and my grandfather followed soon after so I have only dim memories of them. It's my father's parents who are so vivid.

After Oma and Opa escaped the Holocaust, they went first to England and then came to New York in March of 1939. Except for a few relatives on both sides who had already been living outside of Germany and Poland, everyone else in their extended families perished. My grandmother was the youngest of seventeen children and everyone, *everyone*, along with their children, spouses, grandchildren, was murdered by the Nazis. So yes, the family miraculously escaped but they left behind a blazing inferno that consumed humans like the pit of hell itself.

I vaguely understood this as a child. I didn't realize the pull that people outside your own small family can have on your life, your soul. I didn't know that you couldn't just walk away from something so horrific, sigh deeply, and say, "Whew! At least that wasn't me!" So I took my grandparents at face value, not knowing at what cost their lives had been preserved.

They lived in an immaculate brick apartment building in Queens, populated with other Holocaust survivors. They politely greeted one another with *Frau* and *Herr*. My father once asked his mother, exasperated, "Mom, you've known Mr. So-and-So for twenty years. Why don't you call him by his first name?" She laughed, but you knew she would *never* do that.

All these people got monthly checks from the West German government, reparation money for the losses they suffered. The green halls smelled strongly of disinfectant; the gleaming floors reflecting back our echoing footsteps in that unnaturally quiet place. My brothers and I temporarily brought life and youth through its tragic portals when we visited, but even that seemed forced, unreal.

The apartment itself, a tiny one-bedroom, seemed so small after our spacious suburban home on Long Island. That's what grandparents did, I reasoned. They lived in little places because they were old and didn't have kids. Still, I loved visiting them. I loved getting a shiny quarter from my grandfather, *just because*. I loved climbing onto their high bed with its satin coverlet. I loved sitting in the narrow little kitchen and eating a plate of *spungetti* (translation: spaghetti) that my grandmother had tossed with an awe-inspiring amount of butter. I loved listening to the adults talk, my grandmother's voice dropping to a whisper and switching to German when something really juicy was being said ("Speak English, Mom," my father would say, sighing). I loved being treated as a little princess because I was the only girl and had blonde hair like my grandfather's dead mother in Poland. I loved being special.

But I didn't always feel so special. I remember being three years old, at nursery school, and being lonely. I thought I was ugly. Now I look at pictures of myself from that era and think, *What was wrong with me? I was such a cute little girl.* But my perception was darkened; my ability to make and hold friends somehow stunted.

Home was better than school. My mother, one of the more social beings to grace this earth, effortlessly gathered people around her. Jewish holidays, summers, in-between times, invariably found us entertaining family and friends. Unable to maintain much in my own life in the way of a social network, I nevertheless benefitted from the social whir swirling about me, through no labor of my own. Sampling the cheese, crackers, and bowls of nuts that graced the coffee table, listening in to the adults' conversations, playing with my cousins—these things I enjoyed. Home was safe.

Sunday nights, however, I would lie awake for hours, watching unblinkingly as my light-up digital alarm clock clicked the minutes away. Though bright, I felt out of step with my classmates and dreaded the coming week.

When I turned ten, an awful thing happened. My little five-year-old cousin had a terrible accident and lay dying in a coma. My mother left for a week to help the grieving family and I turned to God. Praying fervently night after night, I begged him to heal my cousin. To my great disappointment, the little boy grew worse and eventually died. A part of my heart turned to stone, and I lost my childlike faith.

When re-examining one's life from the vantage point of middle-age, the question is: What is worth telling and what is not? So many events make a story, some critical yet of no special interest except to the subject herself. I know that I veered from a good and righteous path at a young age despite a good and moral upbringing. Why?

Looking back, I can see that I got in trouble through some of my reading choices. *Cosmopolitan*, Jacqueline Susann novels, various other really nasty books that I never should have found, much less read, all contributed to a certain *bentness,* as C.S. Lewis called it in *Out of the Silent Planet.* My concept of sexuality became perverse, distorted, and my taciturn, closed nature kept me from discussing this with those who could have set me straight, had they known.

All this led to an ugly involvement with a young man in his twenties, a friend of the family. At the time, I thought this a great romantic secret; now I see a pedophile abusing a gullible young girl. The upshot of this entanglement was that I grew to hate myself. By sixteen, like many girls today, I became obsessed with being thin, as how much food I allowed myself was the only thing I could control in an increasingly out-of-control world.

In my teen years, I looked for boys to take away my loneliness and magically make me happy. Pursuing the ones who were disinterested and quickly tiring of the ones who did seem to like me, I bounced around like a beach ball run amuck. When I went off to college, as an immature seventeen-year-old, I hoped to start my life over again. Instead, I merely dug deeper and deeper into the sin which by now had an iron grip.

Halfway through that first year of college, I came apart emotionally. My parents rescued me from an ill-conceived plan to fly to London and brought me back home, where I got a tedious job at the local mall and sought to renew myself in the security of my childhood home. But restlessness had a hold on me, and books had a terrific grasp on my imagination.

I read *Zen and the Art of Motorcycle Maintenance*, and suddenly Bozeman, Montana, seemed to me the new Mecca. I had previously met someone on a bus who told me about job opportunities at Yellowstone National Park, so I applied and, to my amazement, was accepted. At eighteen, I stuffed an already oversized backpack and got on a plane for Montana, my longsuffering mother deeply upset at my latest antic but helpless to stop me.

For most kids my age, the job at Yellowstone would have been a dream come true. A group of young adults sharing a rustic house, an older couple cooking and supervising, an easy job at the touristy general store, the breathtaking landscape of lake, woods, and mountains. But I had never learned how to plunge in socially. I was looking for someone else to take care of my needs. I was desperately lonely and unable to find my way out. So I did what I always did: I looked for the perfect boyfriend to take away my pain.

One day, during my time off, I wandered around the lobby of the quaint hotel by the lake. I noticed two handsome young men, one blonde and one dark-haired, early twenties, a little older than me. I went over and introduced myself. It turned out that the blonde one had just graduated from the law school of the university I had attended. I thought this a great coincidence and felt an immediate bonding with these fellows. They were vacationing for a few days on their way further west, where the blonde man had a job waiting for him.

As I got to know these brothers, I discovered that they were born-again Christians. Now, the term *born-again* was just getting highly popularized by 1980 and had all sorts of bad connotations for a Jewish girl. But I was surprised at how normal these guys seemed and also impressed by their genuine kindness. They didn't seek to take advantage of me, which would certainly have been easy enough. Instead, they spoke to me about God. The blonde man gave me a pocket New Testament and told me to start reading the book of John. Though I was a voracious reader, I clearly remember not understanding a word and giving up after less than one chapter. Undaunted, this fellow somehow knew of two Jewish believers at Yellowstone and set up a meeting for me. I still didn't understand anything I was told, but accepted the gift of a New American Standard Bible (a Bible I still have today).

After the brothers left, I fancied myself in love with the blonde one and grew depressed and restless. I moped around for a couple of weeks, then abruptly quit and decided to follow him to his new town. Catching a ride with some people I met who were heading in that direction, I unexpectedly showed up at the blonde's house. He was shocked to see me and quickly enough sent me on my way, disentangling himself from the very difficult situation I had so blithely put him in.

So it was that on a gloriously sunny day in June, with dusky blue mountains in the distance and vibrant wild flowers lining the sides of the road, I found myself standing next to the highway on the Idaho/Oregon border with my thumb out. Since I was only eighteen and had led a very sheltered existence (with the exception of *Yom Kippur*, I had yet to miss a meal), it didn't occur to me to be frightened. Quite the contrary. Though I had not grasped the Gospel message preached to me at Yellowstone, nevertheless the idea of *Jesus* took root.

"He's protecting me," I said. And I'm convinced now that he was.

So began my hitchhiking odyssey, á la *Zen and the Art of Motorcycle Maintenance*, *Even Cowgirls get the Blues*, *Fear and Loathing in Las Vegas,* and probably several other 1970s books I should never have read.

Somehow or other, I went from Oregon to Nevada, to California and down the coast to Los Angeles, always having a clean place to stay at night, never having to pay (with either cash or sexual favors).

When I hitched into Sacramento, California, I got a ride with an older guy whose *schtick* I never quite figured out. He had a modest home and seemed to take in kids who needed a place to stay. That first night he had some errands to do and asked me if I wanted to come along.

"Sure," I said, ever the adventure junkie.

We drove around the city, doing whatever, and then went to a Chinese restaurant for dinner. Halfway through the meal, this fellow (I think his name was Lloyd) motions with his head. "Look over there," he said, lowering his voice. "See those men at that table? The one in the middle is Governor Jerry Brown."

Jerry Brown! Throughout high school, I had taken an active interest in politics. Plus, back in 1980, who didn't know about Jerry Brown? The hip California governor who dated Linda Ronstadt. These were the heroes of my post-60s generation.

"Can I meet him?" I asked, eyes wide.

Lloyd shrugged. "Go ahead."

Immediately, I jumped up and boldly walked right over to the governor's table. "Excuse me," I interrupted. Politely, the men stopped talking and gave me their full attention.

Ignoring everyone else, I held out my hand to Jerry. "I just got into town," I began, trying to look older than my age, although with my wild, waist-length hair, skimpy shirt, and faded jeans I doubt I succeeded. "And I'm thrilled to meet you."

"It's a pleasure to meet you also," said the governor gallantly. "How do you like Sacramento?"

"I haven't seen much of it yet," I replied, amazed with the generous reception I was getting.

"Well, look," said the governor, "why don't you come to the Capitol tomorrow and I'll have Jacques (he pointed to the man on his right) show you around?"

"Wow, thanks," I said. Saying good-bye, I returned to my table.

"I can't believe how friendly he is," I told Lloyd.

"He's a great guy," agreed Lloyd, staring at me in a way that made me uncomfortable.

The next day, I had no idea how to get to the Capitol building and hesitated to ask more favors of Lloyd, so I let the whole thing slide past me.

That night, Lloyd asked me if I wanted to accompany him to a local concert. I went, but decided that this older man was not for me and he was getting on my nerves. As a result, I became demanding and petulant. We came back to the house and I went to sleep in a room with two other girls who were also staying there. We were all in our sleeping bags on the floor.

About five a.m., I suddenly woke up when a hand pressed down on my shoulder. It was Lloyd.

"Get your things together," he said unsmilingly. "I'm going to drop you off at the highway so you can keep going."

Wordlessly, I went into the bathroom, got dressed, and rolled up my sleeping bag. Within minutes I had slid into the front seat of his car. Embarrassed, I knew that I had behaved badly the night before, yet I was also relieved to be rid of this man. Soon enough we reached the entrance to the highway and he stopped the car.

"So long," he said, not looking at me.

"Bye. Thanks," I answered, grabbing my stuff and getting quickly out of the car.

I stood on the side of the road, watching him as he pulled away. Though I hadn't wanted this man, and it had been obvious that he wanted more from me than I was prepared to give, still, I felt mortified at being thrown out of his house. *How difficult am I?* I wondered. Always when things went wrong I assumed it was the other person misunderstanding me. How ugly was my behavior?

I didn't have time to ponder these thoughts, however, because, almost immediately, a battered, old pickup stopped for me. The driver, a bearded, redneck type, had a bumper sticker emblazoned across the glove compartment that read, *Drugs or sex, no one rides for free.* Fortunately, in my case, that proved to be overly optimistic.

I emerged from the truck in the vicinity of San Francisco. Very soon (I never had to wait for long) another car stopped for me. The driver of this vehicle could not have been more different. Clean-shaven and well-dressed, he was obviously a professional of some sort. Pilot, I learned.

Mark invited me to share dinner with his family (he lived with his parents) and spend the night in the guest room. I said *yes*, having no idea what "home" entailed. An hour later, we exited from the coastal highway and drove through the dusty, aromatic hills near San Jose. The bucolic scenery entranced me.

After a while, we turned into a long, gravel drive. A large sign announced the *Sanders Vineyards*. The road snaked up a hill for close to a mile until a long, low, stucco home, reminiscent of a Spanish hacienda, sprang into view. Tires crunching on the gravel, Mark pulled up close to the house and parked the car. He opened his door and got out. I jumped out on my side.

I stood in front of the house and gazed at the view. "You live here?" I asked him, astonished.

Rolling vistas of cultivated grapevines stretched ahead of me as far as the eye could see. Lemon and orange trees perfumed the air with their luscious fruit. Masses of flowers I couldn't identify brightened the air with vibrant yellows, reds, blues and purples. A lone donkey sauntered leisurely off to the right. This wasn't a home: it was a movie set!

"I'll put your stuff in the house and then show you around, if you like," he offered, obviously proud of the place.

"Sure," I said.

I watched as Mark opened the back door and seized my huge backpack. Then I followed him through intricately carved double wooden doors and into a dark foyer, tiled with stones cool to the touch.

A heavyset, smiling Mexican housekeeper greeted Mark, exposing a gold tooth. When she caught sight of me, she frowned, letting loose a string of Spanish. Mark listened patiently and responded, also in Spanish. I didn't understand a word they said, so I focused on looking around.

The house had that rustic, early California look. Dark woods, colorful furniture, artifacts mounted on the paneled walls, pottery bowls filled with freshly cut flowers. I thought I was in *Gunsmoke,* or at least *Bonanza.* I was about to examine an ancient gun more closely when I heard the housekeeper sigh. *"Si signor."*

I looked over as she left the room. "She okay?" I asked.

"Fine," Mark responded, not quite meeting my eyes. "Follow me. I'll show you to your room."

I trailed after him down a long, polished hallway, almost bumping into him when he abruptly turned into a room on the left. He placed the backpack carefully on the floor, like it was a Louis Vuitton suitcase and not something I'd gotten a deal on secondhand.

"This is great," I enthused. "Thanks!"

It *was* great. A high, four-poster double bed boasting a quilt that Grandma on the frontier might have made dominated a small but meticulous room. A long, low dresser with a large mirror could have been at least a hundred years old. Two framed oil paintings with horse and ranch motifs graced the walls.

We walked back down the hall and into a huge kitchen. Mark opened the refrigerator and took out two cold cans of soda, handing me one. Then we went outside and got into something that can only be described as a glorified golf cart.

"This is great for riding around the property," Mark explained, noticing my raised eyebrows. "It's too big around here to walk."

As we rode around the vineyard, and Mark pointed out the various outbuildings, fields, and animals, my heart leaped within me. Immediately, in my mind, I went from being a temporary guest to mistress of the place. I didn't want to work to make a dream come true.

I wanted a ready-made life I could just plug myself into. I wanted to be dropped down into the middle of paradise. I wanted to be taken care of.

Mark's parents were very kind people, and dinner went well. I didn't understand just how unusual a young, Jewish girl from Long Island seemed to this Old California Napa Valley wine-growing family. I didn't understand how preposterous my longings were.

The next morning, after breakfast, Mark offered to drive me wherever I needed to go. With a heavy heart, I realized that my fantasy of *The Princess and the Grapes* was to remain just that: a fantasy.

Later that day, I emerged into the hip, beach town of Santa Cruz. Immediately, I found my way to the ocean, took off my sandals, and luxuriated in the sensation of the warm sand between my toes. Some muscle-bound guys surfed nearby, their boards a bright assortment of colors. I sat and watched them, contentedly breathing in the sun-baked salty air. When they emerged from the blue and white flecked water, I strolled over and engaged them in conversation.

One of the men turned out to be last year's Mr. America. *This is too cool*, I thought to myself, donkey and hillsides and grape arbors forgotten. *How California is it, to meet Mr. America on the beach?* Life had ceased to be life; it had somehow become one of the novels I so greedily devoured.

Nothing turned up in Santa Cruz as far as overnight accommodations, so I restlessly hitched a ride further south. A short drive down Highway 1 took me to the trendy resort town of Carmel. What a magnificent spot! Art galleries and outdoor cafes jostled for position, cascading down a hilly main street that ended abruptly at the turquoise beach. Famed Pebble Beach Golf Course wound its emerald green beauty adjacent to the pounding surf of the ocean. Fashionable-looking men and women in designer clothes, sunglasses firmly in place, rubbed shoulders with equally fashionable-looking tourists.

The longer I walked around, the more I liked the place. *Maybe I should try to get a job*, I thought. I pushed open the door of a clothing boutique. The young Asian girl behind the desk looked at me quizzically, her long, dark, silky hair draped over one shoulder.

"Yes?" she said, with the slightest trace of an accent.

"Do you need any help here?"

"Ah, no." She studied me critically and pursed her lips. "But two doors down is a cookie shop. They are always hiring."

My face lit up. "Thanks! Towards the ocean or away?"

"Towards," she said, her face softening into a smile. "Good luck."

"Thanks," I said again, waving as I left the store (but not before I noticed the $500 price tag on a dress worn by a headless mannequin. *Whoa.*).

Two doors down I smelled that oh-so-familiar scent of baking flour, sugar, butter, and chocolate chips. I looked up. The lettering above the door read *The Cookie Shoppe.* The door opened and an older couple carrying little white bags walked out, talking to each other. They looked happy. The husband saw me standing there and held the door so I could enter.

"They're the best," he said conspiratorially, while his wife, laughing, concurred.

Once inside, I waited on a long line. When my turn came, I asked the teenage girl behind the counter if they needed any help. "I'm looking for a job," I told her.

"Oh, this is a great place to work," she enthused, her ponytail bobbing up and down as she nodded for emphasis. She pointed to a spot against the far wall of the store. "Just wait over there and I'll let Liz, she's the owner, know you're here."

A few minutes later, an attractive, blonde, thirty-something lady wearing a long, white apron emerged from the back of the store. She smiled sweetly when she saw me.

"Come," she said, gesturing to a little round table with two iron grille work chairs. "Have a seat."

Liz asked me a few questions and had me fill out some paperwork. Twenty minutes later, I had a job.

"Can you start right now?" she asked.

"Sure," I said, stunned at how fast things had progressed. "Uh, Liz?"

"Yes?"

"Would you happen to know of any place I could stay? I just got into town today."

"Well," she said slowly, "my ex-husband has a big house five miles down the road from here. Maybe he'd be willing to rent a room to you.

I'll give him a call."

"Wow, thanks!" I grinned. "This is great!"

"I'll let you know by the end of the day. Don't worry; you'll have a place to stay tonight." She then stored my backpack, got me an apron, and introduced me to the fellow who would be training me to bake and sell cookies.

Liz came through with a place to stay, and that evening she dropped me off at a big, beautiful, new home several miles south of Carmel. Set back in the woods, it was at a high enough elevation so you could catch glimpses of the blue sea across the road and down the cliffs. Her ex, Jeff, seemed old to me, though he was probably not yet forty. Thin and wiry with dark hair and a mustache, he perpetually wandered around with a long-stemmed wine glass in his hand. A fluffy-tailed cat purred against one of his legs. I had no idea what he did for a living.

Back in the summer of 1980, even though we were at the end of the hippie era, the world remained an innocent enough place so I didn't fear being left alone in a deserted house with a man I didn't know. If you asked me that night, "Aren't you nervous?" I would have told you that I believed Jesus protected me, not having any clue as to who Jesus was or why he would do such a magnanimous thing. And protected I was. No one bothered me, plus I had a clean room to call my own along with kitchen privileges. The rent was $200/month.

The biggest problem with such a great place to stay was that I had no transportation. Five miles was pretty far to walk. When I couldn't bum a ride off Jeff, I turned to hitchhiking. It was one thing to stand at a major highway and go as far as the person who picked you up would take you, but when there was a specific goal with a time limit it wasn't very reliable.

After the euphoria wore off from such a successful start to my new life in Carmel, old problems re-emerged.

First, I was lonely. I didn't know how to connect socially with the other young people at the cookie store. I could joke around and be friendly, but when everyone left at night, I hadn't made any real friends. I continued to look for a boyfriend to meet my needs instead of getting to know other girls, which would have made me much happier.

The other problem centered on my poor eating habits. After a bout with anorexia in my midteens (I vividly remember barely tipping the scales at 100 pounds and my father demanding that I eat half a sandwich and a banana for lunch. "What?" I shrieked, appalled. "If I eat all that, it will make me fat!" And I really believed it), I had swung the other way my freshman year of college and weighed 5-10 pounds more than what was ideal. I looked just fine, but at the time thought I was grossly overweight and didn't deserve normal food. It was really a sickness. I tried not to eat and then, out of sheer hunger, consumed far more calories on junk then if I had just eaten filling, healthy food.

I didn't have the life skills necessary to go to a supermarket and make decent choices. Instead, I ate haphazardly, always restricting myself. Of course, by the end of an eight-hour shift at the cookie place I was ravenous, so I ate way too much cookie dough and broken cookies. Then I felt nauseated from excessive sugar. This did not help a healthy mental outlook, either.

After two weeks of this juggling act, despite the potential of staying in a town like Carmel and pulling my act together, I had had enough. Restless, discouraged, lonely, I lost interest and told Liz that I was quitting.

"Are you sure, honey?" she asked, solicitously, more concerned for me than I knew.

"Yeah. I have a brother in L.A., and I'm going to head down and spend time with him."

This was actually true. My oldest brother had moved to Los Angeles after he graduated from college and gotten a job in the entertainment industry. I admired him greatly and had called him from Carmel in a fit of loneliness. "Come see me," I pleaded.

"It's not a good time for me," he said. "But as soon as I can, I will."

I was in a frame of mind where "tomorrow" was not soon enough. Suddenly I felt young and overwhelmed. I needed to see a family member.

I did my usual hitchhiking act, this time landing in Santa Barbara. I met a guy who lived on a boat, and he offered me a berth for the night. My divine protection, however, was wearing thin. This fellow tried to rape me, but I somehow managed to talk my way out of it (more unwarranted grace from above). The next morning, as soon as it was light, I escaped, determined to make my way to my brother's.

I got a ride in an old van (old in 1980, that is) with a bunch of aging hippies. They ignored me, which was fine. The world didn't seem as friendly a place as it had a few days ago.

I found my brother's apartment, but he had already left for work. The key was right where he had said it would be, though, and I let myself in. There wasn't very much to do. Jerry's refrigerator reflected his status in life as a 23-year-old bachelor. That is to say, it contained three bottles of champagne, half a gallon of milk, some old lettuce, and a rapidly aging carton of eggs.

When my brother came home from work that night, he seemed less than thrilled to see his irresponsible sister. "Mom and Dad are worried sick about you," he said by way of greeting. "They've already left on their trip to Israel, but Mom gave me her Visa number and I'm to put you on the first plane back to New York."

What could I do? I had no plan. I stayed another two days and then Jerry drove me to LAX. He was very kind, but I didn't fit into his new, exciting life at all. I was a liability.

After finding my way home from Kennedy Airport (an airline employee gave me a lift), I came face-to-face with my other brother, Michael. He thought that he would have the whole house to himself for six weeks while my parents were in Europe but now, within a week, his crazy sister had returned. Suffice it to say that he was not pleased.

I dragged my oversized backpack into the house, aware of the hostility vibes heading my way. "Hey, Mike," I said.

"Hi," he grunted, arms folded.

Then he got more talkative. "I can't believe what you did. Do you have any idea how upset Mom was when you disappeared like you did? Dad had to convince her to get on the plane with him."

"I was fine," I said, completely dismissive of my mother's pain. I didn't believe my actions affected anyone else. It was all about me. "Anyway," I said, my eyes brightening, "I was perfectly safe. Jesus protected me the whole time."

Mike's eyes narrowed. I could tell he was thinking, *Jesus? This was new.* "You're a moron," he spat. "If Dad ever hears you say that, he's gonna kill you."

That's all it took. Just those words, "Dad's gonna kill you." All my newfound, ethereal faith drained right out of me. It would be another five years, five sin-drenched years, until I would have the courage to seek after God.

Nine

That fall saw me back at the prestigious university I had dropped out of the previous spring. I had missed the opportunity to room with the girls from freshman year, so had to take an apartment off campus, by myself. To say I was lonely would be a supreme understatement. I felt detached from humanity. With entirely too much time on my hands, I read constantly. I particularly liked the authors Joyce Carol Oates and Iris Murdoch. Both women were excellent writers, but their work tended toward the dark. I grew more and more depressed.

I started to fantasize about being a wife and mother. *That* would bring happiness, I reasoned. Determined, I sought a serious boyfriend who would lead me toward that elusive goal. Of course, anyone with any sense ran from such a confused, desperate girl. What remained was, well, the jerks. By December even I knew that I couldn't bear anymore. At the end of the semester, on a cold, snowy, winter's day, my father came and got me.

That next semester, I transferred to a state university much closer to home. I wish I could say that life improved once I moved into the dorms among kids who were more from my cultural background, but it didn't. I made some friends, but still went after having *a boyfriend*, as if that would fill the emptiness in my heart. I longed to connect with other people but felt as though some sort of plexiglass wall kept me back. I was blinded to my own actions and how they repelled others. I only saw me and my needs. Other people existed to meet my needs, and they always fell short.

I became an English major. What else does a girl who loves to read do? One semester, I signed up for a class that the other kids said was really easy, an easy *A*. It was called "The Undiscovered Self." I had no idea what it was about, but it seemed interesting.

The professor was a soft-spoken Brazilian. He had a salt-and-pepper, bushy beard and looked to be in his forties. He liked me immediately (the professors always did. It was the boys my own age who backed off). The reading list was exclusively made up of New Age books. Authors like Carlos Castanada and Edgar Cayce; titles like *The Tao of Physics,* and *I Ching.* All of this stuff focused on the supernatural, but not the biblical. I found it intriguing.

I read about occultism, reincarnation, eastern philosophy, and dozens of other things I have since forgotten. I distinctly remember reading some of these books and thinking, *Yeah, this really makes sense.* But then, right after I put the book down, I wouldn't be able to remember the logic of the author's argument. It was as if Someone had wiped my mind clean with a celestial sponge. In retrospect, I was protected from getting overtaken.

The topic assigned for the final paper was reincarnation. I decided that this was a theory just too bizarre for me to believe. With a heavy heart, because I knew the professor would disapprove, I wrote a paper disagreeing with the basics taught in the class. As expected, the professor was not pleased, but still had the courtesy to give me a good grade. I had done the work.

Now I look back on that class and am appalled at what is taught in our universities to unsuspecting and impressionable young adults. I could so easily have been swept into the whole Eastern/New Age Movement; it's a mercy that I was not. Deep in my spirit, I knew that these philosophies, attractive though they might seem on the surface, in actuality were *wrong.* For the next few years, I stepped entirely away from seeking after the spiritual.

After graduating from college, I floated through a series of secretarial jobs. What else did one do with an English degree? By twenty-two years old, I had moved back home and was working for a lady lawyer.

On my twenty-third birthday, my best friend, Patti, treated me to dinner at a fancy Chinese restaurant.

Set back from a winding country road, its intricate walkways lit by small white lights, this particular restaurant was a landmark of elegance. Patti and I were both excited about our night out, looking forward to a great meal and lots of talking.

The slender, well-dressed waiter led us through the large, dimly lit rooms, where round tables boasted glowing candles. He showed us to a small table for two next to a huge window, handed us our menus, and took his leave.

"Order whatever you want," said Patti graciously. "It's your birthday."

My birthday! I always loved birthdays but now it seemed that I was going nowhere fast. Getting older with nothing to show for it was depressing. Here I was, almost two years out of college, and neither my job nor my personal life held any interest for me.

I looked at my menu. The full color page of splashy looking drinks caught my eye. Normally, I'm not much of a drinker; one glass of wine is enough to make my knees weak, but these really appealed to me.

"Hey, let's get one of these rum things with the cute little umbrellas," I said.

Patti scanned her menu. "Sure. I'll have one, too."

We ended up ordering two each, sipping slowly and talking for hours. Patti was a girl from my neighborhood that I had only gotten to know towards the end of high school. It turned out that we had a lot in common and could talk about anything. Generally we walked on the beach or played backgammon. I felt free to be myself with Patti. Nothing seemed to shock her.

Now we shared our hearts regarding our futures. Patti didn't have nearly the level of restlessness with which I was afflicted. She had no desire to get married and liked her job at a local engineering firm. I, on the other hand, was bored senseless.

"My life has to change," I moaned, dizzy from the copious amounts of rum I had drunk.

Finally, full and tipsy, we decided to head home. Staggering out to the parking lot, breathing in the frosty nighttime December air, we followed those cute little white lights back towards my car. The lot was full of cars, but we were the only people outside. That is, except for a very attractive man passing us in the opposite direction.

"Hey," he said.

"Hi," we said back. After he walked by, I said to Patti. "I know him!" And I did. He was a workman who often came through the office where I worked. He looked different dressed nicely.

"Hey," I yelled at his retreating back. "Wait a minute! Don't I know you?"

The man stopped walking and turned around. He came over to where we were standing. "You're the secretary at Rachel's office, aren't you?" he asked.

"Yes. Today is my birthday," I added, irrelevantly. I hadn't noticed before how exceptionally attractive this fellow was. I was mesmerized. "My name's Becky."

"Hey, Becky. I'm Rob. Happy birthday." He smiled a slow, sexy smile.

"Well, Rob, since it's my birthday, why don't you kiss me?"

Behind me, I heard Patti groan. But I didn't care; I was too far gone for that. I threw my arms around Rob's neck and pulled him close. It was a great kiss. I was hooked.

Rob stepped back first. "That was pretty intense," he said impassively. "But I'm meeting my girlfriend for dinner and I'm late." He waved at us. "Good night."

"Bye," I said. When Patti and I were safely in my car, I burst out laughing. "I can't believe I did that."

"Neither can I," snorted Patti, shaking her head. "You are too crazy."

Once the alcohol wore off, the infatuation, which should have worn off as well, switched instead into high gear. I grew obsessed with this fellow, though he was obviously wrong for me on so many levels: Gentile, uneducated, from a broken home, with an addictive personality. He drank too much, smoked too many cigarettes, freebased cocaine. He was my opposite in many ways, plus he was very young, a year younger than me, but extremely experienced when it came to women.

Suddenly, I looked forward to going to work. My senses were on overdrive, listening and watching lest Rob should come through the little lobby right outside my sliding glass windows. I did everything I could to encounter him. The fact that he had a girlfriend meant nothing more to me than an inconvenience. I considered Rob fair game.

It so happened that I met Rob at a time when life's rules had unexpectedly changed for him. The girl he loved and with whom he routinely had sex went one night to a local Baptist church and made a commitment to Jesus. Now she wouldn't sleep with Rob anymore.

Rob was frustrated. He respected his girlfriend and didn't want to push her, but he was a guy used to a high level of sexual performance. He had neither the inclination nor the self-control to be celibate. Then I danced across his path.

It didn't take long for me to get sexually involved with Rob. That clinched it. I was completely hooked, emotionally and physically. Life ceased to hold meaning except for when I could see, or speak to him. I lived for him. I was a woman obsessed.

While Rob was involved with me, he continued to maintain his relationship with his girlfriend. He went with her to the Baptist church and also gave his heart to Jesus. However, unlike the girlfriend, he continued to drink, smoke, do recreational drugs, and see me.

Something about Rob made me throw all caution to the wind. Less than a month after kissing him in the parking lot, I became pregnant. I went to the local Planned Parenthood and had a test done. Then I told Rob.

He was horrified. "I've already had three girls get abortions," he moaned. *Three girls? Was he kidding?*

"Let's not think of it as an abortion. Right now it's a baby," I said.

Rob just stared at me, his face pale.

I went on a campaign to get Rob to marry me. I was too terrified to tell my parents and lacked the courage to have a baby as a single woman. Rob even went and talked to the pastor of the Baptist church, who also recommended that Rob marry me.

"I can't do it," he stated baldly.

"Oh, come on," I urged, all self-respect gone. "I promise you that after the baby is born, you can divorce me if you want. Come on." But he wouldn't budge.

"Here," he said one night, handing me a piece of paper with a name and phone number written on it.

"What's this?"

"It's a woman you can talk to about the baby. My pastor gave it to me."

Okay.

By now I was good and scared. Flipping out, actually. The initial euphoria had worn off and had been replaced by nausea. I should have told my parents but was much too ashamed. Even though I was a college graduate, I lived at my childhood home in an expensive area and couldn't see how I could possibly support a child. I didn't know what to do.

It was about this same time that my grandmother lay dying in a local hospital. She had outlived her husband by several years and was succumbing to stomach cancer. One of the biggest regrets of my life was my inability to spend the time with her that I should have during this period because I was so focused on my own dilemma. I went to the hospital a few times, sat next to her, and held her thin and bloodless hand. I was unaware of the horrible pain she stoically bore, and didn't realize the effort she poured into being kind to me. I loved her, but couldn't focus on her then. All that mattered to me was Rob. Rob and the unborn child I carried.

My grandmother died the way she lived: with great courage. The day of the funeral was one of those brilliantly sunny, clear and cold February days. I was starting to feel like I was going to my own funeral.

I sought out the rabbi after the service, determined to ask him for help. I had known him my entire life, but this was the first time I had actually attempted to solicit his spiritual counsel. "Can I talk to you?" I haltingly asked, not sure even what I would say.

Agitated, he shooed me away. "Some other time," he said gruffly. Offended, I backed off. I have since come to understand that the poor man was suffering from cancer and wasn't himself. But that door still was effectively shut for me.

Later that day, when the whole family sat at my aunt's house, eating and talking quietly, my cousin Mindy casually remarked, "You know, they say that when someone dies, someone is born." Pain gripped my heart; I looked away.

A few days later, alone at home one night, I took out the piece of paper Rob had given me. With shaking fingers, I called the number. A woman answered.

"Hello?" She sounded as if she were eating something.

"Uh, hi. I got your number from Pastor Thomas. He suggested I call you."

"Yes?"

"I'm pregnant and thinking about getting an abortion."

There was the crackling and shuffling of paper on the other end of the phone. "Abortion is murder," pronounced the woman, her tone bland and casual.

Murder! I knew it was bad, but I didn't need to immediately hear the word *murder!* Tears pricked at my eyelids. Irrationally, I grew angry. "Thanks a lot," I yelled into the phone, slamming it back down into its cradle.

The next day, I went back to Planned Parenthood. The girl who worked there took me into a small office. "Here," she said, handing me a small card.

"What's this?"

"It's an abortion clinic. Give them a call, and they'll set up an appointment for you."

Listlessly I fingered the card. "You do it."

She shook her head. "I can't. It's illegal for me to even dial the phone. You have to."

"But why?" I anguished, tears running down my face. "Why can't I just have this baby? I'm too upset to have an abortion!"

The young woman coolly appraised me, her eyebrows arched. "You're too upset to raise a child," she said in a bored voice.

The Planned Parenthood people never spoke to me about other options; they pushed the abortion issue hard. I was too cowardly to resist. I made the appointment at the clinic for three days later. Rob dropped me off.

"Please," I said, before leaving his truck. "We can still change our minds! Let's have this baby."

He shook his head. "I can't do it. I'm sorry." He looked into my eyes briefly. "Call me when you're done, and I'll pick you up, okay?"

Numbly, I nodded, then left his truck and watched him drive off. I entered the facility, a clean, well-kept professional building.

The receptionist signed me in, then asked for the fee. Wordlessly, I handed her three hundred dollars in cash. I sat down in the waiting room and glanced around at the faces of my fellow abortionees. Everyone seemed young and nervous, like me.

Soon another woman entered the waiting room from the inner office. She read several names, including mine, off a list and ushered us into a room. We sat in a circle while she gave a brief teaching on what to expect, and the possible symptoms afterward that would warrant our calling the office.

"Any questions?" she asked dispassionately.

"This is murder," I grumbled.

She glared at me. "You can leave if you want."

But I didn't.

The next two months were hard for me. My mother guessed what I had done but I denied it, unable to accept or solicit her comfort. My relationship with Rob deteriorated, and I spent my time working and taking long, lonely walks on the windswept beach close to my home. All in all, it was a pretty dismal time until April, when I got an unexpected phone call.

My mother's cousin owned an apartment building in Santa

Monica, California. These apartments were very cheap, rent-controlled affairs, a short walk from the Pacific Ocean. Santa Monica tended to be a bit more socialist than the rest of the nation, thus you could live for $300 a month next door to a million-dollar mansion. The people who scored one of these apartments tended to keep them for life. In fact, the reason my mom's cousin called was because the elderly lady who had lived in one of the units for the last seventeen years had just died, so the place was vacant. Betty knew I had expressed some interest in moving to Los Angeles, so she gave me first crack at taking the place.

"Save it for me; I'll be there in two weeks," I told her, overjoyed.

The first thing I did was to approach Rob and ask him to come to California with me. I had my sales pitch all prepared, though in my heart I knew there was no way he would ever say yes. Imagine my surprise when he agreed.

"Sure, okay," he said, stunning me into momentary silence. "It's time for a change."

Next thing I knew, I was dipping into my savings at regular intervals, helping Rob pay off some loans, and enabling him to get his decrepit truck road-ready for a three-thousand-mile trip. I didn't mind; I was so happy he was coming with me, I floated on clouds. I neglected to tell my parents that he was coming until the night before I left.

"I can't believe you're doing this," stormed my father as he angrily helped fit my worldly possessions into the trunk of my '75 Oldsmobile Cutlas Supreme. He turned to face me, blue eyes narrowed. "Let me just say one thing to you: of all the stupid things you've ever done, *and there have been many,* this is by far the most stupid!" He slammed the trunk of the car shut.

I didn't care. Nothing in life mattered except Rob.

The next day dawned bright and clear; a perfect May day. I bade my parents farewell, then eagerly slid into the driver's seat of the big, red car. Rob and I had agreed to meet at his house.

We managed to cram a five-day journey to California into only fourteen days. In that time, I spent nearly half of my $5,000 savings on motels, restaurants, and car emergencies. I was not my normal frugal self. I existed to please Rob.

Various images remain with me from that time: the cool lushness of a spring morning in Missouri; a rowdy bar in Knoxville, Tennessee; the heady, overpowering scent of honeysuckle down a highway divider in Memphis at sunset; lazily watching the Mississippi River swirl by while sipping a pina colada; sharing a sampler plate of buffalo and rattlesnake from a steakhouse in Amarillo; restlessly tossing quarters into a slot machine at a dusty roadside café in Nevada; blinking in wonderment at the beauty of the barren hills of the California desert; overwhelmed by the sudden influx of motorists as we approached Los Angeles County; navigating our way through a bewildering freeway system in the middle of the night so we could find the apartment in Santa Monica.

"I can't sleep here," Rob announced as soon as we had found the key in its designated hiding place and opened the apartment door.

I looked around. True, the walls needed painting and the carpets were junky, but that sleep-a-way couch in the middle of the room looked new. "Why not?"

"It's awful." He scoured the room with the practiced eye of a trained carpenter. "We're going to have to change everything."

Well. This was certainly a side to Rob I hadn't suspected. But right then I was falling asleep on my feet.

"Can we deal with this tomorrow?" I pleaded. But Rob was already ripping carpeting up in a corner of the one-room studio.

"It's hard wood," he crowed. "I can strip this and polyurethane it. You're not going to believe how nice it's gonna look!"

When Rob was finished fixing up that tiny apartment, it did look a lot better, but I was also a lot poorer. I didn't care, though. I would have done anything for him. I was mesmerized by him in a way seemingly incomprehensible to just about everyone else.

Rob got a job right away building McMansions on a construction site south of Santa Monica, past Venice Beach. I started doing temp secretarial work. What I really wanted was to work in the entertainment industry.

Even though Rob had gone with his girlfriend (*wasn't I his girlfriend now?*) to her Baptist church and had given his heart to Jesus, one would have been hard-pressed to realize this as he lived just as wildly now as he had before, the only possible difference being that now he had an occasional bout of remorse. I was shocked when he announced that he was going to find a Baptist church to attend, like the one back home.

"You don't have to come with me," he said.

Wild horses couldn't keep me away from Rob.

"It's okay, I'll come," I said.

We came to find out that the church steeple visible from our kitchen window belonged to a Baptist church. That Sunday morning, we walked down the block and joined the worshipers entering the church.

I felt strangely excited to be doing this. It was so *forbidden!* Even though Rob had reassured me more than once that he didn't expect me to go to church with him, I discovered that I really wanted to see what this was all about. My experiences at Yellowstone from five years ago were not uppermost in my mind, but I did remember them.

I wasn't sure what to expect. The words *Baptist church* conjured up images of a screaming, red-faced pastor with a Southern accent, berating the members of his flock. With some trepidation, I climbed the white stone steps and entered the large, airy sanctuary. Imagine my surprise when the service started and the pastor turned out to be a soft-spoken native Californian, a young man not more than thirty. He spoke intelligently and gently, sharing with us from the book of Ephesians:

"Wives, submit to your husbands as to the Lord. For the husband is the head of the wife as Messiah is the head of the church, his body, of

which he is the Savior. Now as the church submits to Messiah, so also wives should submit to their husbands in everything. Husbands, love your wives..."

A thrill went through me at those words, *submit to your husbands.* It seemed so, well, sexy. More than that, though, it was a confirmation of the proper relationship between men and women. All my life, I had felt pressured by the post-neo-women's lib to perform both academically and in a brilliant career. My desire to be a wife and a mother were considered foolish and lacking by the women academics in my circle of relations and acquaintances. Suddenly I was discovering that the Bible actually encouraged and taught these things that were dearest to my heart. I was blown away!

I filled out one of those little white visitor's cards that were shelved on the pew in front of us and dropped it in the offering. Rob and I said hello to some of the friendly people who came up to meet us, then shook the pastor's hand on our way out the door.

That week, we were surprised by a visit from the pastor. He showed up at our apartment door one evening, seemingly oblivious to the glaring fact of our living together. *Guess it doesn't bother these guys,* I thought to myself.

He sat with us for about a half an hour, asking some questions but mostly listening. Very warm, very welcoming.

"What a nice guy!" I exclaimed, after he left.

Rob was less impressed than me. "It's better back home," he mumbled.

I sighed. This missing home stuff translated to missing the girlfriend I thought he had given up for me. I was soon to find out that he had lied to her about the move to California, pretending that he went alone in an attempt to straighten out his life. I wanted to be furious but couldn't as I dreaded doing anything that would drive Rob away. Instead I concentrated on winning him over. I cooked gourmet meals, catered to his whims, loaned him money. I draped myself around him, telling him how much I loved him. I even bought him a little yellow sports car.

The fellow who lived next door to us was our age, an overweight blonde guy from Malibu. A compadre. We three quickly became friends. Tim owned a Datsun 2000 convertible that he wanted to unload for $1,000. In yet another of an endless series of weak moments, I purchased it for Rob, not understanding that you can't buy love, but you sure can buy disdain.

Despite Rob's desire to go to church every Sunday, he showed no sign of morality the rest of the week. All too soon he fell in with a group of ne'er-do-wells down in Venice Beach. A wannabe actress/cocktail waitress started calling the apartment at 3 a.m., looking for Rob. It was no better than I deserved, but it's all too easy to just see how you've been hurt, and not how you've hurt others.

In the meantime, I began to form relationships with the pastor of the Baptist church, his wife, and some of the other members of the congregation. They were kind and reached out to me in a way I had never before experienced. I was starved for kindness.

Less than two months after we arrived in California, Rob and I decided to visit Rob's uncle in Palm Springs and also go to the Barstow 250 Off-Road Race. We zipped out of town on a Friday after work, top down on the little yellow sports car, doing 100 m.p.h. on the freeways outside the city limits. I only had eyes for Rob.

Later that evening, we pulled up to his uncle's modest bungalow, 7785 Canyon Center Road. The uncle, a nondescript, bearded man in his thirties, lacked the charisma of his nephew but seemed nice enough. He accompanied us to the off-road race the next day, a broiling hot outdoor affair where vast quantities of beer was drunk. I have a picture of myself from that day and my face is bright pink. I survived, though, and that night we sat in the back of the uncle's pickup and gazed up at the explosion of diamond-bright stars in the sky, grateful for the relief from the heat.

The next morning, Sunday, Rob's uncle, a born-again Christian, took us to his church in Palm Springs. The uncle was fascinated by my Jewishness and proceeded to ask all sorts of questions I couldn't answer. I felt simultaneously defensive but also pleased by the attention.

The church was relatively new; a spirit-filled, charismatic, nondenominational one with lots of young people, very different from the Baptist church in Santa Monica. Rob's uncle introduced us to some folks, all of whom were very friendly. We sat in some padded folding chairs and fanned ourselves with our paper programs, as there wasn't any air-conditioning. Two big ceiling fans hummed noisily overhead.

The worship music started. The pastor's wife sang lead vocal and played keyboards, while three guys backed her up with drums, guitar and bass. This was very different from the organ music at the other church! I immediately felt very drawn into the worship through the music. Several songs in, I had a startling realization in my spirit that Jesus is real, that he is who he says he is. Just after this, one of the elders in the church came forward with the microphone and said, "If you believe in Jesus, I want you to stand right where you are."

Now I had never been one to be obvious in a crowd. I never sang out, or anything. I was entirely too self-conscious. I also thought that Rob would think I was faking belief as a way of getting him to commit to me, as he had often told me that one of the reasons why he could never marry me was due to my lack of faith in Jesus. So I was in a quandary. Should I stand? And risk scorn? Or should I sit quietly and sort this out another time? I vacillated.

Something (which I later came to realize was the Holy Spirit) pushed at me from within. *Stand!* Nervously, purposely not looking at Rob, I stood.

About half a dozen other people stood as well. The congregation broke out in applause and shouts of, "Praise God, Thank you, Lord!" Rob's uncle grinned at me while Rob merely raised his eyebrows. Then the pastor took the microphone from the elder and preached his sermon.

I couldn't understand what he said. None of it made any sense to me. In fact, I still didn't really know the Gospel message, or what I believed. All I knew was that Jesus had become very real to me, and that I had irrevocably crossed a line. The date that day was July 7, 1985. Seven, seven, eight, five. The same number as the number on the house where I spent the weekend.

Instinctively, I knew my lifestyle was displeasing to God. That doesn't mean I cleaned up my act; it just meant I started feeling guilty about things that hadn't bothered me before.

At first Rob thought that I had merely pretended to accept Jesus. It took him a few days, but soon he was able to believe me and be happy.

Two weeks after we got back to L.A., a group from the Baptist church drove down to Anaheim in Orange County. They were going to the Billy Graham Crusade and asked me if I would go with them. It sounded interesting so I said *yes*.

As was customary, they had an altar call after Dr. Graham spoke. Even though I had technically "been saved," I went down to the main floor, and met with one of the pray-ers. He led me in a prayer of repentance and then gave me the packet of information that the Billy Graham people hand out. There were several index cards with Scriptures on them that you're supposed to memorize, some teachings with questions to answer, and a Gospel of John to read. When you finish doing all this, you mail it back to their national headquarters in Minnesota and they send you a certificate of completion.

I'm very academically inclined so this was something I could handle. As I processed this information, I understood the Gospel for the first time. I understood that Messiah died for our sins and that he rose again on the third day and is still alive in heaven, interceding for us.

I remember having a week-long temp job at an office down by Los Angeles International Airport and reading that Gospel of John when there was nothing else for me to do. I remember being shocked by the story of Jesus and discovering that the Jews, *along with the Romans*, wanted him dead. This conflicted with what I had been told as a child, which was that the Romans alone killed him. We were all guilty! Later I came to understand that it is only those who take part in the sacrifice whose sins are forgiven.

Once whetted, my appetite for reading Scripture took off like a rocket. I bought myself a leather-bound Bible and began to read in earnest. Soon I knew more than Rob, which didn't help the ailing relationship.

By August, Rob had made plans to return to New York. My tears ran like a river as I begged him to stay. "I can't live without you!" I sobbed.

"Are you kidding?" he protested, staring into my red-rimmed eyes. "You're doing great here. You have friends, a good job. You don't need me."

It was true. I had blossomed that summer since finding Jesus.

Suddenly, through church involvement, I had friends who really seemed to like me and whom I liked. A job with a major film producer had miraculously fallen into my lap. I just loved Southern California! I knew that the relationship with Rob was wrong but clung to it stubbornly. I barraged God with prayers, pleading with him to let me marry Rob. Mercifully, in retrospect, he gave me the proper answer: *No.*

Ten

After Rob left, I shakily and tearfully grew in my faith. My first test came later that month when my parents called and told me they were coming to California for a visit.

"What should I do?" I asked the Baptist pastor. "They don't know that I believe in Jesus and I'm afraid to tell them." I had just recently read the Scripture that clearly states, *Whoever acknowledges me before men, I will also acknowledge him before my Father in heaven. But whoever disowns me before men, I will disown him before my Father in heaven* (Matthew 10:32-33).

"Hmm," said the pastor. He leaned back in his chair and settled his glasses more securely on his face. "I tell you what. Don't lie to them, but don't feel like you *have* to tell them either."

Okay. I liked this advice. I rather doubted either Mom or Dad would say, "So, what do you think, Becky? Is Jesus the promised Messiah?"

Well, I was right. They didn't ask that question, or even one remotely like it. They commiserated with me over Rob's departure but were secretly relieved. Actually, maybe not so secretly. The visit passed pleasantly enough and soon they returned to New York.

In addition to the Baptist church, I was also attending a youth-oriented, rock 'n' roll church in West L.A. I alternated between the two places on Sundays, and attended the youth church's midweek service. It was a very happening place, where hundreds of entertainment industry twenty and thirty-somethings worshiped with all their hearts, gathering to hear the charismatic sermons of the young, hip, jean-and-cowboy-boot-clad pastor. I hoped it would only be a matter of time before I met a guy through this place. I hadn't yet figured out that sometimes the bigger the place, the greater the potential for isolation and loneliness. It was the Baptist church, with its small circle of young people and larger circle of older folks, where I was forming real friendships. The youth church had an exciting service, but I always went home alone.

The youth church held a baptism service, and I signed up to be immersed. I didn't know too much about it other than you were supposed to get baptized after you got saved. So I went. I got a photocopy of directions and went to the house of a church member who had a swimming pool. I wore a leopard-spotted bikini. This was not a church where they handed you a white robe.

I went alone. It seemed that everyone else had friends and family cheering them on. Twenty people must have gotten baptized that day and almost every girl came up out of that crystal-blue chlorinated water sobbing and emotional. Every girl except for me.

There must be something really wrong with me, I thought to myself, disconcerted. I got immersed out of obedience to the Word of God, but felt nothing. Well, maybe I felt a little depressed because I had no family who would support me.

An amazing thing happened the next day. I woke up and, for the first time since giving my heart to the Lord two-and-a-half months previously, I knew I could not rest until I told my parents about my newfound faith. This didn't mean I wasn't terrified; it just meant I knew I had to tell them no matter what.

With shaking fingers, I dialed the phone number to the house back on Long Island. Mercifully, my mother answered the phone. "Mom?" I squawked, my stomach churning.

"Becky, sweetie. How are you?" My mother's pleasant tones floated over the phone wires.

"Uh, Ma, there's something I need to talk to you about."

Immediately, my mother's voice tightened. "Oh, no. What is it? What's happened?"

"Nothing bad," I sought to reassure her. "In fact, it's something really good. It's just going to surprise you." I could feel my mother bracing herself from three thousand miles away.

"Just tell me."

The words came out in a rush. "I've been going to church since I moved out here and I've come to believe that Jesus is God. I'm a

140

Christian now." *There, it's out.*

There was total silence on the other side of the line and then the sounds of soft crying. I felt sick, like I'd purposely killed a baby animal. "Mom, are you okay?"

Shakily, my mother drew a breath. "Are you telling me you've become a Gentile? I don't understand! Isn't our religion good enough for you?"

"I'm not a Gentile, Mom, I'm a Christian. It's different. You can be Jewish and Christian at the same time. A Christian means one who follows the Messiah. That's me. I follow the Messiah."

"That doesn't make any sense. I'm sure we can talk it out."

I gripped the phone. I didn't want to talk anything out. My faith was entirely too new to stand up to pressure. I didn't want to risk it. Stubbornly, I shook my head. "Look, Ma, I'm sorry that this is upsetting to you but to me it's a wonderful thing. I've found God." I struggled briefly with courage, but lost. "Uh, could you tell Dad?"

She did.

I spent days anguishing over my father's reaction. I wasn't sure what he would do so I imagined the worst. The scenario where he hopped on the next plane to L.A. and showed up at my workplace, grabbing me by the back of the neck and forcing me home always caused the greatest *angst.* Reality, as is so often the case, was nothing like imagination.

I got one telephone call and one letter. Both were relatively brief. Basically, he had an ultimatum: either give up this silly idea, or I won't talk to you again.

Fine, don't talk to me, I responded. *It's true, so I'm never going to give it up.*

That was the last contact I had with my father for several months.

That February, my brother Jerry got married. The wedding was held at a fancy hotel perched on a cliff overlooking the Pacific Ocean. I drove down from L.A., apprehensive as this would be the first time I would see my parents since telling them about Yeshua.

I arrived on a stunningly beautiful, crisp, clear day. I swung into the circular drive in front of the hotel, noting with great appreciation the spectacular flowers planted along every walkway. Roses in all hues, orange and blue birds of paradise, lilies, violets...what magnificence. A young, Hispanic fellow in black slacks and a crisp white shirt sprang to attention when I pulled up, insisting on valet-parking my modest car. I unloaded my one small suitcase and checked-in.

Later that day, I was bouncing down the stairs intent on exploring the place. Who should be coming up the stairs, winded from a run, but my father? I don't know who was more surprised when we came face-to-face. I started to say hello, but he turned aside, ignoring me. I felt terribly hurt, but at the same time I knew this was how he felt about Jesus, not me.

About the time I saw my father, I had been a believer in Jesus for a little over half a year. Since Rob left, I had attempted to find a boyfriend who believed as I did. I had a tendency of living out that famous quote from Groucho Marx, "No one wants to belong to a club that will accept them." The men who liked me didn't appeal, and the ones I liked weren't interested.

One day, during my lunch hour, I took a walk around the movie studio lot where I worked. I loved taking walks during my lunch breaks. First, it got me out of the office and into the fresh air. Second, it brought me into contact with all the interesting things that go on in a place where several television series and motion picture films are being simultaneously shot.

I had noticed that the actresses usually hid in their trailers while the actors wandered around, accessible. So I tended to meet the men more than the women because that's who emerged, blinking, into the sunshine. One fellow, who played the father on a hit TV series, was also a believer. He would sit and talk to me about God. I found that really thrilling. This particular day, however, I met an actor I had never seen there before.

I was standing on the steps to the Commissary, shading my eyes with my hand from the glare of the sun, when a shadow fell across my path. Startled, I pulled my hand away and found myself looking into the face of a fellow who had been a regular on one of my favorite shows from my high school and college days.

"Hello," he said.

"Hi," I said back.

He started talking to me as if he expected me to know his name, which of course I did. I introduced myself and we started chatting.

"So, what are you doing here?" I asked him.

"I'm shooting a new series with Hayley Jackson," he said, naming a well-known comic actress.

I hadn't heard about this sitcom. If a TV pilot gets the nod, it goes into a thirteen-week production schedule. That's what they were filming.

"What do you play?"

"I'm the husband," he answered. *Oh, the male lead.* He glanced at his watch. "Hey, look, I gotta go. Why don't you give me your number? I'll call you."

Why don't I give you my number? With all the self-control I could muster, I dictated my phone number while he wrote it down on a little pad that he pulled out of his hip pocket.

After saying good-bye, I walked back to my office in a daze. I was used to chatting with the male stars but not potentially *dating* them! Adrenaline started to pound through my veins. By the time I reached my familiar gray cubicle, I was on supercharge. All my old fantasies about walking into a ready-made exciting life that I didn't help create came crowding back at me. By quitting time that day I was no longer a secretary; I was...Hollywood Wife.

The next few days crawled by at an agonizingly slow pace as I waited for the phone to ring. Nagging doubts sprang into my mind about dating an unbeliever, but I swept them all away, telling myself that I didn't know enough yet to so label him. *It's possible he knows God*, I reasoned, though even through my romantic haze I could see that the odds were slim, if not negligible.

When Byron did call to invite me to dinner, I unhesitatingly said yes. He showed up at my little apartment, ushered me into his trendy sports car, and took me to an upscale restaurant right there in Santa Monica. I felt like Cinderella.

That night I spoke to Byron about my faith in Jesus. He listened politely for a few minutes, argued a bit, then lost interest in the topic. We went on to make that small talk people make when the only thing that binds them together is mutual physical attraction. I realized with a sinking heart that not only was he not a believer, but he wasn't even remotely interested in the things I held most dear.

We dated sporadically for a couple of months. The thrill of going out with a TV star dimmed significantly as I realized just how self-absorbed and nuts this guy was. Once, while wandering bored around his huge loft apartment while Byron was on yet another phone call, I idly picked up some papers on a desk.

"Stop!" he screamed, scaring me such that I jumped. It turned out that I was holding his tax return, and he panicked at the possibility of my knowing how much money he made. I decided I was basically through at this point.

The final nail in the proverbial coffin came a week later. I had gone to a small, worship concert at a Valley church that featured a Jewish believer who sang and played piano. I had heard him before at my youth church, and marginally knew his wife as she worked at the same movie studio as me. I sat in the small sanctuary, feeling the peace of God drench me with its sweetness. I also repented of seeing Byron, of putting him before God and making an idol of his worldly status.

After the service, I walked to the front of the sanctuary and said hello to Max and his wife, Barb. One thing led to another, and soon I confessed to them my loneliness and desperate need to get married and have *someone.*

"You're lucky," Max encouraged me, shaking his head. "When I was a new believer, I already had a girlfriend. I went right from her to Barb." He blew a kiss at his wife, who smiled.

Oh, to have a marriage like that, I thought wistfully.

"But," he continued. "I never had that 'just me and God' time that lets you spend hours with him and only him. Don't lose this opportunity! You're young, you'll get married, but you'll never have quite this freedom again. Don't fight the circumstances of your life. Glory in them. Be with Yeshua." Max and Barb spoke to me for a few more moments and then turned to the next person who was waiting for them.

That short encounter radically changed my mindset. I went home and ended my relationship with Byron (just before he did; I think it was a draw). I won't say that I wasn't lonely anymore, but a good deal of that negative *gotta find someone* energy left me.

That Monday night, when I went to the weekly Bible study at the Baptist church, the pastor's wife took me aside.

"I met a girl in the Christian bookstore in Westwood that I think you would really like," she began.

"Oh, really, why?"

"She's a Jewish believer, like you. I think you'll have a lot in common." Karen, the pastor's wife, pressed a piece of notepaper into my hand. "Give her a call."

"Okay, thanks," I said, folding the slip of paper and zipping it inside my purse. When I returned to my apartment later than evening, I took out the paper and looked at it. *Mandy Brotkin, 779-8081.* I put that slip of paper next to my telephone and thought about it for a few days. I wish I could say that I *prayed* about it, but I don't think I was quite at that place yet, spiritually. By Thursday, after work, I decided to go ahead and call.

One ring, two rings, three ri...

"Hello?" A nice voice; a bit of a Western twang.

"Hi," I said. "You don't know me, but my pastor's wife gave me your name." Briefly, I introduced myself and explained why I was calling.

Mandy was extremely friendly. "Why don't we meet for coffee?" she suggested. We agreed on a place and time.

It turned out that Mandy was a missionary with Jews for Jesus. I had heard the name over the years but had never really understood the dynamics of the organization. I discovered that Jews for Jesus is a parachurch organization, which means that everyone who goes there already has a church that they attend. JFJ is not a church. It employs missionaries who seek to tell Jewish people the Good News of Messiah

Jesus. Their Los Angeles branch operated out of a large office building, and held weekly Friday night services (which they referred to as Bible studies).

A few people from the youth church, plus Max and Barb, were the only Jewish believers in Yeshua I had met. I assumed we were few and far between. I was the only Jewish person at my Baptist church, a unique position that afforded me much attention. I certainly enjoyed the limelight.

I have to admit that when I accepted the Lord I breathed a certain sigh of relief that I was now associated with the majority culture. This was my ticket to acceptance. My first Christmas, I went to the local Thrifty Drugstore and bought fifty dollars worth of the *shlockiest*, most glittery, tasteless, Christmas tree decorations I could find. Happy as a clam, humming "Joy to the World," I decorated a pine-needle-dropping tree bigger than me that took up a hefty percentage of the real estate in my studio apartment. So I wasn't sure if I wanted to be pushed back into a Jewish culture.

With some trepidation, I got to know Mandy better. I enjoyed her company and began to realize that my Jewishness was not something that could be pushed down, like a jack-in-the-box. No. Rather it was the very essence of who God had created me to be. *He didn't make me a Presbyterian from Virginia with country club parents. I'm from Long Island and we* yell!

I started to get involved with doing some volunteer evangelism. Jews for Jesus writes these witty tracts, about the size of a legal envelope, and their missionaries hand them out on street corners and at major events wherever Jewish people are likely to be found. Every so often, I would get together with Mandy and some of her friends from the L.A. branch office and haltingly press these tracts, or *broadsides*, into the hands of strangers.

I felt really good about doing this. It opened up a whole new world for me and got me away from obsessing about my own loneliness and future. I was doing what Max had counseled.

It was a shock then, when Mandy got angry with me one day. "You never come to our Friday night meetings," she said accusingly into the phone.

146

What?

"I'm always telling people about you and you haven't been here once!" She sounded like she was about to cry.

Friday night meetings? True, she sometimes spoke of them, but I had thought they were some type of staff gathering. I hadn't thought to ask for a more concise explanation.

"Give me the details," I said, soothingly.

By the end of the phone call, I knew the Friday night meetings were a type of service for both Jewish and Gentile believers, and those Jewish people interested in finding out more about Yeshua. *Oh.*

I committed to Mandy that I would come that week. Pacified, she hung up.

When I got off work that Friday, I didn't have enough time to drive home to Santa Monica and then go up to Van Nuys. I went from Hollywood straight to Van Nuys, stopping at a little fast-food place for a quick burrito, then drove to the JFJ building.

At this time, I was twenty-four years old. Since I had come from work, I was wearing a trendy, burgundy, tight, long skirt with a matching blazer and burgundy leather high heels (I still have those shoes and can barely hobble around my bedroom in them now though my little girls *love* them!). I looked really good, and I knew it.

Arriving a little early, I sat down in the large, almost empty meeting room. Mandy ran over to me and kissed me hello, but then had other obligations as she sang on their worship team. Soon enough, the room filled up. I glanced about at my fellow meeting attenders, noticing what a Jewish crowd this was as compared to the Gentile churches I had gotten used to.

The service started with a series of worship songs done in a very klezmer-like style. These were not hymns, nor were they the exciting, rock-beat songs of the youth church. Then the leader spoke. He was a short, wiry, former actor with a bushy black beard and bright, twinkling eyes. A very dynamic speaker. I liked him right away.

After the service, Aaron, the leader, invited everyone to stay for the *oneg* (food and fellowship). Never one to turn down free food (especially when I was single), I meandered over to the tables in the back of the room. Sometime during the last few minutes of the service, a few of the volunteers had set out platters of cheese, crackers, chips, dip, cookies, slices of cake, fruit, etc.

I loaded up a little plate, then stood self-consciously against the wall, watching the crowd. Suddenly, a tall, thin, young man with dark hair and a beard whom I had noticed sitting across the aisle from me during the service walked over.

"Hi," he said brightly. "I'm Dave Hermon."

He's kinda cute, I thought. I extended my hand. "I'm Becky Cohen."

"I've never seen you here before."

"No, this is my first time."

We chit-chatted for a few minutes, and then I asked him the question new Jewish believers always ask each other: "When did you get saved?"

"When I was nine," he answered.

Huh?

"I'm from a rather unusual family," he explained, noticing my puzzled expression. "I'm a fourth-generation Jewish believer. My grandfather came to know Yeshua as Messiah in Odessa, Russia, in 1879."

I can't emphasize enough how bizarre that sounded to me. I thought everyone who was Jewish found Jesus in their early twenties, after college, then got ostracized by their family. Obviously this fellow was lying to impress me.

"Wow, that's really interesting," I said, not wanting to ruin the conversation by calling him an out-and-out liar to his face.

It turned out that Dave *was* telling me the truth, and through knowing him I became aware of a whole spectrum of people previously under the radar. We exchanged phone numbers, and within a week went out on our first date. By the end of two weeks, we were inseparable.

This was too good to be true. After years of peering into the face of every man I passed thinking, *Is this the one?* had I really found my soulmate? I was wildly excited.

A few weeks into the relationship, I started thinking about all the awful, intemperate things I had done, like sleeping with too many men and having that abortion. I knew I had to tell Dave about my past in the early stages of getting to know each other, and not spring it on him later. I had racked up too many hours of soap-opera watching not to know that invariably the heroine's ugly secrets get diabolically revealed on her wedding day, leaving her sobbing and alone at the altar.

One day after work I drove over to the recording studio where Dave was a sound tech. Breathlessly, I burst in on him. "Hey," I said.

"Hi," he answered, pleased to see me but confused as to why I had suddenly shown up.

"I need to talk to you. Are you available?"

"Sure," he said. "Let me wrap up a few things here and then we'll go somewhere."

Restlessly, I went to the front office and paced back and forth for the next half hour. My stomach churned. I didn't want this relationship to go south, but I knew God was pressing me to be honest. This was one of my first real tests of obedience as a believer.

"Okay." Dave emerged from the studio carrying a black briefcase and a light jacket over one arm. He held the front door open for me. "Where should we go?"

"How about Wendy's?"

"Sounds good."

Twenty minutes later, we were seated at a table drinking soda and sharing some greasy, overcooked onion rings. Dave looked at me expectantly. I plunged in.

"There's some stuff you need to know if we're going to keep seeing each other," I said nervously. "I didn't grow up in the kind of family you did. I've only known the Lord for a year, and I wasn't very well-behaved. I got into some trouble."

Dave sat there nodding. So far none of this was a surprise.

I started talking. I must have talked for about an hour, going into some detail but mostly giving a broad overview of past sin and its more obvious repercussions. When I finished, Dave looked a little pale.

"What do you think?" I asked, spent.

He took a deep breath. "That was a lot," he admitted. "But Scripture says that when we come to Yeshua, he washes away our sins and cleanses us. You're clean before God. Who am I to judge?" And he took my hand and clasped it firmly.

Wow. I fell in love with him at that moment.

My life changed. Everything I did, I did with Dave. I went to his church, I hung out with his friends, I cooked dinner for him at my apartment, I went on walks to the beach with him, I went every Friday to Jews for Jesus with him...the word *lonely* left my vocabulary.

After two months of this, I just assumed we were getting married. Therefore, it came as a very pleasant surprise one night after a Friday Bible study when we got into Dave's car and he didn't turn on the ignition.

"What's up?" I asked.

He cleared his throat. "Would you," he began, then stopped. He tried again. "Would you be my wife?"

"Oh, Dave," I blurted out. "I thought we had decided that!" I started laughing and crying at the same time. He pulled me close and held me.

Ignoring current wisdom regarding engaged couples knowing one another for a full year before getting married, we immediately tracked down the pastor of the Baptist church.

"Will you marry us?" I asked, praying that he wouldn't stubbornly insist we slow our courtship down. "Please, please, please!"

The pastor pulled out a slim black leather appointment book. "Sure." He grinned. "When?"

Dave and I looked at each other, excited. "Three months?" Dave suggested.

The pastor flipped through the pages of his book...*flip flip flip.* "December 13th?"

"That sounds great!" I enthused. Dave nodded in agreement.

The next thirteen weeks were an exercise in patience for me. I couldn't wait to get married. Looking back with the wisdom of age, I know I should have slowed down and enjoyed every moment. It would be a long time before the future would again shimmer with such glorious brightness.

One of the first things we did after becoming officially engaged was to take a red-eye flight back east to meet the prospective in-laws. Dave's parents met us at the airport in New Jersey after we stumbled, exhausted, off the plane.

"Welcome to the family," smiled his mother, hugging me. Miriam Hermon was an attractive, stylish woman in her midfifties with salt-and-pepper hair, startling light blue eyes, and a throaty voice. Her husband, Philip, greeted me as well. In contrast to his son, he was clean-shaven, white-haired, and wore his crisp oxford shirts tightly buttoned. *They are so different from what I'm used to,* I thought, a slight feeling of unease gathering in the pit of my stomach.

The ride to Dave's childhood house initially passed through sections of New Jersey that looked familiar to me: smoke stacks, gas refineries, congestion, urban plight. Soon, however, the scenery changed.

I had become overfond of saying "what exit?" when Dave spoke of being from New Jersey. Now I saw a side to the Garden State that truly awed me: magnificent homes on winding roads guarded on either side by towering trees, intricately manicured lawns, vibrant flower beds. Lush greenery everywhere dazzled my eye after a standard dry, brown, California summer. Soon enough we turned into a development and drove past house after gigantic brick or Tudor-style house. At the top of the hill, we pulled in a long, narrow driveway.

"This is your house?" I asked Dave, impressed.

"Parents' house," he corrected me, with a twinkle in his eye. "Not bad for Jersey, is it?"

"I'll have to rethink my humor," I said dryly.

I was treated to a tour of the house. I had grown up in a beautiful home with the same number of bedrooms as Dave's house, but we didn't have the additional office, rec room, game room, game room addition, finished attic...well, it went on and on. All available wall space (and there was a lot of it) was covered by exquisitely framed oil and pastel paintings signed by Dave's mother.

"Your mother is a terrific artist!" I whispered loudly to Dave.

"She used to earn her living doing artwork before she got married," he told me proudly.

After the tour, we were given the healthiest breakfast I think I had ever eaten: farm eggs, sprouted multi-grain bread with *real* butter, fresh squeezed orange juice. I had come to think of Dave as a hopeless fast food addict incapable of choosing wisely when it came to food, so this was something of a shock.

Dave's mother showed me to a funky little room upstairs. "This is where my mother stays when she's with us. Get some rest. You'll meet Rachel and Rina at dinnertime when they come home from work." Those were Dave's two younger sisters.

I had recently come across the verse in Mark 10 where Yeshua says that no one who has left home or brothers or sisters or mother or father or children or fields for him and the Gospel will fail to receive a hundred times as much in this present age (homes, brothers, sisters, mothers, children and fields—and with them, persecutions) and in the age to come, eternal life. I had left behind all to follow him, and now I was getting a new family. This, I reasoned, was the beginning of my hundred times as much. I had never had sisters and greatly looked forward to a wonderful relationship with Rachel and Rina.

Soon I was alone in the little guest room. I undressed and got into the single bed with its scrollwork brass headboard. A crushed velour cranberry-colored blanket lay neatly folded at the foot of the bed. I knew that Dave was in his boyhood room just down the hall, also trying to catch up on some missed sleep from the flight in. It was agonizing to know he was so close yet unavailable.

I was very fatigued, yet my brain was too wired to allow me to sleep. After tossing and turning for the better part of an hour, I got up, slipped into my silky green robe, and tiptoed across the plush turquoise carpet to Dave's room. Stealthily, I grasped the doorknob and turned it. It clicked loudly. Quickly, I let myself in the room and closed the door.

Dave wasn't asleep either. He sat up in bed when he saw me. "What are you doing here?" he whispered, alert.

"Shhh." I put my finger to my lips and smiled. Then I climbed in bed next to him and kissed him. We snuggled for a while until Dave extricated himself.

"I love you," he said. "But this isn't right. You need to go back to your room."

"Oh, come on," I coaxed.

Dave kissed me again but shook his head *no.* "Go on," he urged. "Get some rest, and then we'll have hours together."

Sighing, I returned to my room.

That little encounter served as a painful reminder of just how differently Dave and I had lived our lives. Though I had given my life to Yeshua, I still reacted and operated in much the same ways that I had as an unbeliever. I had gotten very used to treating sexual things in a cavalier fashion. Integrating my "new man" in Yeshua was not automatic.

Dave, on the other hand, had grown up in a believing household and had given his heart to the Lord as a young boy. He had kept his purity and not rebelled against God, even as a teenager. I hadn't known men like him existed.

I didn't realize, at twenty-four years old, how far afield from a sanctified believer I remained. Having received a disproportionate amount of praise from both the folks at JFJ and the Baptist church about my rapidly increasing maturity as a believer had blinded me to the very worldly image I still presented. Dave looked at me and saw what God could do; his family, however, had no such vantage point.

I finally fell asleep in my lonely, narrow bed, and when I awoke, it was early afternoon. I pulled on a tight pair of leopard print pants and a clingy shirt, then brushed my long, curly hair. Peering into the full-length mirror mounted on the back of the bedroom door, I carefully applied blue eye liner and matching blue mascara. Then, barefoot, I walked over to Dave's room. The door was ajar, and when I pushed it open, I saw that the room was empty.

Heading downstairs, I followed the sounds of voices to the enormous kitchen. Giant murals of bucolic scenes complete with tiny shepherds and fleecy sheep covered the walls, all done by Dave's mother. *She's good,* I thought admiringly.

Dave and his mother stood by the sink, their backs to me, talking intently. His mother was busily chopping carrots and dropping them into a bowl, stopping every so often to gesture with one hand. Her voice was low, insistent; his, stubborn.

"Hey," I called out, cheerily.

They both spun around, suddenly aware of my presence. Dave's face lit up with a smile as soon as he saw me. His mother smiled too, but it took a split second longer. Her eyes widened as she took in my "hot chick in her twenties living in L.A." outfit, but she wisely refrained from commenting.

Soon enough, Rachel came home. She worked locally as a secretary in a lawyer's office. I liked her right away. Two years younger than Dave and somewhat self-effacing, she nevertheless had an engaging way about her. Tall and dark-haired like Dave but with her mother's round, pretty face, I thought her quite attractive. She had a similar background to me in that she loved to read, had graduated with an English degree, and now found that the only jobs available were disappointing secretarial positions. Unlike me, though, she didn't work at an exciting movie studio but for well-fed, stuffy, rich attorneys. She was desperate for a change.

Two hours later, Rina returned from work. She commuted into Manhattan and took the train back and forth. Rina was a buyer for a major cosmetics company and had a glamorous position. She was tall, dark-haired, and very slender, with artfully applied makeup and a stunning wardrobe. She more than any other member of the family openly exhibited the most fascination with this new believer her brother had brought home.

"You're nothing like Dave's old girlfriend," she confided to me later, when we were alone. "She was very conservative, but you," she said, her eyes sparkling, "wear such *wild* things!"

I took that as a compliment. "Thank you," I murmured, smiling at her. It didn't occur to me until many years later that Rina was commenting on the obvious and not necessarily praising me.

Two days into the visit, Dave and I borrowed the family car and headed across the George Washington Bridge to Long Island. He drove like a maniac, tailgating, slamming on his brakes, zipping into impossible spaces.

"Hey," I shouted, gripping the door handle, "when did you start driving like this?"

Dave grinned, his eyes intently on the road ahead. "You've never seen me drive in New York City," he said. "All my aggression comes out on these roads. It's the only way to drive here."

Only way indeed, I thought dubiously, already less brave than when I had blithely courted death in the little yellow sports car.

We were on our way to my parents' house so I could introduce Dave to my mother. My father had apparently announced that he did not intend to see me or meet Dave. Mom was making us dinner and then we were to drive back to New Jersey that same evening. I was very nervous about the whole thing. My stomach hurt and my hands were clammy.

As we sped further and further east on the Island, the signs reflected the nearness of home. *Syosset, Plainview, Woodbury, Huntington Station, Commack, Sunken Meadow State Park.* Rob's stomping grounds as well. I glanced out the car window as if I expected to see him materialize on the side of the Parkway. The last thing I wanted was to run into him now that I was engaged to Dave. Still, a part of my heart had not entirely healed from that intense relationship. I pushed it away.

"Turn here," I directed Dave as we exited from one highway onto another. "We're within ten minutes now."

As we took the last exit before the state park toll booths, I detected through the open window of the car a faint whiff of the salty sea air from the Long Island Sound. Straight ahead, through the trees, shimmered the hazy blue of the water. We veered right onto a different road.

"Okay, slow down: it's a right just up ahead. Oh look!" I added excitedly, pointing. "Those are my back woods. Turn here!"

Dave downshifted the car and pulled abruptly into the entrance of the development, flanked on both sides by curved brick walls. We rounded the corner and turned up the steep driveway, pulling to a stop just under the basketball hoop. We got out of the car.

"This is very nice," Dave said, eyeing the long, low, brown-shingled ranch house with its meticulously tended landscaping.

"Thanks." I smiled at him, still nervous about what was ahead that evening.

"Come on." Dave held out his hand and I took it, gaining strength from the warm vitality of his fingers. Together we mounted the brick-and-wood railroad tie steps that wrapped around the front of the house and up to the porch. I knocked on the door.

"Mom?" I called. "We're here."

A woman's footsteps clattered over the fieldstones in the front hallway and the door swung wide open. "Becky!" she cried as she hugged and kissed me. "You don't have to knock. Come in, come in!"

We followed her into the entryway. "Mom, this is Dave," I said shyly.

156

Mom gave Dave a hug. "It's so nice to meet you," she said, looking up at him. "I've heard a lot about you from Becky."

"I'm happy to meet you too, Mrs. Cohen," said Dave.

"Oh, please," corrected my mother. "Call me Jane."

"Jane."

They smiled at each other and my stomach relaxed. *This is going to go well*, I thought, relieved.

And it did. We had a wonderful evening with Mom. She served one of her specialty dinners of roast chicken, baked potatoes, and salad. For dessert we enthusiastically dug into her chocolate-covered marble bundt cake. I ate until I was ready to burst. Twenty-four is old enough to be out on your own, but there's nothing like coming back home and having Mom cook for you. I missed it; I missed her.

"So," I said, toward the end of the evening, feigning nonchalance. "Where's Dad?"

My mother's eyes darkened. "He went out to a movie," she answered. "He doesn't want to be here."

"Is he hiding around the corner, waiting for us to leave?" I asked sarcastically, suddenly hurt.

"Becky, you know this whole Jesus thing has upset him terribly."

"So? It's the truth, and he better get used to it!" I was ready to defend my faith to the last gasp, but Dave stopped me.

"You dad needs time, Becky. Don't attack him."

Mom threw Dave a grateful look, and I saw that they were off to a good start. Little did I realize at the time that even though Mom wasn't happy about our being believers in Yeshua, she was infinitely relieved at how stable and sweet Dave seemed after years of my dating all sorts of characters.

By 10 p.m. we reluctantly said our good-byes and got in the car for our two-hour trip back to Jersey. I stalled a bit at the end, hoping my father would get bored, or restless, or curious, and come home before I left. But he didn't.

The next three months were simultaneously the fastest and slowest season of my life. I absolutely, positively couldn't wait until Dave and I could share a bed, an apartment, a life. At the same time, each day was filled with so much anticipation over the imminently glorious future that it all just *flew!* Before I knew it, the wedding was two days off and the out-of-town family started to arrive.

Now that the moment I'd been wishing for since I was twelve had finally arrived, I was a nervous wreck. I worried about *everything:* how much money the rehearsal dinner cost, if I was going to erupt in a cold sore (I was prone to these, and no, I didn't), where everyone was going to eat, how my family was going to act in the Baptist church, what my department at the movie studio was going to think, if Dave was going to do something to mortify me, etc., etc., etc.

As was to happen so often in my life, the Lord worked everything out and my worrying was in vain. The day dawned with a drizzly, gray sky that turned to dazzling sunshine during the wedding ceremony itself. Dave showed up at my apartment at eight in the morning with the last of his belongings (he was moving in with me) plus a load of dirty laundry. Reality and fantasy collide again.

Dave's cousin, Matt, flew in from the Philadelphia area. Matt was a real shutterbug, and he followed me around, clicking a photographic record of this momentous day. Rina and Mandy (she was my maid of honor) showed up just after Dave left. We joked and laughed, made toast, got dressed, and still had plenty of time before walking over to the church for the 11 a.m. ceremony. I was in total hyper-land. Finally, by 10:30, we donned our coats and walked down the alley to the church.

This is the last time I'll be outside as a single woman, I thought, clear-eyed and amazed. My dream was becoming reality. Gray fog enveloped me, and I could have been in London as easily as in Southern California (except for the palm trees). Beside me, Rina held the large hat box that housed my bridal veil. Mandy trudged along behind us, somewhat fatigued by my exuberant spirits. Undaunted by the cold rain pelting my face, I climbed the white, stone steps and entered the church.

Once inside, the pastor's wife quickly ushered us to the bride's room downstairs. It was here that we were supposed to finish getting ready, and wait for the ceremony to begin. I didn't really know what to do. I had already put on the ankle-length ivory silk dress that I had found in Rina's closet ("It's perfect for you!" exclaimed both Dave's mother, Miriam, and Rina, after they pulled it out and had me try it on), a gorgeous pair of intricate lace and pearl pantyhose, and glittery satin shoes. I ran a comb through my hair, then Rina helped me adjust the veil. She and Rachel had bought it in Manhattan and presented it to me as their wedding gift. It was very beautiful. Waves of shimmering veils cascaded down from a pearl and faux-flowered wreath. I felt like a princess.

Women started showing up in the waiting room. My mother arrived, resplendent in pale pink silk, closely followed by Dave's mom, Miriam, regal in periwinkle blue. The two mothers had met at the rehearsal dinner and now did their social best to get to know each other. Rachel arrived, we threw Matt out, and soon the place was rolling. Last but not least, Jerry's wife, my sister-in-law Stacy, arrived.

Stacy and I had been in the process of developing a warm and vibrant friendship a couple of years back. After I announced to the family that I was a believer in Yeshua, she initially cried and then became aloof. A curvy and beautiful woman, she always reminded me of a brunette Princess Diana. I was glad to see her; happy that she had decided to accompany Jerry to my wedding though I knew how much she disapproved of the Baptist church and my spiritual lifestyle.

"Hello, Becky," she greeted me in a low monotone.

"Hi, Stacy," I gushed in return, overly enthusiastic in my attempt toward friendliness.

Stacy looked at me critically, then announced that I needed some makeup. *Makeup? Wasn't I wearing my trademark blue eye liner and blue mascara? What more did I need?* I was grateful for the unexpected attention, though, and patiently allowed her to pull out a cosmetics bag. She dabbed some blush and lipstick on my relatively unadorned face.

As the clock ticked relentlessly toward eleven o'clock, the women headed up to the sanctuary. Soon the only ones left were Mom and me.

"Oh, Mom," I said, standing in front of the floor-to-ceiling mirror and gazing at my bedecked self. "Can you believe that I'm really getting married today?"

My mother coughed nervously. "You know," she said, "it's not too late to change your mind."

"Mom!" I swung around, shocked that she would suggest such a thing. I knew she liked and approved of Dave. Coming alone to California for her daughter's wedding had been harder for her than I could imagine. "You've gotta be kidding! There's no way I'm not marrying Dave!"

My mother sighed, but didn't pursue the matter. I think that she believed my faith in Yeshua was another temporary phase and that when it was over, I would be stuck in a mismatched marriage. She feared for me.

Overhead we heard the strains of Tchaikovsky's wedding march. The pastor's wife tiptoed downstairs and whispered loudly to us, "You're on!"

Mom and I climbed the well-worn, carpeted steps to the upstairs foyer. The white double doors to the sanctuary were closed, and only Mandy, the maid-of-honor, stood outside of them. The pastor's wife nodded at Mandy, held open one of the doors, and we watched as Mandy slowly walked down the aisle to the front of the church.

We listened as the strains of the organ died down. There was a short silence, then the organist forcefully pounded out "Here Comes The Bride." The pastor's wife gently pushed on my back and, side by side, Mom and I walked through the doors and down the aisle. As is the custom in Gentile weddings (which I wasn't used to), the entire congregation stood up and turned around in order to see the bride. It was completely unnerving. I wasn't accustomed to so much attention and felt entirely overwhelmed. Somehow or other I made it to the front of the church where Dave, resplendent in a rented tux, stood waiting for me, a broad smile lighting up his face.

This is all that matters, I thought. *It's not the dress, or the flowers, or the cake, or the guests. It's this new life we're about to enter.* I had no idea what to expect, but I felt more than ready for the adventure. Life was a sparkling treasure, and it stood before me—us!—heaped in great abundance.

PART FIVE

Upstate New York
1989

Eleven

"**O**h, no!" I looked out the window and bit my lip so as not to cry. Big snowflakes lazily drifted down from the leaden sky. At another time I would have thought it a beautiful sight, but not now. I was dreadfully homesick for the palm trees and warm ocean breezes of southern California.

It was the third week of April, and Dave and I had moved to a small university town in upstate New York less than two weeks before. The last two years had passed in a blaze of activity. On our honeymoon, we had prayed and decided that God was calling Dave to seminary. As soon as we returned from our idyllic journey up the California coastline, he quit his job and enrolled in a world-renowned seminary in Pasadena. He had already been accepted before he met me but shelved the whole idea once we began dating. Both of us felt God's hand heavy upon us to prepare for ministry in obedience to Him.

Six months after the wedding, one semester into seminary, at the end of twelve-credit intensive Greek, we moved from my little beach-side studio apartment all the way across the Los Angeles basin to a one-bedroom seminary housing apartment in sunny, smoggy Pasadena. It wasn't until the following winter, when the smog briefly lifted, that I realized there was a spectacular view of rugged mountains from our second-floor balcony.

My job at the movie studio detonated. I was just too maddeningly, annoyingly happy for an office filled with divorced thirty- and forty-somethings. I quickly found another position with a bank in a huge high-rise in downtown L.A. Dave and I lived as frugally as possible on my salary and had enough left over to pay for most of his tuition and books. The Lord showed his faithfulness to us by filling in whatever we needed through unexpected gifts. We were able to make it through without loans, which was amazing.

I loved Dave, and I loved being married, but it wasn't the Cinderella existence I had always envisioned. The prince didn't come and carry me off on his white horse to his gorgeous palace and ply me with dainty treats as he massaged my feet. No. Instead, I was the one off earning the money for my student/husband. I'm afraid that even though I was in full agreement from the start that this was God's plan for us, I still wasn't very gracious to Dave about his lack of income. Sometimes I was downright mean.

I also occasionally flirted with my new, attractive boss at the bank. Fortunately, he was a very solid, nice guy in love with his own wife so nothing happened, but I wasn't acting the way a believer should. About eight months or so into our marriage I hit a time point in the relationship where if we hadn't been married I would have gotten bored and moved on. I realized that I didn't want to lose Dave and didn't want to do something irreparable to our marriage, so I would talk to him about all these things as they were happening. It was the best thing I could have done because sin loves the darkness and hates the light. Once you bring evil into the light, it shrivels and dies. That's what happened, but at what cost to Dave?

Two years into the marriage, we had a baby boy. I was expecting a cute enough baby but was blown away when *absolutely the most beautiful child I had ever seen* popped out! Thoughtful and intelligent, he looked curiously about the hospital nursery while all the other babies howled like, well, like babies.

Dave and I took this precious bundle back to our student apartment, amazed that the hospital staff trusted us enough to let us go. "I can't believe they let totally inept people like us just walk off with real babies," I remarked to Dave as I sat gingerly in the front passenger seat of the car, massaging my still swollen belly.

That day we had our introduction to parenthood as I gamely pushed through the early, painful stages of learning to breast feed, plus forcing myself off the bed and over to the changing table with each successive poopy diaper. I had never experienced physical discomfort before, so this was a real growing time. Dave was also able to say to the baby what he would say to each of our children on their second day of life:

"So," he said, tenderly cradling the baby and looking right into the little red, crying, face, "what's the matter? Were you born yesterday?" We both thought this terribly funny, but of course it only works for one day of someone's life and it's done.

Those first three weeks were very hard as I adjusted to the sleeplessness and constant demands of caring for an infant. I had achieved what I always wanted, but it was hard, so hard! I remember noticing women with multiple children whom I had previously not thought of as anything remarkable but now revered as giants of capability. *How can they handle three* (or two, or four, or five) *children when I'm drowning with one?* I would think, awed.

As the weeks progressed, however, and I regained my strength and learned to nurse effectively and without pain, I grew more confident. I took baby Josiah on stroller walks for miles through Pasadena, into South Pasadena, and even over to the millionaire neighborhoods of San Marino. What a pleasure to wheel the world's smartest and most adorable baby down the broad, smooth sidewalks and breathe in the perfumed scent of flowers while enjoying the warmth of the sun on my face! I loved those solitary excursions.

Baby Josiah also proved to be an inroad into rebuilding a relationship with my father. My parents had moved from Long Island to Southern California the previous year, and we saw them about every six weeks. The visits were not unlike walking across a minefield in that you proceed very, very carefully. My father was willing to meet Dave, and even treated us to dinner, but remained reserved, aloof.

I've always enjoyed God's sense of humor. It so happened that Josiah looked exactly like my father did as a baby! I have a picture of my father as a one-year-old, in an old black and white portrait from Leipzig, Germany, 1931, and he has the same wide, light eyes, startled expression, and curly blonde hair as my son. Needless to say, it's *tres difficile* to maintain an attitude of hostility to the couple who just gave birth to the brilliant, adorable, spitting image of oneself.

By the time the baby was three months old, our income from my maternity leave dried up. The fact that I had the maternity leave salary at all was miraculous in and of itself, for I was determined not to lie about returning to work but to honestly say I wasn't coming back.

Somehow or other, there was a miscommunication with human resources at my corporation and they had to allow me the money. I understand that, after I left, they rewrote their policy in much more explicit language.

By taking extra classes and studying year-round, Dave had managed to finish a Masters of Divinity degree in just over two years. We packed up our household and headed across country to join a small group of people who had been praying for a messianic rabbi. Dave, they all agreed, was the answer to their prayers.

But was I? Ministry, I quickly learned, was not standing on the sun-drenched steps of a wedding cake church and smiling modestly as people streamed out of services and came tripping forward, saying kind things. No, it was more like dodging bullets and arrows as sinful humanity cast about looking for a scapegoat for their woes.

If someone strikes you on the right cheek, turn to him the other also, cautioned Yeshua in the Sermon on the Mount. I hadn't learned that yet. When I saw someone coming for my left cheek, I rushed to meet him with my spear and attacked first.

We had barely started our ministry in upstate NY and already people were murmuring.

Why doesn't your wife work?

You make too much money.

You make too little money.

You're not what we wanted. And on and on.

In those early years, Dave was reluctant to use his authority. He had seen it abused too often in his life and hesitated to aggressively confront people. They in turn saw a power vacuum and were quick to jump in. So the conflicts started.

I would get very emotionally overwrought when I saw people coming against my husband. I was always ready to rip someone's head off. Not a very good shepherdess. Then, of course, would come the flip side of that when I would bitterly repent of my character flaws and throw the position of rabbi's wife back at the Lord's feet, insisting that he had made a drastic mistake in choosing me. But he never gave me permission to walk away.

This trauma came and went in cycles. In-between we had babies.

One incredibly cute and smart baby after another. In three-and-a-half years, we had two boys and a girl: Josiah, Shmuel, and Yohana.

Yohana came in May. When she was twelve days old, I loaded her and the two little boys into a double stroller, crammed the full diaper bag in the basket underneath, and walked over to the town square where Dave was participating with other area clergy in a March for Jesus.

The day was unbelievably hot. Up until then, the temperatures had barely broken into the 70s, but suddenly summer had sprung with a vengeance. I wore a loose white t-shirt, little short shorts, sunglasses, and had my hair pulled back in a ponytail. Even though I wasn't really recovered yet from childbirth, I felt good. I felt...free. The intense sunshine was purifying.

I kept to the periphery of the square, always seeking shade. The various pastors took turns speaking from a makeshift podium, their strong voices booming out into the still, hot air through a borrowed sound system. Dave came up and blew the shofar, its mournful tones reverberating for almost a full minute. When he was done, a great clapping and cheering went up as hundreds of people from all different churches praised God together.

I started feeling like I had better get home and make dinner while I still had the energy when I heard the Lord's voice:

You are aptly named, Rebecca. Your children will possess the gates of their enemies.

Tears filled my eyes. I was not accustomed to hearing God's voice, but I knew it was him. I bowed my head, overcome. I listened for more but that was it: those exciting words of affirmation and prophecy.

Following that, we had a four-year wilderness experience. Dave lost a power struggle with another fellow in the congregation, and we relocated to a small city an hour east of where we originally planted the congregation. Our small body of believers shrunk in size until we could comfortably fit into a humble living room (ours) for Shabbat services. I was so involved with raising three small children that I didn't care all that much. For Dave, who believed that God would do great and amazing things through us, it was crushing.

In addition, money became so scarce that I was reduced to counting pennies at the local dairy in order to buy milk. Then God gave me a special gift that was to bring joy into my life and the lives of those around me. He gave me the gift of bread.

The year Yohana was born, that Rosh Hashanah (which came in September), I was poring over my favorite cookbook when a recipe for challah jumped off the page at me. I had never made anything that required yeast, as it seemed too mysterious and difficult for this suburban Long Island girl raised on Wonder Bread (in those familiar plastic bags with the little red, blue, and yellow dots). I wasn't even all that sure *how* bread became bread. I decided to give it a try.

I went to the store and forced myself to buy the excessively overpriced yeast in the little packages (there must be a cheaper way, I reasoned. There is…). At home, in-between nursing Yohana, diapering Shmuel, and reading to Josiah, I measured out the flour, added the salt and yeast, stirred in the honey, oil, and eggs. Then I gradually added water, kneading as I went along. Once the dough formed a ball, I put it in a bowl, covered it with a towel, and let it rise in my gas oven for one-and-a-half hours. Then, meticulously following directions, I pushed down the ball, rerolled it, and let it rise another hour.

I again pushed the dough down, cut it into three equal pieces, and rolled each one into the form of a snake. Lining up the three snakes, I braided them from the middle out, sealing up the ends with wet fingertips. I placed the unbaked challah on a greased cookie sheet, covered it with a damp towel, and let it rise again. Then, with my fingers, I smeared beaten egg all over it and sprinkled it with sesame seeds. Excited and anticipatory, I reverently slid the whole creation into a preheated oven and baked it for close to an hour.

The aroma that permeated the house was unbelievable. My little boys showed up in the kitchen. "What's that smell?" they wanted to know. Baby Yohana woke up and started crying, looking to nurse.

When I finally ascertained that the bread was done, after much tapping, poking, and prodding, the boys and I stood back, awed.

It was a masterpiece. In the dark, hot confines of the oven, the bread dough had doubled in size, and the beaten egg turned the challah a rich, golden color. It was literally the most beautiful bread I had ever seen.

"Oh," I breathed.

"Oh," breathed my two little boys as well, their eyes round and happy.

"Can I eat some?" asked Josiah, already pulling himself into a kitchen chair and settling down expectantly.

"Me too! Me too!" chimed in Shmuel, pulling at my leg.

I stooped down and lifted Shmuel, holding his soft, squirming body close to my chest. I kissed the top of his curly brown head. "Not yet," I said reluctantly. "Let's wait for Daddy so he can see it."

Josiah nodded obediently, slid back off the chair, and wandered off. Shmuel was not so easily mollified. "No!" he yelled, reaching for the bread.

I bought him off with a yogurt, but it took some negotiating. Finally I had to take the kids on a stroller walk to the library so we could all get away from that tantalizing scent.

Early that evening, when Dave came home, I proudly took him into the kitchen and showed him the bread.

"Wow!" he exclaimed, dumbfounded. "*You* made this?"

"Don't sound so shocked," I said.

"I'm just amazed." Dave looked from me to the bread and back to me again. He put his arms around me and kissed me. "I have married an extraordinary woman."

"Oh, pshaw," I said. But I was very pleased.

The challah tasted as good as it looked. Very soon, Dave presented me with a gift of a bread book. I loved that book. I studied every recipe carefully and made several: bagels, pizza dough, whole grains, black bean and raisin, buttermilk, sunflower seed and raisin, rye, sourdough, sprouted, plain whole wheat. There were nights in which I would lie in bed and think about the new bread I wanted to try in the morning and I would be so excited it would take me a half hour to fall asleep instead

169

of my usual exhausted five minutes.

Soon word spread and I began to be known as the "bread lady." Friends offered me money to bake them bread. I started a cottage industry and sold about twenty loaves a week, hand-kneaded and baked in my simple gas oven. The money I made went right into buying food for our growing family. I experienced a great deal of satisfaction from being able to help out like this, doing something I loved, while still being completely available to our three small children. I read in my Bible about the Proverbs 31 woman, who,

> ...selects wool and flax and works with eager hands.
> She is like the merchant ships, bringing her food from afar.
> She gets up while it is still dark;
> she provides food for her family
> and portions for her servant girls.
> She considers a field and buys it;
> out of her earnings she plants a vineyard.

Meanwhile Dave, a trumpet player from his youth, took up the bass guitar. "Someone needs to keep the beat on the worship team," he explained *sans* apology. It was a challenge for him, but also a much-needed creative outlet. Soon he was writing songs as well. They all had a strong bass *thump* rhythm.

"I love your songs."

We were lying side by side in our queen-sized bed. The three children were all asleep in the room they shared, and Dave and I were able to quietly talk and reconnect with each other. This was my favorite time.

"You do?" His surprised, vulnerable tone touched my heart.

"Yes, I really do. They're different, interesting. So much music sounds the same, it ends up being background noise after awhile. But your stuff is clean and dynamic."

Dave drew me close to him. "Your approval means everything to me," he whispered, right before he kissed me.

170

Our wilderness experience ended in a completely unexpected way. One day Dave got a phone call from another messianic rabbi in a city about an hour away.

"Would you be willing to help me out with a new Jewish believer?" Rabbi Lanny Goldstein's fast-paced New York accent emanated from the receiver.

"Of course," answered Dave. "What's going on?"

"Well, it's very exciting," said Lanny quickly. In sharp contrast to Dave, Lanny did everything quickly. "There's a fellow in the town next to you whose wife just became a believer. They came here for our service and the husband, Marty, gave his heart to the Lord."

"That's wonderful!" enthused Dave, always thrilled to hear of a Jewish person meeting his Messiah.

"You haven't heard the really exciting part," said Lanny. He paused dramatically before continuing. "He's the director of the Jewish Community Center."

Dave's mouth dropped open. This was big. "You're kidding," he said, though of course he knew there was no way Lanny would make up something like this.

"If you could meet with Marty once a week to teach him and help him get grounded in his faith, that would be wonderful."

"It would be an honor," replied Dave.

Dave made contact with Marty and started driving once a week to Marty's spacious home. He pulled out a Bible and began in Genesis.

171

Soon Marty's wife, Lana, joined them. After a while, we came to find out that Marty had a Jewish believing friend named Phil.

"What's this I hear about a Bible study at your home?" asked Phil. Soon Phil started showing up.

"How come you haven't invited me?" demanded Phil's sister, Madeline. She came too.

"Can I come?" pleaded Molly, a distant cousin of Marty's who had recently gotten saved at the local Nazarene church.

"I'd better see what you're up to," declared Marty's rabbi, from the conservative synagogue.

"I better make sure the doctrine is sound," determined the Nazarene pastor's wife.

"We're going with you," chimed in several members of her church.

"Take me with you," I urged Dave. "This is too good to miss." And I piled our three little children in the van since we couldn't afford a babysitter and took them, too.

The weekly study at Marty's home was fabulous. For Dave and me, being in the midst of a group of interesting and interested people, on fire to study God's Word, was like drinking sweet, cold water after a bout in the scorching sun. We lapped up those times thirstily.

Soon there were so many people in Marty and Lana's house that Lana said, "Okay, this needs to move." So Marty found an office suite in a building he co-owned and *voila!* we were no longer a small group that met in our living room but an official new congregation.

Unfortunately, a marriage is more than the honeymoon, and a relationship between a person and his church community is more than those first few months of intoxicating happiness. Marty and Lana found out that we were not as wonderful as they had first erroneously surmised. Still friendly, they nevertheless decided to make their spiritual home the congregation sixty miles away, where Marty had accepted Yeshua.

"What?" I sputtered, completely exasperated by this upsetting turn of events. "They're going to drive *sixty miles* when they have something great right in their own town? Why?"

"Becky," said Dave, also sorry to lose this couple but much more savvy about human nature than me, "they're used to a certain level of authority, plus they're new believers. It's hard to accept guidance from us. Praise God they know him and they want to worship somewhere. That's a big deal."

"Maybe," I conceded. Meanwhile, we still had the office suite and our congregation slowly but steadily grew. In about a year, close to a hundred people would crowd into our rapidly shrinking space. "This is it," we reasoned. "This is the time when God is going to do amazing and mighty things through us."

What happened instead shocked us. One of the women who attended was the mother of three small children; her husband was incarcerated in one of the local prisons. Every couple of years, Gary was released, only to get back on drugs, do something illegal, and bounce back into the slammer. Dave did everything he could to befriend Gary and show him godly love. At one point, we were even willing to let him live with us for a season so we could more fully help him.

"I would never approve that," said Gary's parole officer, shaking his head as he sat in our living room and explained his denial of the request. "You people have young children. They need to be protected."

We thought our kids would be just fine, but it turned out that the parole officer understood Gary better than we did. While on probation, Gary broke into the office building where we had our congregation and robbed us and another business. He made off with a piece of sound recording equipment Dave had spent a whole summer earning and which was probably worth around $8,000. Most likely, he had sold it for drugs and gotten almost nothing for it. An angel of God blinded his eyes so he didn't notice the valuable musical instruments as well. It would have been devastating to lose the guitars and the bass.

The orthodox Jewish guys who co-owned the building with Marty used this opportunity to throw us out. They had never been happy having a messianic Jewish congregation on their premises but hadn't done anything rash out of respect for Marty. Now they could say we were a liability.

A very nice church across town told us that we could meet there on Friday nights for almost no money, but the damage was done. In no time at all, our numbers shrunk back down. We were to see this pattern a lot over the next dozen years. The attendance at services would gradually increase only to spiral back down. Again and again, we gave our hearts away, only to have them hurled back in our faces. Whenever Dave and I sought the Lord on whether or not we could do something different with our lives, we always got the same resounding *NO*. Both of us knew it would be sin to pack up and go somewhere else. We stayed.

At the end of that summer, two events happened that significantly impacted my life. Both came out of the same evening.

Dave and I had been invited to the annual fund-raising banquet for our town's Crisis Pregnancy Center. This was an opportunity for hundreds of local people to raise money and awareness for alternative options to abortion. Frankly, the program could have been about raising money for farm equipment, for all I cared. I was just happy to be able to dress up and go out to dinner with my husband, even if it was in the company of six hundred of my closest friends.

By the time I had arranged the bedtime routine with the babysitter and kissed the three kids good night, we were already a few minutes late. Dave pulled into the crowded parking lot and found a space in the far corner. Holding hands, we strolled over to the front door of the country club where the dinner was being held.

Little white lights were strung gaily around the entranceway. Inside, deep red carpeting muffled our footsteps as soft lighting from polished brass fixtures cast a romantic glow on the walls. "How nice!" I murmured, holding tightly to Dave's arm.

He grinned at me. "It's good to be out with you."

We found our seating arrangement and settled ourselves in, greeting our table mates. Just then, Dave spotted two couples entering the dining hall.

"Oh, look!" he whispered to me, gesturing discreetly. "There's Bob and Emily Matthewson, the doctors I did that sound job for, and their friends, the Sweets."

I glanced up. Twenty feet away, unaware that we were watching them, were two couples. One I didn't know, and the other I had met briefly. Bob and Emily, the ones I had met, were doctors about the same age, maybe a little older, than Dave and me. They were both believers who loved music and had gotten along great with Dave. Bob had some Jewishness in his background, plus he was from New Jersey, so he seemed like a familiar type. His wife, Emily, on the other hand, was a tall, striking redhead from Alabama. Her good looks, professional degree, charming Southern accent, and significantly higher income bracket all combined to intimidate me.

Dave excused himself and went over to say hello. In a few minutes, he came over and got me. "Come on," he said. "I want to introduce you."

A little nervously, I accompanied him to the other table. Cordial greetings were exchanged with the Sweets, while Bob and Emily expressed delight at seeing me again. They couldn't have been more gracious, but still I felt unsettled, and out of my element.

After we returned to our seats, I heard God speak to me: *Ask Emily to pray with you once a week.*

Oh, Lord! She won't be interested in me.

Ask her.

So I did. Shakily, I stood up.

"Where are you going?" asked Dave, munching happily on a salad drenched in bleu cheese dressing.

"God just told me to do something," I replied enigmatically. "I'll be right back." I threaded my way through the mobbed dining hall and over to the table where Bob and Emily sat engrossed in conversation.

"Well, hello again!" said Bob jovially, upon noticing me.

"Hi," I said. I looked at Emily. She looked back at me, a question in her eyes.

"Hey," I said, "this is probably going to sound strange, but I believe that the Lord told me to ask if you would be willing to get together with me once a week to pray. Take some time to think and pray about it before answering," I added hastily.

Emily flicked a strand of long red hair away from her face and smiled. "I don't have to think about it," she said in her gracious Southern accent. "I'd love to."

"Wow, great," I said, not sure where to go from here. "Uh, why don't we exchange numbers and I'll call you?"

I walked back to my table on clouds. I was so thrilled that a woman as dynamic and interesting as Emily would want to spend time with me. *Thank you, Lord!*

I didn't realize it at the time, but that was the start of one of the most significant and enduring friendships in my life.

The other thing that happened that night had to do with the program. The featured speaker was a young girl who had survived a botched abortion attempt while in her mother's womb. She testified to the mercy and kindness of God. Both she and her mother shared the platform. This beautiful girl walked with a cane, having endured a lifetime of surgeries and hip-related problems due to the trauma suffered during the abortion. It was a three Kleenex evening, particularly for me. I had repented of my own abortion, and thought it was behind me, but this brought out all sorts of emotions I hadn't even known were lurking there.

When Dave and I left that night, we felt very, very close to one another. He was as pleased as I over the encounter with Emily. He also understood how the intense abortion talk affected me. I felt like I could trust my husband with anything.

That night we conceived our fourth child. I believe that Shira ("song," in Hebrew) was God's way of restoring in my life what the abortion—due to my own sin—had stolen.

Shira was an exceptionally beautiful child. She had a very round head, big blue eyes, and curly blonde hair. She also was a screamer.

She yelled and squirmed and cried and nudged and carried on. When she was an infant, and all my attempts at nursing, pacifying, and stroller walks remained unsuccessful, Dave would blast D.C. Talk's "Jesus Freak" on the stereo while dancing with her and *that* would work. Otherwise, nothing. This was a child who drove us to our knees again and again. At literally the drop of a hat, Shira would throw herself onto the floor and indulge in a wild, endless tantrum. It wasn't until the age of seven that she began to get a handle on her emotions and exercise some level of control. After that, she turned into the most delightful, happy girl. It was the grace of God that we made it to that point.

When Shira turned eighteen months, I gave birth to my fifth and final child: Leah. Those first few months were a bit unreal as I mentally adjusted to the fact that I had such a large family. I have to admit that when I discovered I was pregnant with Leah I was concerned since I could barely handle the four kids. The Lord spoke to me, however, and assured me that this child would be easy.

And she was. Cute as a button, with dimples in both cheeks and soft, brown hair that from birth stood straight up like it had been spiked with mousse, the newest Hermon baby enthralled us all. Shira, in particular, seemed to think we had given her a gift of the world's most interactive doll. It was gratifying to think that these two little girls, so close in age, would always have each other as friends.

The November before Leah turned one, we were invited to a family bar mitzvah on Long Island. We decided to combine the event with spending Thanksgiving down in New Jersey with Dave's parents. I really looked forward to a break from my routine and a chance to get away and be treated. I thought I would contribute to the Thanksgiving dinner and brought ingredients for a decadent sweet potato and marshmallow casserole that I knew would please both my family and Dave's father.

We stuffed our family of seven in our Plymouth Voyager minivan and gaily headed off on what we expected to be a rollicking adventure. Five hours later, nudged and cramped, we arrived at Dave's spacious childhood home. His parents greeted us warmly, and we made it until dinner by eating endless clementines, supplied in huge bowls by Dave's mother.

That day was fine. The next day, Thanksgiving, got ugly.

I could tell right from the start that Miriam was not happy with my casserole idea. It combined two things she hated: relinquishing control in her kitchen and serving unhealthy food. She had spent forty years trying to get her husband, a junk food *aficionado,* to eat right. I think it was the marshmallows that kicked her over the edge.

Thirteen years of tension exploded that day. I stomped over

Miriam's territory, convinced that I was a wonderful woman trying to make everyone happy. Miriam, in turn, bristled at my attempt at being helpful. The sweet potatoes made it to the table but not without a power struggle. The joy was lost.

I endured the meal but then pulled Dave upstairs for a hurried, private conference.

"What is it?" he asked wearily, sick of these emotionally loaded female conflicts.

His attitude put me on the defensive. "It's your mother," I hissed, blinking back tears. "I can't get along with her! I just wanted to do something your father would enjoy and now she's mad. I'm so upset!"

Instead of comforting me, Dave withdrew even more. "Look, there's nothing I can do. Why don't you just try to get along? We're only here for one more day."

I should have taken his advice, but I didn't. I felt hurt that my husband was incapable of protecting me. I felt unloved and unappreciated. Furious, I retreated from Dave in anger.

Needless to say, the rest of the visit was hideous. Miriam and I were coldly polite to each other, and the children seemed tentative as to why everyone was so upset.

I have a picture from that visit, snapped by an unsuspecting relative. In it, Dave and I look drawn and worried. I, in particular, have that look of women in pictures from 1870 taken after they have been schlepped over the prairie and forced to suffer for years in order to build a working farm: it's that grim, relentless look.

By the time we said our stilted good-byes, Baby Leah had come down with some sort of mysterious illness, the main symptoms of which were unrelieved crying and sleeplessness. We strapped her into her car seat and headed east to Long Island. It didn't take long before I succumbed to total abject self-pity, mixed with an unhealthy dose of self-loathing. I felt hopeless as a wife, mother, daughter-in-law, rabbi's wife, follower of Messiah. Instead of consoling me, Dave seemed to be in some sort of somnambulist shell-shock. Who could blame the guy?

Less than two hours later, we arrived at my cousin Ted's house. Staying at his spacious, four-bedroom home, already occupied by him, several cats, and a wide selection of *objets d'art* gleaned from international traveling, were my own family of seven plus my parents, in from California. I attempted to pull myself together long enough to eat dinner, be social, and get the children into their makeshift beds. The baby, however, wouldn't stop fussing.

"I'm going to call Cousin Howie," decided my mother, a concerned look on her face. Cousin Howie, married to one of my mother's relatives, was an excellent doctor who lived about a half hour away. "Maybe Leah has an ear infection."

"Maybe," I numbly agreed. I was so worn out from emotions that all I wanted to do was fall into bed and pass out. But there was obviously something wrong with Leah.

Leaving Dave behind to relax, my parents drove Leah and me to Cousin Howie's. He and his wife were exceedingly kind and made a fuss over how cute the baby was. Leah, for her part, acted better than she had all day. She stopped crying and babbled a few baby words to her appreciative audience.

Cousin Howie looked in her ears, nose, and throat. Confused, he shook his head. "I don't see any sign of infection or illness. All I can tell you is to give her Tylenol and let her sleep it off."

Relieved, we stayed for several more minutes chatting, and then bundled the baby up and headed back over to Ted's. All the kids were asleep when we got in. I said good night to my mom and dad and entered the room I shared with Dave and Leah. As soon as Leah got in her bed, she began to cry again.

"Shhh," I hushed her, conscious of all the people who could potentially wake up or be disturbed. She cried harder, though, and I was forced to take her into my bed and nurse her to sleep. Every 45 minutes, all night long, despite Tylenol, she would wake up. By the following morning, I was beyond exhausted, my reserves of strength depleted.

The next several days of our visit were horrendous. Leah just wouldn't sleep properly. She needed enormous amounts of attention. After the bar mitzvah, Dave left on a prearranged trip to a rabbi's conference in Florida. When we made these plans, I envisioned a wonderful time with my parents on Long Island. In actuality, it was probably the worst week of my life. All I wanted to do was go home, but I had to stay until Dave returned from Florida so I could pick him up at Kennedy Airport.

Two days before Dave's flight was due back, my parents left for California. My mother felt terrible going as she saw what a tough time I was having with the baby. "You'll be okay," she assured me as she was leaving, but her eyes were worried.

We would have just made it through, except that on the last day, Leah started feeling well enough to crawl around and investigate the house. Until now, she had not shown much interest in anything more than her immediate surroundings. Now she crawled out of our bedroom and moseyed down the upstairs hall. Warily, I kept my eye on her from the open doorway as I simultaneously pulled clean laundry from a basket and folded it into suitcases. Too late, I saw her pause on the landing next to an antique Chinese vase perched proudly on a specially designed holder that extended from the top of the landing over the foyer below. She pulled herself into a seating position and stretched out her chubby baby arm.

"No! Stop!" I shouted uselessly.

Leah glanced at me, then proceeded to reach for the brightly colored and infinitely appealing vase. She stuck her hand through the bars of the bannister and pushed at the side of the vase. I raced over but wasn't in time. The vase rocked on its pedestal, then plummeted to the tiled floor below, ricocheting off a marble-topped table before rolling to a stop. It sounded like a gunshot going off.

"What was that?!" All of the children emerged from various corners of the house, eyes wide. I grabbed the baby and raced downstairs to inspect the damage. Fortunately, my cousin Ted wasn't there. It turned out that the vase was slightly dented, and there was a ding on the marble table. Heart pounding furiously, I explained to the kids what had happened.

They all thought it was pretty funny. I didn't see the humor in it at all. My cousin, nice as he was, wouldn't be pleased and I felt very alone and unprotected without either Dave or my parents around. (When we had first arrived, he had sat the older kids down and warned them not to touch any of the art treasures, or "I'll kill you," he said. Exaggerated, but effective nonetheless. We were all extremely careful.)

180

"Why, oh why did I ever agree to this crazy trip?" I moaned aloud. I thought about calling Ted on his cell phone and explaining what had happened, but after the week I had been through, I just didn't have the courage. Instead I wrote him a note and left it in a prominent place. Then I packed up the car and drove to the airport with the kids.

I was so happy to see Dave! I told him what had happened. I was calmer now that I had escaped with my life and was on my way home. About an hour into our drive north, Leah fell peacefully asleep. By the time we reached home and unpacked the van, she had reverted to her normal, cheerful self. That night, she slept ten hours without waking.

When I look back on that Thanksgiving week of 1999, it looms in my mind as the week from hell. I had no idea of the difficulties that lay just ahead.

PART SIX

Cancer

The wading bird, the Godwit, flew more than eight days non-stop without food, water or rest, crossing the Pacific Ocean for a total of 6,230 miles in order to reach her winter home in New Zealand. Amazing what is possible for God's creatures!

Twelve

When Leah turned a year old, I decided to wean her. I cut back on the nursing and, as is often the case, experienced some engorging in my breasts. A day or so into this new regime, I was checking myself and noticed a little lump under my left arm. I figured it was from the weaning process and expected it to go away the next time Leah nursed, as these little lumps have a tendency to do. Three days later, it was still there. I mentioned it to Emily, when she came over to pray.

"You should check it out," she advised. "But don't worry, these things are usually nothing."

I hadn't been worried before she said, "Don't worry." Now I wasn't so sure. *Hmm.*

It took me over a month before I made an appointment to see my ob/gyn. Dr. Prinsky, a Jewish man whose family had survived the war in Poland, was a cultured and sensitive fellow for whom I had great regard. He felt the lump and frowned. "Get an ultrasound and a mammogram."

"That sounds like such a pain in the neck," I responded.

Dr. Prinsky flared. "Becky, you are the mother of five children. Get the tests!"

I thought he was being a bit of a drama queen, but I had the tests. The ultrasound showed the necessity of the mammogram. After the mammogram, the radiologist said, "I'm ordering a biopsy, but don't worry. Eighty percent of these lumps turn out to be nothing."

The surgeon Emily recommended for me said the same thing: "Don't worry."

I really wasn't worried, but this line of medical professionals advising me against it was, well, *worrying.*

The night before the biopsy surgery, the Lord told me, *Do not fear.*

I am with you.

That was it. That was all He said, but it was enough. I felt a strong sense of peace. I also knew the news I was to get the next day wasn't going to be good. God generally doesn't say not to be afraid before *good* news.

"I'm sorry to inform you that you have cancer."

Both the surgeon, Dr. D'Angelo, and Emily sat with me in a little room off to the right behind the surgery area. Only moments before, Dr. D'Angelo had finished removing the lump from my breast under a local anesthesia. Now all three of us sat in a little circle, facing each other. Emily, her hand clasped in mine, looked very concerned.

Dr. D'Angelo was grave as he shared the news. "I knew even before Dr. Matthewson checked this under her microscope that it was cancer. It was giving me a devil of a time cutting it out."

Emily cleared her throat. "Unfortunately, it's a very aggressive cancer. I have the name of an oncologist I recommend that you see right away."

"Yes," said Dr. D'Angelo. "But first you have to schedule a surgery date with my office. I'll need to cut out everything associated with that tumor and have one inch of clean margins all around the area."

"One inch!" I exclaimed, the first thing I had said since they broke this cancer news to me. "There'll be nothing left!"

The two doctors smiled at my attempt at humor. I could tell they were relieved I was taking this so well. What they didn't realize was that God had already warned me this was going to happen and had assured me of the ultimate outcome. All I had before me now was the journey.

Dr. D'Angelo and Emily laid it out for me: first, surgery. Then, either radiation or chemotherapy, depending on whether or not the cancer was contained. If there was any question as to the possibility of the cancer spreading, I would need chemotherapy.

Emily drove me home and told Dave the news while I stood quietly in the kitchen with them. Then she left, and Dave hugged me. Neither of us knew what to say.

I was absolutely terrified going into surgery. I feared I would wake up in the middle of the operation, experiencing horrible pain. When they wheeled me into the preop waiting area, the anesthesiologist put some valium in the IV. That helped. Then they rolled me into the stark green operating room with all the sharp, shiny instruments and unidentifiable machines. Two male nurses lifted me from the rolling bed I was already on over to the operating table.

Dr. D'Angelo entered the surgery room, much as the star actor comes on stage during a Broadway play. He strode right over to me, his crinkly, brown eyes kindly above his surgical mask.

"You'll be just fine," he assured me. "Once we start the anesthesia through the IV, count backwards from 100." He motioned to the anesthesiologist.

I smiled weakly at the doctor. "Okay. One hundred, ninety-nine...." That was it. The next time I opened my eyes and experienced any memorable level of consciousness, I was back on the rolling bed, heading to a regular room in the hospital. I had a large bandage on my chest and it was over. Just amazing. *Thank you, God.*

My mother flew in from California to help with the household as I recovered. She stayed about a week. Two weeks after that, I started chemo.

I had heard the term *chemotherapy* for years, but it was one of those vague, undefinable words that held no real meaning for me. I had never been interested enough to ask what precisely it entailed. Nor had I been close enough to someone going through cancer to find out. The whole process was vaguely mysterious.

I arrived in the transfusion room of the hospital at the appointed time. By now, I was getting a little more familiar with needles in my arm, so it was no big deal when the nurse put the IV in. I was even, I must admit, somewhat proud of my bulging blue veins on the inside of my arms. *Easy to get a needle in me,* I thought.

I chatted with Jenni, the nurse on duty, very aware of the fact that I was a lot closer in age to the nurses than many of the other patients. Cancer seemed to be predominantly a senior citizen disease. Or at least it looked that way to me from eyeballing the transfusion room at my local hospital.

I was there for about three hours and received two chemo meds through my veins. One was a bright red liquid called adryiamycin, and the other a clear chemical solution known as cytoxan. It wasn't so bad. I went home and felt pretty good. I told Dave that he could go back to the office and that I was fine. He looked doubtful but left anyway. I then took a stroller walk with my two babies over to the elementary school to get the older three kids. It was a warm April day, and it felt good to be alive, walking past the myriad green lawns enclosed by their pretty flower gardens. We came back to the house and I gave the kids a snack. The phone rang and it was my mother-in-law, Miriam.

"How are you feeling?" she asked.

"Pretty good," I replied. "I walked to the school and got the kids."

"You did?"

Yes, I started to say, when it hit me. A huge wave of nausea, unlike anything I had ever experienced, slammed into me, starting with my head. My whole body shook.

"I don't feel good. I'll talk to you later," I just managed to whisper into the phone before hanging up. I had never felt so sick in my life. I crawled up the stairs to my bedroom and lay down, curling up into a fetal position. After about five minutes, I groped my way to the bathroom and threw up in the toilet.

This is awful, I groaned into the mirror while hurriedly brushing my teeth. I went and lay back down.

"Mommy?" My sweet seven-year-old, Yohana, stood next to my bed. "Mommy, are you okay?"

"Mommy doesn't feel well, honey. Could you call Daddy and ask him to come home now? Tell him Mommy needs him."

"Okay," she said, bouncing off downstairs in search of the phone.

Meanwhile, my head felt like someone was knocking a hammer against it from the inside. *If I can only keep still, maybe it will feel better,* I thought. Then, *Oh no, I have to throw up again!* I forced myself to flee the bed and go back into the bathroom. Again, I threw up. This was to happen eight more times over the course of the next twelve hours. Soon all I had was the dry heaves. I couldn't keep even a sip of water down. All I could do was cry out to God to help me.

Early the next morning, I phoned the doctor's office and told them what was happening. "Better get right over to the hospital," said the doctor. "I'll get some saline solution in you and order an anti-nausea infusion."

A friend drove me to the hospital while Dave stayed home with the kids. He pulled the car up to the admittance entrance. "Do you want me to come in with you?" Pete asked, concerned.

"No, it's okay," I answered weakly. "I'll be fine." I staggered out of the car and into the hospital. At the check-in desk, they took one look at me and ordered a wheelchair, despite my protests. In the transfusion room, Jenni inserted an IV line into my arm and immediately started the anti-nausea med.

Within moments the sick feeling receded. When the saline solution followed, I could literally feel the strength pouring back into my parched body. Soon I was sitting up straight instead of slumped over. "Can I eat something?" I asked.

Two nurses brought me some chicken soup. Starved, I ate with gusto, spooning it down. I noticed that they were staring at me. "What?" I demanded, looking up.

The nurse who wasn't Jenni smiled. "We just love seeing people with an appetite here," she explained.

Oh.

Two weeks later, my hair fell out. First, my scalp ached and then clumps of hair just fell off in my hand. It was freaky. At first I tried to disguise the bald patches, but within a few days I stood at the hall mirror with a pair of scissors and cut off as much of my hair as I could. That way, less would fall out. I found that losing my hair was nothing compared to extreme nausea. The American Cancer Society hands out free wigs to cancer patients. I took the kids and we went over to their office one day. They had a ball trying on the wigs: long red ones, short black ones, curly ones, straight brown ones, afros, you name it. I finally settled on a short brownish/blonde one. It was okay most of the time, though on hot days I simply tied a bandana around my head and looked, as my brother Michael said, like a biker chick.

I never for one moment entertained the thought that the cancer would lead to death. When I told the kids what was going on, I was quick to point out that I had cancer, but it wasn't the type that led to death, so don't worry.

"I didn't know there was another kind," said my oldest son.

Despite the cancer, I was young and strong and strove to maintain my normal lifestyle. On bad days, I dragged myself around the house, forcing myself to clean and make dinner. Many people prayed for me and helped out with food as well. Eight treatments and five months later, I made it through.

After chemo came 32 radiation treatments. They were a walk in the park, in comparison. I schmoozed with the doctor and the nurses, rejoicing in the fact that the cancer finish line loomed just ahead. When I did finish, it was anti-climactic. I had gotten used to lots of attention from medical personnel and congregants. Now I was a weakened, bald woman, expected to function on all levels. It was rather disconcerting.

It took nearly five months after chemo ended before my hair began to grow back. When it reached a length of 1/8 inch, I tore the wig off, thrilled to have "hair."

A year later, I began to have pain in my right hip area. I went to the chiropractor and we both thought it was some sort of sciatica. Several weeks later, I had my yearly gyn check with Dr. Prinsky and mentioned the hip pain. His reaction shouldn't have surprised me.

"Get it checked out!" he barked. "I'm sending you to an orthopedist."

Again, he was right. The cancer had spread to my hip bone. I was shocked. I didn't realize that breast cancer could return via bones (lungs and liver are other popular routes) and I certainly never expected to see it back. The treatment was radiation alone.

"You'll have a hole in your bone the size of a golf ball," explained Dr. Stevenson, the radiation oncologist. "It'll take anywhere from 1-2 years to come off the X-rays."

At this time, a woman at the congregation shared a vision she believed was from God. "I saw Yeshua standing between you and Dave," she told me. "He had his robe wrapped around both of you and your right hip was glowing red."

I was greatly encouraged by that word. It confirmed for me that God held me in his hand and would indeed heal me.

What happened next was miraculous. Six weeks after the radiation treatments, I had my first x-ray and *the hole had disappeared!* I took the X-ray to another radiologist, a friend's husband, and asked him what he thought.

"If I didn't know anything about you, and if someone handed me this film and said to take a look at it, I wouldn't even think there was a fracture here," he replied.

Wow.

Emily, who had been praying with me all along, pointed out that when breast cancer returns in the bones, it tends to show up in several places at once and usually kills. For this cancer to return to just one spot and then to be healed was stunning. "It's a miracle," she affirmed.

I told everyone what God had done for me. I shared my story as often as I could, I was so excited. I lived Isaiah 63:7:

> *I will tell of the kindnesses of the Lord,*
> *the deeds for which he is to be praised,*
> *according to all the Lord has done for us,*
> *yes, the many good things he has done*
> *for the house of Israel.*

The next few years were a time of growth for our young family. We saw God work in our lives on many different levels. Although our income continued to stay low, the Lord blessed us beyond abundantly.

For years we had driven a Plymouth-Voyager minivan. A gift to begin with, it had gotten rusty and decrepit and was starting to need more and more repairs. It would have been great to buy a new car, but we barely had the money for the auto mechanic, much less a car.

One day I said to the kids, "Let's start praying and ask the Lord for a new minivan." I hesitated to say "new" as I didn't want to be greedy, but the Holy Spirit impressed on me that I should pray for a *brand-new* minivan. The kids were excited and we prayed daily for about two months. Nothing happened, and I thought, *Our car is good enough. We'll be fine.*

That was in the summer. The following spring, someone walked up to me at the congregation and handed me a sealed note. I opened it.

The Lord wants you to have a brand-new minivan. Please use this money for that.

Folded inside the envelope was a banker's check for *eighteen thousand dollars!* The person who gave the money wanted all the glory to go to God and desired to stay anonymous.

Dave, the kids, and I were just thrilled. It seemed like an enormous amount of money to us. Additionally, someone else added another $2,500. So now we had $20,500 for car shopping.

Immediately, Dave researched the best cars. He soon came to the conclusion that almost every one had a fatal flaw: one brand was too small, another regularly had transmission difficulties after a certain mileage, a third got low fuel economy ("gas is only going to get more expensive," I prophesied all-too-accurately), and on and on.

"So what should we get?" I asked, dazzled by all the slick, color brochures that Dave came home with from the car dealerships (you know, the ones where there's a zoom-in shot of a leather headrest, and another glossy color shot of the car somewhere in New Mexico).

"A Toyota," Dave promptly replied. "The best car out there is the Toyota Sienna."

"Then let's get it."

Dave shook his head. "It's way too expensive, Becky. They're at least $26,000."

"Look," I said, "this is what we'll do. Let's pray about it, go to the Toyota dealership, and see what God does."

Dave looked at me. "Okay, Becky. You're on."

The next day dawned soft and clear, a mild, beautiful day in early May. We drove to the Toyota dealership and test-drove a silver 2002 Toyota Sienna. It was elegant and smooth. I loved it.

"Do you like it?" asked Dave.

"Love it," I said.

Afterward we sat with the salesman and I watched admiringly as Dave negotiated the price further and further down. Finally, after three trips to the sales manager's office, the salesman gave us a figure after sales tax that was the lowest he could go: $4,500 more than we had.

"How long can you hold that price for us?" asked Dave.

"I'll give you 24 hours," said the salesman, "but you'll have to put a nonrefundable $50 deposit down."

Dave and I looked at each other. I nodded.

"It's a deal," said Dave, reaching for his wallet.

Later that day, I called my mother, and she offered $2,500, the maximum amount she could transfer over the phone on her Visa. Also, we borrowed $2,000 from Josiah, who was the richest person in the family since celebrating his bar mitzvah five months previously. "We'll pay you back as soon as we get our tax return," we promised him.

The next day, we returned to the Toyota dealership and triumphantly paid cash for our gorgeous new car.

Four weeks later, when we got our tax refund in the mail, it wasn't the $2,000 we had expected from our return but a surprise $4,000! Uncle Sam was in on the blessing!

A year after God blessed us with our new car, interest rates for mortgages hit an all-time low. "You really need to buy a house," urged my brother Michael.

Dave and I had rented ever since we got married. Part of the reason was we had no money for a down payment. Also, we always felt that we couldn't be tied down to an area by an unsaleable house if the Lord told us it was time to move on. However, it had been fifteen years in Central New York with no end in sight.

"Michael's right," said my father. "Find something reasonable and I'll give you the down payment."

Could this be the man who didn't come to our wedding? I was so pleased by the new depth in our relationship with my father.

Additionally, I had been homeschooling the older children for three years, and Josiah was in ninth grade. "I want to go to public high school," he told us. I thought it was a good idea, but was reluctant to send him to the inner-city high school in our current district. After praying about it, I believed the Lord wanted him to go to the high school in the adjoining town.

Dave and I did some research. Then, on a snowy day in January, we met with a realtor and took a look at three potential houses.

The first one wasn't in the right school district, but the picture looked so good and the price was so low we couldn't resist. Set far back on a sparsely populated country road, surrounded by an acre of land that looked like the setting for a Jane Austin novel, was an enormous, three-story yellow house. I felt excitement growing inside me as I walked up the gravel drive to the front door, trailing behind Dave and the realtor, Matt. I hadn't had any real desire to own a home before, but now that it was a possibility I found that there *was* a landowner lurking in there somewhere. Now, in anticipation, I walked from the bright, winter day into the house and saw...gloom.

Ugh! It was horrible. Dark, dingy, junky linoleum floors, peeling orange and green flowered wallpaper, ancient fixtures. The worst though, was that everywhere smelled like mildew. Once a house turns mildewy, it's very hard to get it out, and it's extremely unhealthy. Scripture even says in Leviticus 14:43-45 that "if the mildew reappears in the house after the stones have been torn out and the house scraped and plastered, the priest is to go and examine it and, if the mildew has spread in the house, it is a destructive mildew; the house is unclean. It must be torn down—its stones, timbers, and all the plaster—and taken out of the town to an unclean place." Dave and I thought this house might be in that category.

The next house was also huge: a towering Victorian-style home on a small side street by the railroad tracks in a so-so section of town. It had virtually no land, but was an easy walk to the library and several other critical Hermon destinations. Like the first house, it was cheap but needed an enormous amount of work: new roof, siding, insulation, interior work. Unlike the first house, it smelled clean. Dave estimated it would take at least $30,000, though, to make it habitable.

Tired by now, and a bit discouraged, we drove with the realtor to the third and final house on the list. Driving up and up and up a hill, we arrived at a nondescript white farmhouse perched on a corner overlooking the city. Perked up by the spectacular location, we nevertheless entered the house with some trepidation. Inside, we were pleasantly surprised by the functionality of the place. True, it would need some cosmetic touches, but the downstairs was spacious and light, with big picture windows. It also looked a lot bigger on the inside; the pantry alone was the size of a small bedroom.

The older couple who were selling the place had an iron wood-burning stove in the kitchen, and the fire crackled and popped, dispelling the chill of the day. The snow outside in the field across the street looked virgin and untouched; not sooty and filthy like the snow in the city. What a pleasant and peaceful place! I liked it immediately. The best part was that it was in the school district that I wanted, but just over the county line so the taxes were significantly less.

"And," said the woman who lived there, pointing out of the kitchen window to the end of the driveway, "the school bus stops right there. You can stand here in the morning and wave good-bye to your kids."

Sold! I thought to myself. I had reached the end of my desire to homeschool. Josiah was self-disciplined, but the other two needed competition from other kids to spur them on. I was not cut out to be a home-school mom either. If the laundry needed to be thrown in, or I had a great but time-consuming dinner idea, I would do that first and leave the kids to (ha ha) teach themselves. It hadn't worked.

We made an offer on the house; the people counter-offered, we accepted, and the deal was made. Three months later, we moved into our first home, just in time for an absolutely spectacular spring.

The following year, a friend gave me a tape by a Christian evangelist. This was recorded by a guy who had determined to know God better so he spent up to twelve hours a day in silent prayer, waiting for God to show up. Soon visions of Yeshua appeared to this man. I listened to this tape and I had two reactions: disbelief and longing. Disbelief because, though I heard God speak to me and had seen his power in my life, I had never "seen" him with my eyes. Longing because I longed to experience the Lord in a heightened spiritual way. I didn't want to wait for death to see him; I wanted to see him now!

I made a commitment to Yeshua. I asked him for a visitation. *I can't spend twelve hours a day in prayer*, I told him (obviously the guy on the tape didn't have five children and a household to run), *but I can get out of bed earlier and be with you as often as possible.*

So with God's help, I did. My youngest child, Leah, was about to enter kindergarten and I no longer had babies who kept me up at night. Every morning, at 6 a.m., my eyes would open and I would have a choice in front of me: do I get out of bed and sit in a chair and pray or do I settle back into delicious sleep? More mornings than not, I got out of bed. It was a wonderful time of getting closer to God.

That same summer, Emily gave me a book which was a parable on following one's dream. "This is a great book," she said. "You'll love it."

The book talked about shaking oneself free of the common and ordinary and seeking after that which one had a passion for, no matter how difficult the road. I read it in a thoughtful mood.

Hmmm. What's my dream? I remember always wanting to be a wife and a mother and that's been achieved. Do I still have a dream? Is there something else? Maybe it's moving to Israel. Is that my dream? I didn't know. I prayed and then left it alone.

Right around Labor Day, I took my almost daily walk down the hilly, tree-bordered country road that wound past my new house, silently talking to God about this and that, as I have a habit of doing.

All of a sudden an idea so alien to what I had been thinking about popped into my mind and I was convinced this had to be from God.

I want you to write a biblically centered book about modesty for today's woman from a Jewish perspective.

A book about modesty? Me? Are you sure?

Write a book about modesty.

By the time I returned home, I was bubbling over with excitement. What a fascinating assignment God had given me! I couldn't wait to get started. Immediately, I got a spiral notebook and made a list of references on modesty from the Bible. I looked up their Hebrew meanings and began to get a sense for exactly what God was saying. A week later, I sat down at the computer and started to write. I found that if I was faithful in arising at 6 a.m. to pray and read Scripture, that the Lord would guide me and I could write about 2 pages a day. I had no outline and nothing more than a vague idea as to how the book would go other than what the Scriptures said, so I depended on God to give me direction every step of the way.

A few weeks into this process I realized that *this was my dream.* This was what I had dreamed of as a young girl. I wanted to be a writer! I always wrote well, but I never tried to do anything that wasn't assigned at school. I talked about writing, I dreamed about writing, but I did not write.

Until now.

A British science fiction novelist, Terry Pratchett, once said that he read, and he read, and he read, and when he was so stuffed with reading that the words began to leak out of him, he started to write. I felt like Terry. I had spent my whole life consuming vast numbers of books and now they were pouring out. I had a sense from God to keep my pleasure reading to a bare minimum during this season of writing so as not to get distracted.

I loved writing the book. It brought me closer to God. If I wanted the writing to go well, I really needed to pray more, read Scripture more, hear from him more. It occurred to me that God had answered my prayers to see him not in the way I had anticipated but in a totally different way that nevertheless thrilled me.

God spoke to me several times about the book. He said that he was writing it *with* me and it was something he intended to use to move forward the kingdom of heaven. *It's going to be published, and it's going to sell,* he said. *I'm going to use it to open doors before you so that you will speak my words with boldness and clarity.*

These remarkable words watered my parched soul. The congregation was going through yet another reversal, and I desperately wanted to accomplish something significant. I knew that there are many ways to move forward the kingdom of heaven, and many of those ways are not immediately apparent, but still the idea of a successful, Bible-centered, holy lifestyle book was immensely satisfying.

It took about a year to write the book, during which time my right hip caused me more and more pain. It wasn't cancer, but rather a degeneration of the hip bone caused by the extreme amount of radiation used on the previous cancer. One week after I wrote the final page of my book, I checked into the hospital for a hip replacement. After hobbling to pre-op, I stretched out on the bed and held my arm up to the doctor.

"Just stick the IV in and cut this thing out," I told him, attempting to laugh. "I can't stand it anymore."

I had a great attitude about the surgery and the four week recuperation period. I was so jazzed about finishing my book that nothing bothered me. I felt a sense of God's urgency about getting the book out and was confident that it would move forward immediately. I even had a contact with an agent in New York City who agreed to read the manuscript as soon as I could get it to him.

When the agent finally got back to me, via email, it was to say that he found the book good in parts but "not marketable." Thanks but no thanks.

I was crushed! I had expected him to sign me and find a publisher right away. All my cheerful optimism failed. I crumpled up the email and threw it on the floor, hurt.

"Relax," encouraged Dave. "You gave them first crack at something wonderful and they turned it down. Do you really want someone who has no vision for this book trying to sell it? How successful do you think that's gonna be?"

When I calmed down, I realized that Dave was right. But where to go from here? A friend owned one of those huge manuals, *How to Get Your Christian Book Published*. I borrowed it and got even more depressed. It seemed that it was virtually impossible for a first-time author to get published. I prayed about it and then listed my book with a Christian review service. Maybe a publisher would contact me.

Alas, I didn't get a single response. Discouraged, I even thought about self-publishing, so eager was I to see my book in actual book form. I asked Emily what she thought.

"Absolutely not," she immediately said. "I just know that God wants you to have a royalty publisher. Don't give up."

Sigh. She was right. I had to have the faith that God would keep the promises he had made to me. In the meantime, I was writing a second book. This one was a novel: the saga of a Jewish family. It was harder to write than the first book, though. With the first book, I was flying high on God's promises to me, glorying in the new and wonderful life he had literally dropped in my lap. With this second book, I needed to trust that even though I couldn't see anything happening in the natural, through perseverance and faith I could achieve the promise. Some days, I felt like the pages were squeezed out of me.

The congregation wasn't going well. A fellow who had been coming for years and with whom Dave had a close relationship suddenly grew angry. The reverberations spread out into the congregation and it dwindled. I coped by diverting my energies to writing.

That spring, I developed severe pain in my lower back, and then in my neck as well. It never occurred to me that it could be cancer so I didn't talk about it with my oncologist. I just put up with the pain until it got too severe to ignore. By the time I had an MRI, cancer was diagnosed in my lower spine.

Dave and I went to see a neurosurgeon. Upbeat and cheerful, he told me that he could easily fix the fractured vertebrae in my spine with a procedure called kyphoplasty, which involved pumping the collapsed vertebrae up with an acrylic balloon-like substance. It sounded too good to be true.

"What kind of post-surgical care is involved?" I asked.

"A Band-Aid™ and an aspirin," he said.

I couldn't wait to have the procedure done and be out of pain.

That next week, Dave said to me, "Why don't you get an X-ray done of your neck? Find out why it's been hurting you?"

"It doesn't really hurt anymore," I said.

"Check it out anyway," he advised.

I was getting radiation on my spine for the cancer, so I told the radiation oncologist about my neck and he sent me for X-rays that day.

Later that afternoon, I was in the kitchen preparing dinner when the telephone rang.

"Hello?"

"Becky?"

"Yes? Is this Dr. Stevenson?"

"Yes. Look, Becky, you need to get a cervical collar *right away*. I just got the results of your X-ray and you have fractures in your neck." He sounded highly agitated.

"What does that mean?"

"There's cancer in your neck and it's caused the fractures. It's critical that you get support for your neck immediately. I'm going to arrange an MRI for you tomorrow and I'll call the neurosurgeon. You'll need to see him as soon as possible."

"Sure, thanks," I said, shocked.

"Take care." He hung up.

Trembling, I hung up the phone and reached for the yellow pages. I called the local medical supply place and found out that they were closing in twenty minutes. "I'll be there in fifteen," I shouted into the receiver. I grabbed my purse and my car keys. "I'll be back as soon as I can," I yelled to the kids as I hobbled to the car.

Early the next week, with the results of my latest MRI tucked under Dave's arm in a big manila envelope, we arrived back at the office of the neurosurgeon. No longer jovial, he tacked the X-rays up on his examining room wall and turned to face us, mustache bristling on his florid face.

"Has anyone informed you people of what's going on?" he demanded, almost angrily. "You have cancer in *every vertebrae.* Do you realize how serious that is?"

"Is there anything you can do for my neck?" I asked him.

"No! A neck is not a spine. I can't do kyphoplasty on a neck. It's much more involved. Frankly, you're in danger of severing your spinal cord and being paralyzed for life. There's no way to do surgery on you now, you're much too fragile. I'm putting you in a stiff neck brace. Get it right away and take it off only to shower." He was writing a prescription as he spoke and didn't look up.

"So what do I do?"

"Come back to me when the cancer is gone and maybe I can fix the neck. But it's a very involved procedure and you would need to wear the neck brace for at least two months after the surgery."

My voice shook. "How long do I wear the neck brace?"

"At least six months." The doctor stood, and I realized that the appointment was over. Dave, white-faced, pocketed the prescription while I balanced myself with my cane (by now, I used a cane and was on several painkillers a day). We said good-bye and made our way to the car. Next we found the orthopedic place where I was fitted for the neck brace.

It was huge, ugly, and terribly annoying. I resembled a frail, middle-aged football player in full regalia. Designed to immobilize one's neck, it made looking down virtually impossible. Tears sprang to my eyes and I blew my nose. I looked like a freak. Dave and I returned to the car.

I stared out the windshield, utterly in despair. Dave reached over and squeezed my hand. "Don't worry," he said gently. "We'll get through this."

Suddenly a warrior spirit rose up in me. "It's too small a thing to merely ask God to heal me of this cancer!" I said. "I'm going to ask him to heal my neck and spine as well, without surgery. The Lord is our doctor." We drove the rest of the way home in silence.

Thirteen

The next two months were brutal. I ramped up my pain meds, went daily to radiation and weekly to chemo. The spine radiation actually gave pain relief, but the angles on the neck radiation meant that my esophagus took a hit. My throat hurt terribly, my mouth burned, my tastebuds got mixed-up. I couldn't eat, I couldn't move, I was in agony.

Dave's sister Rachel telephoned. "I'm coming to help," she announced. "My job is giving me time off for a family emergency."

I cried with relief. Unlike Dave's other sister, at the time Rachel was still single. She worked as a teacher in a private Jewish day school down in New Jersey. She had a real servant's heart and I knew that her help would be invaluable. The kids adored her, and she could keep house and cook with the best of them. Also, since wearing the neck brace I was on driving restriction and Rachel could take me to all my many and sundry doctors' appointments.

One weekend, two women friends of Rachel's who ministered in a healing room drove up from Jersey. They anointed me with oil and prayed for God to heal me. Many others prayed as well. About the same time, one of the women from my prayer group, Connie, came over during Sukkot with a friend of hers and the friend saw in the spiritual realm what was attacking me.

"This cancer is a serpent wrapped around your spine and it's trying to kill you," said Marguerite, her intense green eyes focused and one hand upraised. "That neck brace you're wearing, it reminds me of the open mouth of the snake. It's ready to devour you and only the hand of the Lord is holding it back."

Both Marguerite and Connie urged me to repent of any unforgiveness or bitterness. I felt a weight of conviction as I realized just how angry and distressed I'd become over the many people who

202

had been in and out of the congregation over the years. I had no right to hold anything against anyone. God had forgiven me so much!

I realized that there were people I had said I had forgiven but really hadn't. The mention of their names still brought an *uhh!* to my stomach. If I heard misfortune had befallen them, I thought they deserved it. I set myself to really, truly, forgive and love people. They may not deserve it, but then neither did I. We have all sinned and fallen short of the glory of God. It is only through the blood of Messiah Yeshua that our sins are covered.

So why did I get breast cancer? Was it my fault? Did the sins of my youth, forgiven by God when I came to him as a 23-year-old, still hold sway? I've thought about all this carefully, and I can only surmise that the breast cancer came as a result of many different things, all intertwined so tightly that extricating one string and claiming *that* as the cause is impossible. Environment, nutrition, and genetics are on the physical side. Spiritually, past sin, though forgiven, can still have consequences that reverberate for years. Bitterness, unforgiveness, stress, and family upsets also play a part.

I think in my case that the horrible Thanksgiving week when Leah was a baby triggered something and gave the enemy an open door. I allowed myself to be shaken instead of resting in the joy which as believers in Messiah is ours for the asking. Ultimately, though, I have come to realize that the enemy of my soul wants to destroy me because I belong to God and am determined to move forward the Kingdom of Heaven. God has control over everything that happens to me and he has allowed this cancer and will use it to bring glory to himself. He and only he can crush the head of this serpent and save me.

At the end of October, Dave and I drove down to West Virginia for a spiritual and prayer retreat camp where Dave was scheduled to be one of the speakers. A few days into our being there, they called me up during the evening program, wrapped me in a shawl that had been prayed over, and over one hundred people held their hands out toward me, praying for God to touch me. I stood there facing this sea of upraised hands and felt as if waves of restoration were crashing over my head.

The next day, I reached for my pill bottle to take one of my regular narcotic pills. I heard God's voice:

Why are you taking that? Are you in pain?

I thought about the question. No, at the moment I wasn't in pain. I surmised that God was ramping me down off the pain pills. How wonderful!

No, I replied. *I'm really not in pain right now.* I put the bottle back on the dresser. I didn't take another pill that day.

By evening, when I went to lie down in bed, the neck brace that I had worn for six weeks suddenly frustrated me terribly. I couldn't stand it, so I took it off. Lying back down, I desperately wanted to curl up on my side like I used to, instead of lying like a statue on my back.

Is this okay, Lord? I asked with great trepidation.

You will not be paralyzed, came the response.

Cautiously, I folded the pillow under my head and lay motionless on my side. *Ah, that felt good!* Still, I was fearful.

Are you sure I won't be paralyzed? I asked him again.

Again, he responded: *You will not be paralyzed.*

Five more times that night I asked the Lord the same question and each time he gave me the same response. Hope, a tiny seedling in my heart, grew roots and pushed its happy head above the soil of despair.

The next day, after I dressed and prepared to leave the room for the morning sessions, I went to get my cane.

You don't need that, came the Lord's voice. *Put the cane away.*

Excitement welled up inside me as I propped the cane in a corner of the room and went out into the soft sunshine of a glorious fall day. Drifting maple leaves floated gently through the sky, lazily finding their way to the pine-needle-covered dirt trails that crisscrossed the mountain resort.

"Oh, look at you! No neck brace!" observed one of my fellow campers. "Are you...?" She paused, not sure if she should say it.

I smiled back at her. "God is doing an amazing healing work in me," I said, not entirely sure if I had a release from God to come right out and say, *I'm healed.*

Dave was cautious, too. "Are you sure you don't want to wear your neck brace in the car?" he asked as we drove out of the camp grounds that Friday morning and headed toward home.

"I'll pray about it," I said. I closed my eyes and asked the Lord, *Should I wear the neck brace in the car?* I heard a *no* in my head immediately.

"No," I said to Dave.

He glanced over at me, eyebrows raised. "That was fast."

"Yes," I affirmed. "It was."

I didn't know what to do about chemotherapy. I hadn't actually heard the Lord tell me to stop going. But if I was healed of cancer, then I didn't need it, right? A few days after I returned from West Virginia, I was scheduled to see my oncologist.

"I'm going to tell him that God healed me and ask him to run a diagnostic test," I told Dave.

"Don't do that," warned Dave. "You can't just spring this on him in the examining room. Send him a fax the day before. It's the only way to do this."

The day before my appointment, I sat down at the computer,

thought for a while, then pounded out the following letter:

Dear Dr. Smith:
As you know, I have a strong belief in God's ability to heal. I went to a prayer and spiritual retreat camp this last week and firmly believe that I've been healed of cancer! I've stopped taking pain pills as I no longer have any pain. Would you please send me for an MRI so we can stop chemo?
　　　Sincerely yours,
　　　Rebecca Hermon

The next day, Dave took me to the doctor's (I was still on driving restriction) and we waited together in the exam room, not quite sure what was going to happen.

Suddenly the door to the office opened and Dr. Smith strode in. Mincing no words, he placed my bulging manila file on the stool by the little counter and said, "I got your note."

"Oh, good!" I answered. "What do you think?"

"I threw it away."

"But Dr. Smith," I protested. "God has done an amazing thing in my life! I haven't had a pain pill in over a week, I'm walking without a cane...why don't you order a diagnostic test for me?"

"I'm not ordering any tests," he said abruptly. "They wouldn't do any good right now. It's too soon to tell."

"Well, maybe something will show up that will surprise you," I countered. "I probably don't need chemo anymore."

Barely controlling his aggravation, Dr. Smith ignored Dave and focused his next comments on me. I had never seen him so upset. "You have a very serious and aggressive form of cancer," he told me through clenched teeth. "If you choose to stop treatments, I can assure you that you will die a horribly painful death. Let me know what you decide." He nodded a curt good-bye, then turned on his heel and left the room.

Dave and I looked at each other, shocked.

"It's a good thing you sent that fax," allowed Dave.

I was too shaken to laugh. I didn't know what to do. The extreme pain I had recently undergone, especially the nerve pain as the tumor ate its nasty way through my spine, was too recent in my memory to be dulled by time. Tears welled up in my eyes and overflowed down my cheeks. I sat sobbing in the car as Dave drove us to the synagogue, where I had an appointment with my women's prayer group.

The four women who gathered with me each Wednesday at noon to pray for the congregation, our own lives, and Israel, immediately reached out to me. There were a couple of men who were also around doing other things and they came over. Everyone prayed over me for healing and wisdom.

"I don't know what to do," I sobbed, sitting on the couch in the prayer room, clutching a sodden tissue in my hand. "If God has healed me, then subjecting myself to chemo would not only be a lot of extra agony for nothing, it would also be a lack of trust in what God has done. On the other hand, if he hasn't told me to stop chemo and I presumptuously stop, then I can't expect protection and the cancer could come raging back at me." Shakily, I reached for another tissue.

No one, including Dave, could make that decision for me. They surrounded me with love and prayed that I would hear from God.

I cried the rest of that day and throughout the night. The next morning, I got out of bed at 6 a.m. and sat in my yellow chair next to my bed and prayed.

"Oh, Lord, I'm so frightened," I whispered. "I just want to please you, but I can't make the wrong choice. I can't face that terrible pain again. Please help me!"

I sat silently for a while, and then I heard him:

You can go to chemo.

Are you sure, Lord? It's not a lack of faith, is it?

You can go to chemo.

Vastly relieved, incredulous that I would ever be happy to go to chemo, I woke Dave up and told him what I had heard God say.

"Are you sure?" he asked, hating what chemo did to me, hoping we could just put all this behind us *now*.

"Yes. I'm going to give Dr. Smith a call later and get back on the schedule."

"Okay."

When I reached Dr. Smith and told him I would continue

chemotherapy for the time being, he was bland and professional. I knew he was still upset with me. *Save him, Lord*, I prayed. *Show him you're real.*

The concern Dave had that chemo would debilitate me was not an unreasonable one. Therefore, I was immensely encouraged when a friend of mine phoned me from Connecticut.

"I was praying for you," she said. "And God gave me the Scripture from Mark 16:17:

> *Yeshua said, "And these signs will accompany those who believe:*
> *In my name they will drive out demons;*
> *they will speak in new tongues;*
> *they will pick up snakes with their hands;*
> *and when they drink deadly poison, it will not hurt them at all;*
> *they will place their hands on sick people, and they will get well."*

Well, I thought, *chemo is nothing if not deadly poison.* When I went to my weekly sessions at the hospital and got my double dose of herceptin and navelbene, I would pray that Scripture over myself. God did an amazing thing, too. I didn't get sick from the drugs, nor did I lose any hair!

As the weeks progressed, I regained more and more strength and my faith grew. Many people confirmed for me that God had indeed healed me. One fellow in particular was recently remarried to a Jewish believer whom I had known for years. His first wife had died from breast cancer-gone-into-the-bones. He marveled at how well I was doing and shook his head in wonderment. "You're a walking miracle," he said again and again.

A member of our congregation, a beautiful, faith-filled red-haired lady, came to my house and spent a day with me. "God told me that you need to read these books," she announced, handing me two books so tiny that they resembled glorified pamphlets. One was *God's Creative Power for Healing*, by Charles Capps, and the other was Gloria Copeland's *God's Prescription for Divine Health*. Both booklets shared a similar message: the Word of God (the Bible) is a powerful medicine which, when routinely and consistently taken in (read AND spoken audibly), will lead to healing. The authors suggest speaking to one's body and rebuking illness.

I did that mostly at night. As I lay in my bed, I thanked God for healing me from cancer and for strengthening my bones. I also told any cancer, arthritis, osteoporosis, or bone disease of any kind to immediately leave my body as I am covered by the blood of Yeshua and am healed.

I wanted to stop chemo, though. I constantly barraged the Lord: *when can I end these treatments?* One night I had a dream: I was talking to Dr. Smith and asking him how many more treatments. He smiled and said, "Normally, four to six but with *you*," and here he paused dramatically before saying, "eight to ten." Now realistically, with my condition, the normal treatment would go for another eight or nine months. I had a strong sense in the dream to just trust him.

At my next monthly appointment, I asked Dr. Smith (who had warmed up considerably) to estimate how much longer my treatments would last.

"Oh, a lot longer," he quickly answered. "I may take you off the navelbene this spring, but the herceptin will go on for quite a long time."

I refused to get discouraged. I made a conscious decision not to allow the doctor's words to pierce my soul. Determined to follow God, and God alone, I threw myself on his mercy and took life one day at a time.

The following month, weary of chemo, I returned to the doctor's office for my checkup.

"How are you feeling?" he asked.

"Really good," I answered. "Except that the chemo is getting to me. I think my immune system is taking a beating."

The doctor studied me for a moment. "Are you in any pain?"

"Pain? No, none."

"You wouldn't lie to me, would you?"

"Of course not! I haven't even taken an aspirin in months!"

Dr. Smith leaned against the counter and folded his arms. His mouth twitched at the corners. "I'm going to make you a compromise," he said. "You've been telling me that you're healed, so this is what I'm going to do...."

Take me off the navelbene, please, please!

"I'm going to stop all chemo treatments."

I stared at him in amazement. *What? That's a compromise?* "Really?" I sputtered.

"Really." He smiled. "But I want you to go back on the Arimidex (a one pill a day treatment) and call me immediately if you have any pain."

"Oh, yes, thank you, thank you!" I exclaimed, feeling like I had just won the lottery.

"See you next month," said the doctor as he left the room.

When I exited the exam room, two of the nurses were standing in the hall waiting for me. "What did he say?" asked the one named Mary, curiously.

"Dr. Smith took me off all chemo treatments," I told her, still in a daze.

"Oh Becky, that's wonderful!" Crying and laughing, Mary and the other nurse hugged me.

Later that day, when I got home, I took my calendar and counted chemo treatments from the time I got the dream until that day. Three months had gone by, but allowing for missed treatments at holidays, I had undergone exactly ten treatments since my dream.

While I was still slogging through the weekly chemo, I had a breakthrough getting my book published. Linda, the friend from

Connecticut who had received the Scripture from Mark16, had edited the manuscript. She also mailed me a list of agents who handle spiritual literature. I checked off several of the names that looked like possibilities, put together an introductory letter, and wrote to five of my top picks. I ended up getting some interesting responses just as a fascinating email popped up on my computer screen.

A fellow by the name of George North, along with a woman named Rona Wicker, had just put together a Christian publishing company. These two people were long-time publishing professionals who had a desire to see new, talented authors break into the tightly sewn-up world of Christian lifestyle books. They had apparently gone into the archives of the writer's service I had used and found the synopsis of my book from the previous year. It looked good to them and they contacted me.

By this time, I was used to getting solicitations from self-publishing groups. Basically, that means you give them thousands of dollars and they turn your manuscript into an actual book which you can then sell at conventions, conferences, out of the trunk of your car, etc. Most people get a little desperate to see their book look like a real book after it's been sitting gathering dust for a while so this can be quite tempting. It's like being pregnant for years.

I read George's email and was intrigued. This sounded like the real thing. I quickly wrote him back and electronically sent my manuscript. Hours later, he sent me a message that said, *I love this so far; it's just what we're looking for...we'll get back to you soon...have you written anything else? etc. etc.* That night, I kept Dave up for hours as I eagerly anticipated the realization of my dream.

Two long weeks later, I received another email from George. He and his partner, Rona, had both read the book and were offering me a contract. They also wanted to see my second book. In three months, I would have a finished product, marketing information to follow. I prayed and the Lord said, *This is it.*

"I told you," said Emily. We were sitting on the eggplant purple leather couch in her living room. Winter sunlight streamed through the French doors and lit up the various multicolored glass knick-knacks that were artfully arranged on various tables. Emily's white husky,

Essie, nudged my hand with her wet nose. My kids were all safely at school, and I was able to sit and relax while Emily and I met for our weekly prayer time. I cupped my hands around a mug of steaming herbal tea.

"You were right," I said, taking a sip of tea. "Had I known that the Lord was in the process of forming the publishing company, I would have been a lot more patient this last year." The truth was that I felt somewhat ridiculous about all my fretting now that I saw more of God's plan revealed. All along he had reassured me and reminded me of his promise about this book. Countless times I had gotten down on my knees and repented of ascribing too much importance to *the book, the book, the book!* I knew this project was important to God, but I also knew that my putting him first was of the utmost importance.

"It's a great book," said Emily, one of my staunchest supporters. "I can't wait until it's out! I'm going to buy fifty of them and give one to everyone I know."

Ah, life was good. First a healing and now the realization of a published book. *A season of blessing,* the Lord said. *You're entering a season of blessing.* Soon I had a signed contract for my second book as well.

When the first book made its debut, everyone I knew bought copies from Amazon.com. That first day my ranking went from 250,000 to about 40,000. I figured at that rate I should be #1 in a few months.

How wrong I was! Once the initial excitement died down, my stats shot up into the 800,000s, only to dip back into a moderate 150,000 range if someone somewhere in the world bought a copy. What to do?

"We need a marketing strategy," Dave helpfully suggested one evening as I was bemoaning the fact that the book wasn't selling very well. We were sitting in front of our upstairs computer and checking online stats.

"Isn't that the publisher's job?"

Dave swiveled around on the computer chair and faced me. "I know he's got some ideas," he said, "but in the meantime we need to move forward on our end."

So we did. On a local level, we solicited publicity and set-up book signings. Some of the libraries I had frequented for years bought copies and put them on the shelves. Word spread in the community and more and more people were interested in reading the book. God's hand was on it, and I got only positive responses. The people who only said they liked it and it was well-written paled in comparison with the ones who said that it was one of the best books they had ever read on the subject. The most tremendous response was when people told me that it helped them in their spiritual walk and that they were encouraged to make changes in their lives in order to be more holy before God.

He had given it to me, every page. His Spirit had led me every time I sat down at the computer. If I hadn't spent enough time in prayer and in reading Scripture, I would have been a dry well, unable to produce. Writing the book was an awesome experience.

Fourteen

A few weeks after the book was published, I went to Israel for the first time in almost thirty years. My aunt Renate had made *aliyah* way back in 1947. She was my father's oldest sister by eight years. Her three children were all born and bred Israelis, or *sabras* (an Israeli cactus that's sweet on the inside and prickly on the outside).

My father, Isaac, and his family had escaped from Nazi Germany at the end of 1938, traveling initially to Belgium, then England, and finally settling in New York. By 1946, Renate, his older sister, had joined a Zionist training camp in Upstate New York. She subsequently met her husband, a Hungarian Jew, at a kibbutz and had four children, one of whom died young in a tragic accident. Divorced by 1960, she stayed in the Land, working as a postwoman to support her family.

I greatly admired her pioneer spirit and love for Israel. On multiple occasions, I shared with her about the truth of God that I had found in Yeshua. She very nicely claimed not to be interested. At seventy-two, Renate sold her comfortable home in a beautiful suburb of Haifa and bought a house in one of the settlements in the occupied territories, or West Bank. It was accessible only through guarded checkpoints manned by attractive khaki-clad Israeli twenty somethings. After the security check, one drove past the ubiquitous shuffling elderly woman leading a donkey on a rope and then through the dusty, dilapidated Arab village with the rotting produce precariously perched on crates outside the small, dank grocery store. Palestinian men and boys glared sullenly into the vehicles marked with Israeli license plates. You didn't want to stop here for any reason, nor did you want to drive through on a day when someone had a gun and itchy fingers.

It so happened that one of Renate's granddaughters was getting married in May, right around Shavuot (the Feast of Weeks). I hadn't been in Israel since 1981 when I was nineteen.

"Come on," my father generously offered. "It's time you saw the Israeli family again. Your mother and I are going to Hannah's wedding and would like to treat you. But only you," he added. "It's just too expensive to also take Dave and the kids."

I prayed about whether or not to go. I had never been away from my children for over a week before and Israel was so far away! But, on the other hand, my heart had yearned to go for years now. Every time it seemed financially possible we had another baby. Flying seven people to Israel was a miracle that God would have to work out. I had thought that the Lord would move the family there permanently, but so far we were still in America.

I heard the Lord say, *Go!*

"Go," confirmed Dave. "I'll take care of the kids." He noticed my dubious expression. "The house may not be as clean as you keep it, but we'll be fine."

Once I had a *yes* from God in prayer, plus Dave's blessing, I felt free to be excited. The kids were remarkably complacent about my going without them.

"We'll miss you," they said, "but have a great time."

"I wish I could go," said Shira, blue eyes wide. "I want to see Israel!"

"I wish you could go too, sweetheart," I told her. "Let's pray that God would arrange for the whole family to get there really, really soon."

I left on a cool, rainy day in May. I had a suitcase stuffed full of copies of my book and was ready to tell everyone I met about my miraculous healing from cancer. Four of the kids were at school and my oldest, Josiah, was finishing up his freshman year of college. Dave drove me to the airport.

"Don't come in with me," I cautioned him as he pulled up to the Departures gate. "I'll be fine."

"Why don't you want me to come in with you?"

"Because you always leave your car in the *no parking* area and I'm nervous the whole time that we're going to get a ticket. Just kiss me good-bye here."

Dave looked annoyed. "I can't even escort my wife safely to the airline counter?"

"No," I said firmly, puckering my lips. "Kiss me."

"Fine," he huffed, but he kissed me. "I will see you in eleven days."

"I'll really miss you," I told him, my voice catching slightly.

"I'll miss you, too."

Dave got my suitcase out of the hatch of the van and carried it to the curb for me. We hugged and kissed good-bye again, and then I grabbed the strap and pulled the suitcase behind me into the terminal. Once safely inside, I looked back through the big glass windows. Dave was pulling away from the curb, merging into the airport traffic. I waved, but he didn't see me.

I flew to JFK Airport in New York, where I had several hours before my El Al flight left for Tel Aviv. While waiting for the El Al ticket counter to open, I started chatting with two women who stood behind me in line. They were Christians from Chicago on their way to Israel to join up with a tour.

"I have a book you would love," I exclaimed, unzipping my suitcase and pulling out a copy of my book. "It's just the thing to read while you're on the plane."

Both women seemed intrigued. They carefully examined the book, reading the back cover copy.

"I'd like to buy it," the shorter woman with dark, curly hair announced, flipping open her wallet.

I told her the price.

She handed me the money. "Could you sign it?"

I pulled out a pen and scrawled an inscription, thrilled to see the work God gave me going out to the four corners of the globe.

Once I had my boarding pass, I slowly meandered through the airport, casually looking into the various kiosks that lined both sides of the terminal. I found my gate, sat down, and took a look at my boarding pass. The seat number, I noticed, was 24K. How funny, I thought. That's the symbol for the purest gold purchasable. Then I heard God's voice:

That's you, he said. *Refined by fire and brought forth as pure gold.* Malachi 3.

Excitedly, I pulled my Bible out of my canvas tote and thumbed through it until I came to Malachi. There it was:

But who can endure the day of his coming?
Who can stand when he appears?
For he will be like a refiner's fire or a launderer's soap.
He will sit as a refiner and purifier of silver;
He will purify the Levites and refine them like gold and silver.

Lord, I prayed, my heart warm and full to bursting, *if going through cancer brings me closer to you, it's totally worth it.* I couldn't wait to see what he had for me next.

Israel was...well, Israel was suspiciously like Southern California, only the road signs were in Hebrew and Arabic as well as English. My parents had flown in the day before and were with my aunt so my cousin Lira (the mother of the bride), picked me up and brought me back to her home.

"This is beautiful!" I exclaimed, as we turned off the main road and through the gates of the town. Shohem, a trendy suburb five minutes from the airport, instantly appealed to me. It was a lot like a wealthy area of California, only more exotic. Jacaranda trees, their purple, white and lavender flowers gorgeous against the blue sky, lined both sides of every street. Red-tiled roofed stone houses, each with their own gate, jostled against each other, pushing up and down gently hilly streets. I caught glimpses of fruit trees and flower gardens through the iron grilles and intricately carved wooden fences. I later discovered that paths ran behind the houses to a common wilderness area. Pomegranate trees (*rimon*, in Hebrew) blossomed orange, their precious fruit not ripe until later in the summer. Berry bushes grew in great abundance, and the people of the town could come and gather the fruit as they desired.

Unlike America, parking in Israel was a more casual affair. Lira pulled up to her house and zipped into a space in the opposite direction of a car already there.

"Is that okay?" I asked, aware I would never park like that at home.

"Becky, don't worry. Ees fine," she reassured me in her charming Israeli accent.

Mollified, I got out of the car and stood by helplessly while Lira insisted on getting my heavy suitcase out of the trunk of her VW sedan.

It was good to see her. It had been close to thirty years, but I would have recognized her anywhere. True, her long, brown hair was now short and blond, and her face more lined, but she was still my older cousin that I so admired. When I was ten and Lira sixteen, she had come from Israel and spent a year with my father's other sister, who lived on Long Island not far from us. Lira had gone to the high school where my father taught English, along with our cousin, my aunt's daughter Mindy. Lira came home with my father every weekend to our house, and it was so much fun to have her with us. Her wide cheekbones and almond-shaped eyes, long straight hair, and foreign accent was so *exotic*. Years later, when I turned nineteen, I went to Israel and stayed briefly with her. I hadn't seen Lira since.

Now I felt more like a teenager on an adventure than a grown woman with five children. I followed Lira through the black iron gate, past the big white dog, and up the stone steps protected from the sun by the shade of several enormous palm trees. A charming outdoor patio boasted a small table and two wooden benches. Several flower boxes overflowing with plants I didn't recognize bordered the perimeter of the patio. Lira swept past, ignoring my cries of "How pretty!" and pushed open the massive wooden door that led into her house.

"*Ani habaytah* (I'm home)," she called out, pausing briefly to drop her keys on the kitchen table.

I walked into the marble-tiled foyer. Lira's eleven-year-old son, Moti, together with a white cat, raced down the stairs.

"*Ema!*" shouted Moti. He looked at me curiously.

"*Shalom. Ani Rivkah* (hello, I'm Rebecca)." I hugged Moti.

"*Ah, shalom Rivkah. Aht m'daberet ivrit?* (Hello Rivkah. Do you speak Hebrew?)"

"*K'tsat* (a little)," I answered, smiling. Though officially Hebrew

218

teacher at our congregation, I was by no means fluent. I knew enough to teach up to an intermediate level. When Josiah and Shmuel were babies, I had ordered a set of Hebrew books from a Jewish publisher in New Jersey and had worked my way through them. Occasionally I got stalled, then I would pray and the Lord would bring clarification to my mind. Never having had the opportunity to dialogue with Hebrew speakers, I was really looking forward to trying out my limited Hebrew on real Israelis.

I spent the rest of that day hanging with the family, accompanying them on various wedding-related errands. I loved walking through the sun-drenched outdoor mall area in the center of the town, haltingly translating the signs over the stores. It occurred to me that this would be a good venue for a suicide bomber, but I knew in my spirit that God had not allowed me to come to Israel only to be blown-up by a terrorist. As I walked with Lira and her daughter Hannah into the grocery store, it was nevertheless comforting to be stopped by the elderly security guard who peered into my purse before giving permission to enter.

I noticed that about Israel: everywhere, *everywhere*, people were checking for hidden bombs. It was as natural as breathing. I found myself scanning the crowd, asking the Holy Spirit to prompt me if there were any problems lurking.

The next morning, Lira and I got back in the VW and drove to the airport to meet Mindy and her family, who had flown in from Long Island for the wedding. They rented a car and then caravaned with us up to my aunt's home in biblical Ephraim. It was the first time I was to go there and I observed with fascination the rocky scenery, gnarled olive trees, vast blue sky, and manned checkpoints. Lira drove quickly and carefully through the dusty Arab village.

"I don't like going to my mother's," she told me, hands gripping the steering wheel, eyes focused on the road.

"Will those soldiers come help us if there's trouble?" I asked, motioning with my thumb in the direction of the laughing boy and girl soldiers we had just passed.

"Sure they will," answered Lira. "But by then it may be too late."

"Do you mind if I pray for protection?"

Lira glanced sideways at me. "Okay," she said cautiously.

I closed my eyes and breathed deeply. It was always a little difficult praying with an unbeliever. The waves of resistance tended to be palpable. Lira seemed relatively open, which was very good.

"Adonai," I began, "we put ourselves under your protection and ask that you would keep us safe both coming and going. Rebuke any terrorist attacks that may be planned against Israel. We bless you and praise you, *b'shem Yeshua.* Amen."

"Amen," agreed Lira.

Twenty minutes later, we pulled up to my aunt's house. This was not nearly as upscale a location as Shohem. Indeed, my aunt had sustained a big hit in her standard of living in order to move to the occupied territories. It didn't bother her, though. She's a real pioneer.

The house, I noticed, was pink. So were the roses planted alongside the front path, the mailbox, the various knick knacks on the front porch, the living room walls, and the dress that clad Aunt Renate as she came forward to hug me. ("If you need to borrow anything while you're in Israel," my father had told me, "you can get it from Renate. You just have to like pink.")

"Becky! So good to see you after all these years!" She kissed and hugged me, her sun-darkened face, wizened from sixty years in the desert sun, wreathed in smiles. After she released me, she went to hug Mindy and I greeted my parents, who were standing there.

"Mom, Dad, great to see you!" We hugged and kissed, everyone in the house doing the tumultuous dance of several people all greeting each other at the same time. I presented my aunt with a copy of my book, which she clasped to her chest like a precious jewel. After a while, Mindy, her husband Gene, their two twenty-something sons, Lira, Renate, Mom, Dad, and myself all gathered around the dining room table, drinking tea, eating apple streudel, tuna fish, olives, and the ubiquitous humus. Mindy pulled a large, flat, black manila folder out of her suitcase.

"Aunt Renate, I found these pictures after my mother died," she said. "Could you tell me who some of these people are?"

"Let me see, darling," said my aunt, putting on her glasses and peering closely. The pictures were black and white shots taken in pre-

World War II Europe. I recognized the first one.

"Dad, that's you!" I exclaimed.

He looked at it and shook his head. "No, it's not," he protested.

My mother took a look. "Yes, it is, Isaac."

"No," he said again, "it's not."

"Let me see." My aunt took the picture and studied it. A little boy of about two stood precariously on a flowered carpet in some long ago photographer's studio. He grasped the leash of a toy horse as he stared with large, clear eyes and a trembling little mouth into the camera. A long-sleeved, white lacy shirt with cuffs that almost covered his tiny hands was tucked into a pair of black shorts. White knee socks and brown leather shoes completed the outfit.

"Isaac, that's you," said Renate.

My father stopped protesting, but I could tell he was unconvinced. I took the picture from Aunt Renate and looked at the other side. Imprinted on the top in tiny letters it said: K. *Plathen. Leipzig N22, Hallischestr.* Yes, definitely from my father's childhood.

Meanwhile, Mindy and Aunt Renate were poring over other pictures. "Oh, yes," said Renate, her face brightening, "this was Uncle So-and-So, and Cousin So-and-So...." It went on like that for several minutes. A photograph of a beautiful young woman with luxuriant dark brown hair caught my attention.

"Who was this?" I asked.

Renate's face darkened when she looked at the photo. "That was Pop's sister Sullie," she said sadly. "The Nazis murdered her."

"*That's* Sullie?" Mindy snatched the picture and studied it. "I hadn't realized this was her!"

"I never heard of her before," I said.

"Oh, yes," said my father. "She was my father's sister, and she lived in Holland with her husband and three children. They had two daughters and a retarded son. They had an opportunity to escape to England, but they weren't allowed to take the retarded boy."

"So what happened?" I asked.

"The husband took the two daughters and Sullie stayed behind with her son. When the Nazis invaded Holland, they were shipped off to a concentration camp and killed."

"Oh how terrible!" I shuddered. "What a choice! And how awful for those two girls to lose their mother like that. What happened to them?"

"They eventually wound up in Canada," said Renate.

"And the husband? Did he remarry?"

"No, he never did."

We were all silent for a few minutes, the atrocities of the Holocaust overwhelmingly present. Soon other pictures were studied, other stories told.

"Oh, that was Cousin Manfred. The Nazis took his factory, but he escaped to Switzerland and built another."

"He was our token millionaire, wasn't he?" I asked.

"Yes," said Lira. "He had no heirs and wanted to leave his money to Ema, but she took too long to write back to him and he had already died."

"Is that true?" I gasped.

My aunt waved a hand in the air. "I was sure they could find someone else," she said. "We don't need it." *Wow, Aunt Renate put believers to shame. She was untouched by the things of this world. Unless they were pink, that is.*

Lira had a pained look on her face. "The rest of us could have found a use for it," she remarked drily.

My aunt responded in Hebrew, and then a rapid-fire Hebrew conversation I couldn't follow ricocheted between them.

Later, Aunt Renate took me upstairs and showed me the view from her bedroom window. Gently rolling hills, brown dotted with green, fell away from us as far as the eye could see.

"I wanted you to see this," she told me, gripping my hands in hers. "This is biblical Beit El." Her eyes lit up and she spoke fast in her enthusiasm, her German/Hebrew accented English a little difficult to follow. "This is our land. This is where Jacob met with God. This is where the Prophetess Devorah came from. I have to tell you, sweetheart, that I consider myself blessed to wake up each morning and look out my window at such a fantastic spot."

I nodded in agreement. How I longed for Aunt Renate to understand about her Messiah. How I wanted her to realize that Yeshua was her Jewish Messiah and not some Gentile god she couldn't comprehend! I had sent her the manuscript from my book the previous year, praying that her eyes would be opened. She loved the book but wasn't ready to believe in Yeshua. What could I do? I would continue to pray for her.

The wedding was held on a cool, windy evening at a kibbutz by the sea. Unlike the black and white pictures of kibbutzim from the 1930s and 1940s where bronzed men and women leaned on pitchforks and against tractors as they squinted into the sun, this one rented itself out at night for parties.

In a large, grassy expanse, basically in the shape of a rectangle, were all the accoutrements necessary for a big shindig. A large bar wrapped around one end while several serving stations manned by smiling, smartly dressed young people (members of the kibbutz) dotted the area. Alcoholic and non-alcoholic drinks alike were ladled out of cut-glass punch bowls by waiters, while waitresses circled around with trays of fried mushrooms, little hot dogs, potato knishes, and cheese balls. Close to thirty round tables, each seating ten, covered in white linen and adorned with sparkling wine glasses and silver flatware, stood empty, waiting for their chairs to be occupied. At the opposite end of the field from the bar was a makeshift dance floor boasting huge sound speakers and a small booth for the DJ. Next to the dance floor was the *chuppa,* a flowered canopy held up by four poles under which the marriage ceremony was to be performed. Two dozen wooden folding chairs were lined up in front of the chuppa for guests.

"Why not more chairs?" I asked my father. "There's going to be at least 300 people here."

"It's because at Israeli weddings most of the people just crowd around the couple," he explained. "Not that many people want to sit during the ceremony. It's much less formal than American weddings.

You'll see."

I had come early with Lira and my parents. More guests filtered in around 7 p.m., with the chuppa supposedly taking place at 8. I wandered around, a glass of cold grapefruit juice in one hand and in the other a little plate of half-nibbled hors d'oeuvres. Besides family, I didn't know that many people. I made conversation with several folks, but at one point I just sat back by myself and watched the crowd.

The choice of clothing by the young women really shocked me. Even the bride wore such a low-cut revealing gown that I could barely look at her. *Did I wander into her bedroom and catch her in her nightie by mistake?* I thought wryly. The lack of modesty saddened me. I knew that as a young girl I had also paraded around in public in outfits that were entirely too sexy, and now I deeply regretted that behavior. *Don't they realize how it makes them look?* I thought. I wish I could take some of these girls aside and explain the value of modesty. *Don't sell yourselves short,* I wanted to shout at them. *You're way too valuable in God's eyes.*

The 8 p.m. chuppa took place at 9 p.m. I was learning that Israelis are much more relaxed about time than Americans. My parents and I sat down while, true to form, the vast majority of the guests stood close to the about-to-be-wedded couple. Hannah's older brothers and sister were at the front of the crowd, their eyes glued to the thrilling spectacle of their sister's marriage.

It was a very short service. The rabbi made some endearing comments regarding the young couple, Hannah circled her groom seven times during the *shevat brachot,* the seven blessings, the two sets of parents stood beaming under the chuppa with Aunt Renate, the grandmother, resplendent in pink, between them. The couple shared some wine, the groom eagerly stamped on the glass, the crowd cried out *mazel tov!* and it was done: they were married.

After congratulating the new couple, the guests surged toward the dinner buffet. Table after table groaned under platters of barbequed chicken, steak, pasta salad, a grilled medley of eggplant, onions, and peppers, roasted sweet potatoes, baskets of bread, and salads galore. We were allowed to eat peacefully for about half an hour, and then the DJ fired up the sound system and the party started to roll.

Disco music reminiscent of the U.S. in the '70s poured relentlessly out of the cranked-up speakers. Twenty- and thirty-somethings made their way to the dance floor. Perturbed, I watched as men and women hardly out of their teens practically had sex in their drunken desperateness to *party*. I tried not to be judgmental; after all these were not believers and I had no right to hold them to that standard. At the same time, I knew what it was like to give myself over to lasciviousness in an attempt to fill that void that only God can fill. It never works; it only leads to greater and greater unhappiness.

I missed Dave. Feeling alone and disconnected, I meandered around the property, praying silently for the salvation of everyone I saw. *This is crazy, Lord*, I prayed. *I have wanted to come to Israel for the longest time; now here I am, and suddenly I just want to go home to Dave and the kids. What's wrong with me? Am I getting old?* I listened but didn't hear him say anything. Sighing, I returned to my table and sat down, reviving only when the dessert tables opened.

Two days later, much of the Israeli family (not the bridal couple) and all of the visiting American relatives drove up north for a hiking jaunt in the Banyas. The Banyas is a rugged wilderness area at the foot of Mt. Hermon in which the melting snows cascade down into a spectacular waterfall. All along the hiking trails are rushing streams of the coldest, purest water in Israel. Three rivers merge to form the Jordan.

It was an extremely hot day, but bearable under the shade of the many trees that jutted up against rocky walls. I wore a lightweight cotton skirt and a short-sleeved blouse and still stopped regularly to dab water from my water bottle on my neck in an attempt to cool off. Partway through the hike, a busload of Arab children descended on us. They yelled and pushed, running through the narrow trails and forcing us off to the side. My cousin's little boy, a tanned, sinewy ten-year-old, made a point of taking off his shirt and tying an orange bandana around his waist. Orange is the color one wears in Israel to show solidarity with the settlers.

I was fascinated with the female chaperones of the Arab children. Under the broiling sun, they wore heavy, black pants outfits and close-fitting head scarves. Their faces showed, but not much else. *How can they possibly bear it?* I thought. *How incredibly uncomfortable I would be!* Praying for the eyes of these Muslim women to be opened to the knowledge of the Messiah Yeshua, I cautiously greeted one of them.

"Shalom," I said. *"Cham loch? Aht b'seder?"* ("Hello. Are you hot? Are you okay?")

The woman stared back at me, her eyes hard. Wordlessly, she moved away.

After the hike, we loaded back into our separate cars and drove to a kibbutz high up in the Golan. From there we could see across the UN demilitarized zone into Syria and over to Lebanon. It was amazingly beautiful. Dark and light shades of green interspersed as fields and groves of trees alternated like a patchwork quilt. Cobalt blue mountains ringed about in all directions. I stood where the fenced-in lookout point jutted out the most and gazed out over the valley, the wind whipping through my hair. It was then that I heard the Lord speak to me.

This is my Land, he said. *I will not allow it to be given away. The Gentile church looks at the Shoah (Holocaust) and thinks that I'm done with the Jews. They couldn't be more wrong. I am deeply affected by what happens to the Jews. It's very close to my heart.*

But what about salvation, Lord? I asked. *How does that work?*

There is only one path to salvation, and that is through my Son. My promises to the Jewish people regarding Eretz Yisrael stand apart. What each individual person chooses to do in relationship to me is a separate issue.

"Oh, Lord," I prayed, "use me. Use me to reach your people with the Good News of Messiah Yeshua."

The rest of the time in Israel was anticlimactic. The day we went to Jerusalem was extremely hot and crowded. I insisted on going to the *kotel* (wailing wall), having promised a close friend that I would write out a certain prayer for her and stick it into the cracks between the ancient stones. My parents, Lira, Aunt Renate, and Lira's son Moti waited for me in the shade off to the side. They had all been to the wall and were not in a rush to go again.

Threading my way through literally thousands of people, I approached the women's side. I squeezed into a place at the very front, where I could touch the stones. Carefully writing out both a prayer for my friend and myself, I looked for a tiny spot to push the prayers. It was virtually impossible. So many little scrolls of paper were inserted up, down, and across the cracks in the stones that cascades of them had fallen out, littering the ground at my feet. Finally, I was able to find a spot and pushed the prayers firmly in. The teeny, rolled-up papers were somewhat precarious so I left hurriedly in case they fell and I had to repeat the whole procedure.

To my despair, I found myself growing agitated. Here I was, at Judaism's holiest site, and I felt anything but spiritual. I was hot, hungry, tired, and annoyed at the vast hordes all around me. *God is everywhere,* I thought. *He's not confined to one spot. All these people should go home.*

The rest of the afternoon wasn't much better. Aunt Renate and Lira didn't agree about directions, and we took a long, convoluted walk around the outside of the Old City until, exasperated, my mother flagged down a city bus.

"I'm not supposed to let people on where there's no stop," protested the driver.

He had mercy on us, though, and let us sit down. The air-conditioned interior was absolutely heavenly. We got off close to the part of town where we had parked the car. More haggling over directions and confused wandering finally resulted in a restaurant. Although technically we were going out for lunch, it was already 4 p.m., and we were wilting fast. I was so nudged that for the first time in years I felt more like the teenage Becky and less like the woman of God. It wasn't until I had consumed a delicious tortilla-wrap sandwich made of smoked salmon, cream cheese, and avocado slices that I could bear to even minimally converse with my traveling companions.

On the drive back to Shohem, upset with myself that I let heat and hunger take me out, it dawned on me that Jerusalem is arguably the most hotly spiritually contested place on earth. The dark spirits that reigned here could hardly be expected to ignore me. The city was a constant battlefield between God's army and the legions of hell.

The rest of the time in Israel passed pleasantly, though uneventfully. Before I knew it, I was on a plane, heading home. A couple of hours from JFK, somewhere over the Atlantic, I used my Hebrew to translate the breakfast menu (decidedly ignoring the English translation). It was to be my last foray into the world of Hebrew for some time.

PART SEVEN

Prelude

Fifteen

That summer marked the beginning of a completely new life for me. I heard God say, *Your life is irrevocably changed.*

My book took off like a rocket. There's no other way to describe it. It went from being something of a local phenomena to a national success. Suddenly, every potential avenue for marketing the book caught on fire at once. I watched in utter amazement as the heady promises whispered to me by the Lord took shape before my eyes in an even more spectacular fashion than I could ever have dreamed possible.

Dave and I had sent several dozen books out to different people whom we thought would be able to move things along in one way or another. At first it seemed like a series of dead ends as we heard nothing, but then everything happened all at the same time.

I had gotten used to email being the vehicle by which anything interesting came my way, so it caught me off guard to have an actual phone call. I was sitting at the computer, putting the finishing touches on an article when the *rring rring* interrupted my thoughts.

"Hello?" I said, somewhat absently, eyes intent on the flickering screen in front of me, a sentence half-written, suspended, as it were, in cyberspace.

"Is this Rebecca?" asked a woman's voice on the other end.

"Yes, can I help you?"

"Hi," she said warmly. "I'm Shanna Levy and I'm with *Jewish Ministries Today*. Your husband sent me a copy of your book."

Suddenly, I was all ears. "Yes, nice to talk with you."

"And with you," she said. "I wanted to thank you. This is one of the best books on the topic of modesty I've ever read. We'd like to buy some and feature them in our magazine. Is that all right?"

"Shanna," I said, "you've made my day!"

By the end of the next week, I had received two more phone calls.

The first came at 9 p.m. one evening and was from a lady in Toronto who had her own radio show. "I have to tell you that your book is phenomenal!" exclaimed Dr. Joy, a well-known family counselor. "I read it every chance I could get for three days. I couldn't put it down!"

Dr. Joy, a striking brunette with deep roots in the close-knit Jewish community of her Canadian city, had multiple marketing ideas, several of which she planned to implement herself.

"You definitely need a website," she informed me. "Something simple like www.rebeccahermon.com. Then you can get links to all sorts of places. For instance, I can post it on my website under the title, 'Dr. Joy's favorite reads.' And," she added, "I get over 100,000 hits a month."

Wow! By the time the phone conversation wrapped up, I was flying. I couldn't wait for Dave to get home from the congregation. When he did show, just before 10 p.m., I was waiting for him downstairs in the kitchen.

"Dave," I squealed, "you won't believe the phone call I just had!"

I fixed Dave a late supper and nuked it for him in the microwave. Filling a glass with ice from the freezer, I topped it off with water, and placed it in front of him. Then I pulled up a chair and filled him in on what had happened as he hungrily consumed his dinner.

"That's fantastic!" he said as he swallowed an enormous bite of meatloaf. Next he speared a baby tomato from his salad bowl and gestured with it as he spoke. "This is great, Becky, really great. If your book does well in Toronto, it can spread to other cities. We need to be on top of this."

I nodded in agreement. "Yes, that's just what the Lord showed me. He said there would be all these little fires that would build around North America and then—*whoosh!*—they would connect and the book would positively explode."

Dave and I talked for hours that night about the possibilities that were opening up in our lives. It was a heady time.

Later that week, I got yet another phone call.

"May I speak with Mrs. Hermon?" asked a female voice.

"This is she," I responded.

"Oh, you sound so young!" The woman laughed. "I'm Betsy Bright, personal assistant to Dr. Bill Roberts. He asked me to contact you."

Dr. Bill Roberts! Senior pastor of a California megachurch and one of the most influential evangelicals in America! I had mailed him a copy of the book several months back as his church was known for its keen desire to bless the Jewish people. Now his office was calling me! This could only be good.

Apparently, Dr. Robert's wife had read the book and been so enthralled that she absolutely insisted her husband—despite his hectic schedule—read it as well. He resisted for a time, then got a sense in his prayer closet that God wanted him to read it. He did, and was every bit as taken with it as was his wife.

"Dr. Roberts would like to order several thousand copies for both his church and his worldwide ministry," said Betsy.

"Would you be able to directly contact the publisher?" I bubbled.

"Certainly," agreed Betsy, her tone friendly yet professional. On my end, I struggled not to break out into a "Hallelujah Chorus." I immediately phoned Dave.

"Absolutely amazing," he said when I reached him.

A few weeks later, a major newspaper in Toronto decided to review my book in their pre-Christmas Sunday supplement. The reviewer happened to be one of those people who fell in love with the book. She gave a generous and glowing review. Dr. Joy arranged for me to be interviewed on her radio show the same week the review came out. Suddenly, I had visibility in Toronto.

Dave and I were invited to go up and do a book signing and a few radio and TV interviews. We arranged for someone to stay with the kids and had a delightful time driving up, just the two of us.

"It's really happening, isn't it, Dave?" I murmured as the gray, winter scenery on 90 West flitted past my window.

Dave glanced over at me, then back at the road as he swung into the left lane in anticipation of passing a tractor trailer. "It is," he agreed.

"Are you okay with my success? I think your music is going to do great, but this seems to be the first thing down the pike...."

Dave didn't answer at first. I turned my head and looked at him. His once black hair had turned almost entirely gray, his beard more salt than pepper. He had put on weight and was no longer the skinny young kid I had married twenty-two years ago. *We're really getting old,* I thought to myself. A pang struck my heart.

Finally, Dave responded. "I'm very happy for you, Becky."

"For us," I said.

"For us," he conceded.

Toronto proved to be the stepping stone for North America. Once I had achieved success in one city, it spread across Canada and down into the United States. My publisher hired a top-rate marketing firm and we were off and running. My life changed radically. The season of waiting ended, and now it was a season of trying to catch up. I did as many phone interviews as I could, but there were still book signings and in-person interviews that made it necessary for me to travel. Suddenly, I was in demand as a speaker on this topic that had hit a national nerve. Most of the time, I went to the out-of-town events by myself.

Not everything was perfect. Success brought its own set of problems. Dave needed to be reassured of his importance in my life, and the kids complained loudly about my lack of availability.

"You've just been so spoiled," I chided ten-year old Shira when she refused to eat lunch because the bread was store-bought and not homemade. I hadn't had time to bake that week and had purchased two loaves of yummy-looking twelve-grain bread.

"I hate this stuff," she scowled, pushing her tuna sandwich off the plate and onto the table. "Anyway, you're never home!" Her big, blue eyes stared at me accusingly.

"Shira, even mothers who are home all the time don't bake bread," I said in an effort to defend myself. "Besides, I've only been gone three days in the last two weeks. That's not bad."

"Yes, it is," she yelled, then burst into tears.

"Oh, sweetheart, let Mommy kiss you!"

"No! You don't care about us anymore. You just care about your stupid book!" She leaped out of her chair and ran upstairs, slamming her bedroom door.

I sighed. My wildest dreams were coming true, but life was unraveling in other ways. *Help me, Lord,* I prayed. *Show me the balance.*

Slowly, I got up and wrapped Shira's sandwich in plastic, then put it in the refrigerator. I cleaned the kitchen and walked upstairs. I knocked on Shira's door.

"Go away!" came the muffled response.

"Honey, Mommy loves you. Please open the door and let's talk about things." I stood there silently, hand upraised to knock but not touching the door. I heard a mattress squeak, some footsteps, and the sound of the door unlocking. I turned the knob and walked into the room.

Shira sat on her bed, eyes wet, glowering. She stared hard at me.

"Honey," I said, sitting down beside her and putting my arm around her unyielding shoulders, "I'm sorry that you feel ignored. Will you forgive Mommy?"

"All right," she snapped, angry.

"I mean *really* forgive me? Not just saying it."

"It won't do any good. You'll just go away again."

"Maybe we can work out a plan and every so often I can take you on a trip with me. What do you think about that?" *Oh my goodness, I can't believe these words are coming out of my mouth!*

Immediately, Shira's whole demeanor changed. "Really? You mean that?"

Oh no. "Yes," I said, in it up to my neck now. "I mean it."

"Oh, Mommy, I love you!" Excitedly, she threw her arms around my neck and hugged me.

In February, the Los Angeles Barnes & Noble invited me to do a booksigning. It was a wonderful opportunity to see my parents and sell books at the same time. True to my word, I arranged to take Shira with me.

My oldest son, Josiah, was off at college and didn't care, but the other three children and Dave were all unhappy.

"You're taking her? That is so not fair!" cried Leah, the younger and highly competitive sister.

"I want to go. You'll have so much more fun with me!" exclaimed my fifteen-year-old daughter, Yohana.

"I can't believe you're taking *her*," bemoaned Shmuel, the high school senior.

"You should have discussed this with me before promising a trip of this magnitude to Shira," chided Dave.

"Enough! Enough! Each of you will get a turn," I promised, not sure if I had made a terrible mistake.

Shira herself was so thrilled that she was completely impossible. She became so bouncy and tigger-like that I threatened to leave her home if she didn't calm down.

"I'm calm, I'm calm," she assured me and ran upstairs to decide yet again what she should pack.

Happily, the trip went very well and Shira felt much more loved by me. She was my assistant at the booksigning and won people's hearts with her infectious high spirits, ready smile, and youthful exuberance.

While all this was taking place, the Lord was teaching me how to stand in my healing from cancer. Occasionally, my back and neck ached, and the tumor marker numbers on my blood tests rose a bit more at each successive doctor's appointment. At first I got nervous, but the Lord spoke to me forcefully.

You can't allow fear to get in, he said. *I have given you my promise that you are healed. Do not doubt! He who doubts is like a wave of the sea, blown and tossed by the wind. Stand firm in your healing and understand that the enemy of your soul wants to destroy you, but I am stronger than he. There may be more battles ahead, but the war is won.*

I clung to that word from God. Whenever I felt myself weaken, I picked up my Bible and read Scripture. The Word of God buoyed me up. I noticed that when I refused to give way to fear, the doubts and the aches eventually gave up and retreated. However, it was a constant battle.

A year after I had stopped chemo, my blood tests were looking ominous though I felt great. My new doctor (Dr. Smith had since retired) demanded that I undergo several tests, including a CT scan. He was convinced that cancer was in my body and it was only a matter of time until it manifested.

"I don't want a CT scan," I told him, shaking my head. "They're dangerous."

"What do you mean?"

"I heard that one of them is equivalent to 400 X-rays."

"So?" he said.

"So that much radiation can cause cancer."

"You already have cancer!" he exclaimed, exasperated. "Look, the two most likely places for the cancer to go are your lungs and your liver. If we wait until you're symptomatic, your liver will be full of cancer and it will be too late."

I left the office discouraged, my faith shaken. *Lord*, I prayed. *Should I get a CT scan? Do I have cancer in my liver?"*

His voice resounded clearly in my ears. *You do not have cancer in your liver.*

But what about these other tests? I cried. *If I'm healed of cancer, why are my blood tests so negative?*

You wanted to get off of the Arimidex, didn't you? You're off now.

It was true. The doctor had stopped the pills, saying it was obvious they weren't working.

I got a sense from the Lord to pay more attention to my nutrition. I started taking CoQ- 10, a supplement, and sprinkled ground-up apricot seeds and flax seed over my breakfast cereal. Cutting back on sugar, I redoubled my efforts to eat lots of spinach, sprouts, and leafy greens.

But I also made a decision that I would trust in my healing as a supernatural act from God and not try to earn it myself through a compulsive and meticulous food regimen. "My healing is from God," I told Dave again and again. "I will not turn food into an idol."

I dusted off the two booklets on healing that I had been given when I last went through cancer. Rereading them, I found all sorts of pearls of wisdom that I had missed or not fully understood the first time. I spoke aloud to my body, proclaiming it healthy. "Thank you, Lord," I said, "for healing and delivering me of cancer, arthritis, osteoporosis, bone disease of any kind. Thank you for cleansing my blood. Thank you for keeping diabetes, heart disease, and all other illness far from me and my family." I read Psalm 103 and other healing Scriptures aloud, *in Hebrew*, as the power of the spoken word is far greater than we realize.

Verses 3 and 4 of Psalm 103 say:

He forgives all my sins
and heals all my diseases;
he redeems my life from the pit
and crowns me with love and compassion.

In Hebrew, the same two verses are:

Ha soleach l'chal ah von eh chee
ha rohfeh l'chal ta cha loo aye chee
ha goel mee sha chat chai yai chee
ha m'aht reh chee chesed v'ra cha meem.

How significant are the words we say! The power of life and death is in the tongue.

As I stood in my healing, I began to receive more telephone calls from area churches, and then churches farther from home, to speak on modesty, but also to testify about my healing (and to sell books). I offered prayer at the end of my talking time and rejoiced when people streamed down from the pews. I routinely prayed for hours over men and women suffering from physical ailments, desperate for relief. More and more, I saw the power of God transform their deep pain to deep joy.

Late that spring, my book came to the attention of a well-known female TV talk show host. A member of Moriah's staff called and invited me to be on the nationally syndicated and enormously popular show.

"You're kidding, right?" I said to the briskly professional male voice at the other end of the line.

"No, I'm not, Mrs. Hermon," he said, in the practiced tones of one who regularly has to convince noncelebrities that they *really are* invited to be a guest on *The Moriah Show.*

There was pause. "So then are you able to accept?"

"Yes," I gushed. "Of course!"

"Fabulous. I'll email you all the information. Which airport would you like us to fly you out of?"

I told him the name of my local airport, my brain already in overdrive.

After I hung up, I paced around the house, too excited to calm down. Then I threw myself down on my knees and bent my head to the floor. *Oh Lord*, I breathed, *thank you for this opportunity. You are so faithful in keeping your promises to me, your maidservant.*

I heard his voice. *Speak my word boldly*, he said.

"Of course I will. You are my life."

I heard him say *speak my word boldly* again, and then a third time. Now he had my attention fully focused on him and off *The Moriah Show.*

"Lord," I said, "do you think there's a chance that I won't honor you?"

Silence.

Agitated, I slipped on my shoes and went for a walk down the block. It was late May, and the warm air and soft green color of the new leaves combined to make it just a lovely day. I breathed in deeply as I strode along.

"I think I understand this, Lord," I said aloud, as I walked past the empty houses of my neighbors who were all off at work. "You're trusting me with success, but I have to be completely faithful to use any and all forums to proclaim the truth of who you are to a lost and dying world. I can't allow myself to be seduced by rich and powerful people into complacency." I kicked at some loose gravel as I made my way up a slight incline toward the golf course. "It's not as easy to be outspoken to someone when they've paid for your plane, your hotel, your gourmet dinner, and you're sitting on their velvet couch with their TV crews filming you." I kicked some more gravel as I struggled to work this out.

"But, ultimately, everything on this earth belongs to you. And if you see fit to place me in a position of favor, it's not so I can get personally stroked. It's so that the word of who you are can go forth. It's so that an understanding of the Jewishness of the Gospel can go forth, and hopefully fight anti-Semitism. It's so that the voice of Truth can be clearly heard in a world that has lost all sense of righteousness and morality."

As the opportunities in my life opened up, the world plunged deeper into chaos. A week before my scheduled appearance on *Moriah,* the Iranian president came to the U.S. and spoke at a major college campus. This is a man who had a surface veneer of humility but underneath seethed with rage toward Jews and those who believe in Messiah.

He was asked how he could deny the Holocaust when the factual evidence was incontrovertible. Instead of answering the question, he went on and on about how we should always delve deeper into science. Americans who should have known better—including many Jews— treated him as if he were some nice guy they could have a reasonable

240

conversation with and not a Hitler clone. I listened to some of the commentary on the radio and felt sick to my stomach. It was as if I were living in Germany in the 1930s! This is a man who openly admits his desires to possess nuclear weapons and who broadcasts his hatred of Israel and his plans to annihilate her, yet he's being welcomed in this country as a legitimate statesman. It was all too easy to foresee a path at the end of which would wait another holocaust—the likes of which the world has never seen.

I thought back to some of the stories I had heard from Oma when I was growing up. She always said that Opa had seen what was coming as soon as Hitler took power in 1933, but that getting visas for the family to leave Germany had taken a miracle. Again and again, she told about Opa's deportation to Poland, my father's illness, which prevented the whole family from leaving, the astounding turn of events when the British ambassador cleared the way for emergency visas. Even before I came to know Yeshua as my Messiah, I had a certainty in my spirit that God had his hand on my family in a special way. Once I knew the Lord, I was absolutely convinced that it was him and only him—not some bizarre string of coincidences—that kept my father's family out of the horrors of the Shoah.

Although we trusted in God's protection for ourselves and our children, Dave and I grew more and more concerned over what could happen in America. It was all too easy to foresee a scenario in which the U.S. suffers terribly at the hands of terrorists who claim it's because of our connection to Israel. The aftermath could very well be intense flaring of anti-Semitism.

These issues, mixed with less weighty thoughts along the lines of *do I look all right? Modest enough?* swirled in my head while I waited in Moriah's famous "green room." Only the day before, Dave had dropped me at the airport, and it had been loads of fun on the plane, in the limo, at the hotel. I had a productive time of Scripture reading and prayer and had even written a couple of pages of my new book in the hotel room. Now, even though I knew it was God who had led me here and that he was with me, I still found my stomach queasy and my palms moist.

Help me, Lord, I silently prayed. *Don't let me disappoint you.*

Suddenly, the door clicked open and my heart skipped a beat. One of Moriah's many assistants, this one a collegiate-looking young woman with glasses and a Blackberry™, poked her head in the room.

"You're on, Mrs. Hermon," she said gaily, smiling wide.

Taking a deep breath, I stood up and ran my hands through my hair.

"No, don't!" she cautioned. "Leave your hair the way Makeup had it." Then, "Don't be nervous, you'll do great."

"Thanks." I smiled weakly, wondering if she was going to be this friendly *after* the interview.

Rosa—for that was her name—led me over to the side of the sound stage. Moriah was finishing up a segment with a television actor I didn't recognize. This fellow was promoting his new show. All too soon, Moriah was thanking him for coming. Then she turned and looked directly into the camera.

"Next we have a woman who has written a fascinating book about feminine modesty. When we come back, Rebecca Hermon will join us."

After she finished speaking, Moriah sat still for a moment, smiling. As soon as the light on top of the camera went off, five assistants all sprang at her at once. One fixed her hair, one checked her makeup, one smoothed out her clothes, one handed her a glass of water, and one made sure everyone else was doing their job. Suddenly, they all flew back to the side of the stage and she was speaking again.

"Not very long ago," she said, holding up a book (*my book!*), "we received this book in the mail and a member of my staff read it. Patrice came to me, very excited, and said, 'Moriah, you have to read this book. I just know that you're absolutely gonna love it!' And you know what?"

"WHAT?" yelled back the trained studio audience.

Moriah laughed, then continued. "I DID love it! I was so jazzed that we immediately contacted the author and asked her to be on the show. Ladies and gentleman," she extended her arm toward that side of the stage where I stood, waiting, "Rebecca Hermon!"

Rosa gave me a gentle push and I stepped onto the stage, somewhat dazed. Applause reached my ears, and I lurched over to Moriah, who expertly grasped my hand and gave me a quick hug.

"Thank you for coming," she said.

"Thank you for having me," I forced out, trying not to squint in the glare of the TV lights.

"First," she said, gesturing to herself, glossy black curls bouncing slightly as she moved, "what do you think? Am I dressed modestly enough?"

Hmm. Long-sleeved red silk suit, pearls, dangly earrings, matching red Manolo Blahnik shoes with diamond buckles.... "You look great," I said.

The audience cheered.

"So," said Moriah, after the audience settled down and we had seated ourselves on the studio couch, "tell me where you got the idea for the book."

I had a moment of panic. *Should I describe how I heard from God on national television? Will I sound crazy?* As I wrestled with these thoughts, I heard the Lord say, *Tell.*

"Well, it was like this," I began, somewhat hesitantly. I started talking about having a dream and taking the walk. When I got to the part about hearing God's voice, I thought maybe I should say, I had this *sense,* or this *impression,* but even as the words formed in my mouth, I knew it would be sin.

"God spoke to me," I said quietly.

Moriah's eyes got wide. "Whoa, wait a minute! You say, *God spoke to you?*"

"Yes."

"Why should I believe you? Why shouldn't I just dismiss you as a crackpot?"

"You can," I replied, smiling at her. "But I also heard him tell me he would heal me from cancer. Want to hear about my miraculous healing from cancer?"

"One thing at a time, girlfriend. Let's keep talking about the book."

"Okay." To my surprise, I found I was no longer nervous. I felt as if God had poured an anointing out on me and my mind was clearer than it had been in months. Words just poured from my mouth. "He's real, Moriah. He's real, and his name is Yeshua. He's often called Jesus, but I call him by the same name his mother used: Yeshua."

Moriah waved her hand dismissively. "I've known Jesus since I was born."

"Have you?"

To my left, at the edge of the stage, I heard several gasps.

Moriah herself looked at me with narrowed eyes. "What do you mean by that?"

I took her hand and looked into her eyes. No longer was she the terrifying celebrity with huge amounts of power. No longer was she the consummate entertainer to whom I owed a wonderful opportunity to promote my book. No. She was a lost child of God who needed to find her way back to Abba. *Tell her*, urged the Lord.

"Yeshua is infinitely loving, infinitely patient," I said. "He knew both your mother and grandmother intimately. But we cannot take our own ideas and pretend they're his. If what we think spiritually is in conflict with the Bible, then we're wrong and we need to discard those ideas, no matter how good they sound or how much we've grown to like them. You need to read Scripture the way a parched man drinks water. It's your life."

Her deep brown eyes looked intently back at me. I could discern wetness at the corners. Abruptly, she picked my book off the glass-topped coffee table in front of us. "Very interesting," she said, professionalism coming to the fore. "But now tell our viewers just enough about your book to whet their appetites."

The rest of the interview proceeded quickly and pleasantly. Before I knew it, my seven minutes were up and Moriah was announcing her next guest (a local chef) as she hugged me good-bye. When the cameras went off, she said to me, "Can I talk with you more after the show?"

"I would love it," I assured her, smiling broadly.

Rosa escorted me back to the green room, glancing at me curiously. "I'll come get you when the show's over," she said.

I sank down into an overstuffed armchair and mindlessly watched the program proceed from a TV monitor. The tension that had mobilized into adrenaline relaxed and I felt limp. I didn't even have the mental energy to attempt to start a conversation with the pretty, blonde, twentysomething actress in the corner who gnawed at her fingernails and stared fixedly, with furrowed brow, at the index cards in her cupped hands.

Soon enough, Rosa came for the actress. After she bounced out, I had the room to myself. Thirty minutes after that, Rosa came back for me.

"Follow me, Mrs. Hermon," she said, the ever-present Blackberry™ clutched in one hand, the other holding the heavy, metal door ajar.

Picking up my purse, I walked slightly behind her down several narrow hallways until we got to a door with—yes, it was—a five-pointed, gold star.

Rosa rapped on the door. In response to a muffled "Come in," she swung the door open. Sitting cross-legged on a beige, velour couch, wearing a silky robe and filing her nails, waited Moriah.

She looked up. "Ah, Mrs. Hermon, please come in."

"Call me Becky," I said.

"Becky."

Rosa unobtrusively disappeared and I sat down in the chair opposite the couch. The whole scene felt more than a little surreal. Stifling my natural desire to prattle, I waited. Moriah continued to file her nails and the stillness in the room took on a dreamy quality. Just when I was wondering if I should break the silence, Moriah put down her nail file and looked me in the eye.

"I couldn't decide whether to be upset or intrigued when you said what you did during the interview."

"Said what?" By now, the whole thing was a blur. I already planned on asking for a DVD of the show.

"Honey," she drawled. "You practically came right out on national television and told me I wasn't a Christian. What was that all about?"

I took a deep breath and leaned forward in my chair. "The Gospel is very simple," I said earnestly. "But in its simplicity is a message that can't be tampered with. In the Book of Romans, Paul says all have sinned and fallen short of the glory of God. It is only through our faith in the redemptive blood of Messiah Yeshua—Jesus—that cleanses us and allows us into the presence of our holy God."

"I know lots of sincere, kind, well-meaning Jews, Muslims, Buddhists," countered Moriah, her voice edgy. "Are you telling me that God ignores their hearts and sends them to hell if they don't specifically believe only in Jesus?"

I sat back in my chair. "Moriah, the prophet Jeremiah tells us that the human heart is desperately wicked, who can know it? None of us—no matter how kind and wonderful—is clean in God's sight. His holiness is overwhelmingly, blindingly pure. In his infinite compassion and mercy, he has made a way for us to enter into his presence, and yes, it's only through the sacrificial blood of Yeshua. There's no other way on heaven and earth for men to be saved."

"What about those people who haven't heard? What about them? Are they just gonna be unceremoniously dumped into hell?"

I raised my hands and shrugged. "I have no idea what happens to the people in deepest, darkest wherever. I do know that we worship an infinitely merciful God and I can trust him that he's made the right decision with those who have never directly heard of him. However, Romans 1 testifies that since the creation of the world, God's invisible qualities—his eternal power and divine nature—have been clearly seen, being understood from what has been made, so that men are without excuse.

"Besides," I continued, before she could speak, "ultimately, this isn't about those native tribes lost in the bush somewhere. This is about you, and you *have* heard. You will be held accountable for what you know."

I stopped. A heavy silence hung in the air as Moriah absorbed the deluge that had come her way. Suddenly, I felt weary. The excitement of the day had caught up to me. I also wanted something to eat.

Moriah seemed to have had enough as well. She stood up, which signaled me to stand up as well. Clasping my hand, she flashed me her million-dollar smile.

"You've given me a lot to think about, Becky," she said in her throaty voice. "You've written a beautiful book, and I'll let people know it's one of my favorites."

"Thank you," I murmured gratefully.

"Rosa will help you with whatever you need," she said, picking up her flip phone, pressing a button, and saying briefly into it, "Mrs. Hermon is ready."

Almost instantly, there was a knock on the door. Moriah pulled it open, graciously said good-bye, and I left with Rosa.

"I have you scheduled on a 2 p.m. flight back to New York," said Rosa, after glancing at her Blackberry™. "In an hour, Jerry the limo driver will take you to the airport. Can I get you anything in the meantime?"

"Food," I said hungrily. "How about a tuna melt with tomato on whole wheat and a kosher pickle?"

"Done."

Sixteen

The success of my book opened up many doors for Dave and me. The extra money enabled Dave to record, produce, and distribute CDs of his worship songs. Marketing savvy we had picked up along the way made the move from publishing to recording a snap. Christian radio stations played the CDs and a website provided a venue for sales.

Purchasing a secondhand RV at an incredible deal, we pulled the younger girls out of school for extended periods and toured the country. Basically, we sold books and CDs, led worship, spoke at churches regarding the importance of Israel, and prayed over people for healing.

My boys were both off at college and Yohana either came with us or stayed with a friend when she couldn't miss school. Shira and Leah took stacks of schoolwork, made friends at every stop, and had marvelous adventures.

Dave seemed like a new man. He had been truly pleased for me when my book did well, but the recording and distribution of his worship songs was the realization of a dream that had been with him for over thirty years. When we played his songs in different churches, the Spirit of God fell heavily in the room, and when the power of God came down such that people were healed, saved, and delivered from all sorts of addictions and difficulties, tears would stream down his face.

"Lord, I am in awe of your deeds," he would exclaim, kneeling down with arms stretched wide.

One crystal-clear night in February we were parked at a campgrounds in Palm Springs, California. That evening we had ministered at a large, nondenominational church right in town. The Lord had allowed us to be part of amazing worship and we had witnessed several people healed from debilitating illnesses. Afterwards, close to midnight, exhausted but thrilled, we staggered back to the RV. All of us fell heavily asleep.

Suddenly, at 3 a.m., my eyes sprang open. The darkness around me was heavy and alive.

Is that you, Lord? I asked silently. I sat up, propping my pillow behind my back. Dave and the girls were sound asleep, their soft, rhythmic breathing punctuating the quiet air inside the RV. I closed my eyes in prayer and instantly knew that the presence of the Lord was coming so powerfully, with such holiness, that I needed to be on my knees before him. Slipping out of the makeshift bed that I shared with Dave, I knelt on a cushion and leaned with my elbows over the bed.

Speak, Lord, I prayed. *Your maidservant is at her post and is waiting to hear your words.*

Do you remember, my daughter, your desire that led to the writing of the book and the beginning of this ministry which I have given you?

Oh, yes, I exclaimed. *I wanted to have a vision of you. I want to see you, and hold you, and be yours.*

I have not forgotten, answered the Lord. *It is my wish to answer your prayer tonight, in the same place where you first pledged yourself to me almost twenty-five years ago.*

Tears sprang to my eyes. The Lord! The Lord of all the Universe held dear the memory of my salvation! "O Lord Yeshua," I whispered aloud. "You have stolen my heart with one glance from your eyes."

The air around me took on a strange, swirly quality. Nighttime blackness pulsated. Suddenly I saw myself crouched over the bed as if from a distance. Immediately, I was above the RV, and somehow could still see through the roof into the vehicle. My own figure grew quite small, while Dave and the girls were barely discernible. I felt myself being pulled backwards up, up, up, into the glittering blackness of the predawn sky.

250

I should have been cold this far up, but instead my body felt warm, tingly. A sense of extreme well-being came over me. I was gliding through space with my right hand extended up. Massive amounts of energy flowed into that hand. As I looked to see why, I saw with a thrill that *Yeshua was holding my right hand and pulling me with him up toward the heavens!*

I looked below and the earth had become a tiny speck in the distance. Amazingly enough, I had no fear or dizziness. Minutes passed—the most blissful minutes I had ever experienced—and then we burst through some sort of watery membrane-like substance, only we didn't get wet. On the other side, the blackness of the sky abruptly vanished and a soft, golden light stretched in all directions as far as the eye could see.

Yeshua released my hand and I sank to the ground at his feet in adoration. The floor shimmered pale blue and looked like smooth ice made from sapphires. The Lord's feet glowed bronze. I knew they were feet, yet they were unlike anything I had ever seen before.

"Arise, my daughter." Yeshua's voice, commanding yet filled with love, resonated through my soul. Trembling, I stood up and slowly moved my eyes up to his face.

Brilliant white robes covered his legs. A wide sash, made of a soft, mesh-like gold, encircled his waist. His chest was broad, and his arms were like polished chrysolite. Snow-white hair framed a face dominated by fathomless eyes. Those eyes drew me in. All the hurts, frustrations, angers, upsets, rejections, disappointments of my life burned off under his gaze. What remained was a small nugget of gold comprised of every selfless deed and noble thought, prayer times, and immersion in the Word of God. My body felt as if it had been freed from prison. Tearing my eyes from his beloved face, I glanced down at my feet and saw that I was hovering inches above the ground.

Yeshua encouraged me to notice my surroundings. He stood, relaxed, while I looked about in wide-eyed wonder.

The blue-gem pavement stretched on for miles in all directions. Dimly visible at the edges of the horizon were towering mountain ranges, their summits lost in clouds. Below us was the earth and all the galaxies. Merely by focusing in any one direction, the desired object, no matter how far away, came into view. When I looked toward California, I was able to see into the RV and observe the sleeping forms of Dave and the girls. Oh, and there was me, slumped forward on my knees.

I turned back and the earth receded into blackness. All around me, going about their business in the most brilliant and radiantly light surroundings, were angels and, and...glorified people! Singly, in companionable pairs, in groups, striding about, laughing, talking, singing—all had purpose.

One sight in particular dazzled me even in the midst of all that glory. A man and a woman, both seated on horses—he on a great brown stallion and she on a splendid white mare—surrounded by a throng of saints and angels. The man, tall and respondent, resembled an ancient king, though he looked no more than thirty. A high gold crown inlaid with blue diamonds sat on his head and long white robes flowed behind him. The woman, his queen, had the most extraordinary hair I've ever seen: all the colors of precious metals when the sun reflects off them—and it streamed in ripples past her hips. She also wore a gem-studded gold crown, though this one was dainty as befitted such a one as she, and gossamer-like robes glittered about her. Both the man and the woman exuded the most spectacular mix of solemnity and joy. They obviously took great delight in both each other and in those around them.

"Who are they?" I asked the Lord, awed.

"Do you not know then?" he responded, his eyes dancing with mirth. "It is your father and mother. Your original father and mother—Adam and Eve."

Adam and Eve!

I looked and the scene before me changed. I saw that I was now standing in the outer courts of the heavenly temple. Items I recognized—chairs, tables, archways—materialized. They were fashioned from pure gold, unbelievably large pearls, rare woods. I took a deep breath. The air smelled like the early morning of a glorious summer day.

Next I looked at the distant mountains in the same way that I had focused on the earth. As I stared at them, they emerged into view,

252

much as if I had suddenly been given access to a powerful telescope. Now I could make out streams, rivers, dark green groves of olive trees, vineyards, endless fields of brilliant wild flowers. Everywhere, up and down, in and around those glorious mountains were houses. They were all sizes and colors and varieties. Some resembled Mediterranean villas; others were the prototype for brick English Tudor. Painted clapboard multistory homes that could have been perched on a cliff in Maine somehow seemed appropriate next to French chateaus. Colors dazzled the eye: red, orange, yellow, green, blue, indigo, violet, white and everything in-between. New colors I had never seen before startled me by their intensity.

The homes evoked feelings of complete contentment: I looked at one of the white stucco homes with a red-tiled roof and an image of reclining on an outdoor balcony with loved ones while enjoying gourmet Italian food—freshly grown tomatoes, mushrooms, garlic, onions, artichoke hearts, peppers, olives mixed with cheese over pasta—presented itself.

"Would you like to see the mansion that's waiting for you?" asked the Lord.

Yes, I nodded.

He took my hand—o bliss!—and in what seemed like three quick strides, we came to a large, white home with yellow trim. It had a big wrap-around porch in front and flowers grew in abundant profusion everywhere. Gorgeous roses in multihued tones wrapped around porch pillars. Inside was just lovely—light and airy—but what caught my attention the most was a high-ceilinged library with mahogany bookcases loaded with books.

"There are books in heaven?" I asked wonderingly. "What kind?"

"Take a look," answered the Lord.

I walked over to the nearest shelf and tentatively pulled out a volume. It was *Prince Caspian,* by C.S. Lewis. I reached for another: *The Two Towers*, by J.R.R. Tolkien. Excitedly, I checked a third: *Life in Heaven*, by an author I didn't recognize.

"It was written here," explained Yeshua. He then handed me a book from another portion of the bookcase.

It was my book.

"My book?" I exclaimed. "My book is in a library in heaven?"

Yeshua took the book from me and replaced it. "Come," he said. "I have much more to show you."

I don't know how much time went by next: it could have been minutes, hours, days, months. My concept of time was completely undone.

We traveled up the steep, winding paths that led from one town to another in those glorious mountains. They were high, so high, but unlike the mountains on earth, these did not make you cold or dizzy as you ascended. I found that I could easily leap up impossible chasms and over perilous cliffs without a care (*Hannah Hurnard was right*, I thought).

Eventually we came to a deep ravine. "Look!" commanded the Lord.

As I stood on the edge of the cliff, I suddenly knew that it wasn't heaven anymore but had changed into the edge of the North American continent, somewhere on the California coastline. I looked out over vast expanses of ocean, and in the far distance could see the shadowy outlines of Southeast Asia. Volcanoes exploded, spewing forth lava at a fantastic pace. Vibrant against the black sky: hot pinks, neon greens, bright oranges, lemon yellows—day-glo colors—lit up everything for hundreds of miles.

"What is this, Lord?" I cried, alarmed. "What's happening on earth?"

"Just watch," he replied. "What you're seeing now is still in the future. You are seeing the end of days."

He clasped my hand and I fell against him, ready for the vision. I would have been afraid to see what was to come, but when one was with Yeshua, the word *fear* held no meaning.

Now my vantage point shifted from California. I looked down and saw the entire United States below me. Sky-rocketing fuel and food prices combined with worldwide famine precipitated by a deadly combination of greed and natural disasters had lit the fuse for a depression of legendary proportions. In their desperation for relief, the American people had elected a president of unknown character, whose wickedness was now being unmasked. Islamic terrorists had succeeded in nuking a major city and I saw the black smoke reaching up toward heaven. The people who had survived this brutal attack streamed out in all directions, scarred beyond recognition. The horrors of what they had lived through appalled me, and tears streamed down my face.

Then I saw a new wave of natural disasters pound the entire earth. Hurricanes, tsunamis, volcanoes, tornadoes, floods, earthquakes, famine, drought. Overnight, prosperous countries shriveled up and poor countries dwindled to a fraction of their populations. Intense misery descended on the nations of the earth, but I saw that they did not turn to the living God, maker of all that is. Instead, they cursed him and continued to worship false gods and idols their hands had made.

The enemy of our soul, that serpent, that ancient dragon, HaSatan, stoked the fires of fury in angry and miserable people. He whispered to them that it was the fault of the Jews, that if only Israel were taken from them, none of this would have happened. In America, anti-Semitism reared up as the Jews were blamed for the destroyed city and the economic collapse.

"The terrorists would have left us alone," they wailed, "if only we had stood against Israel!"

"Go!" I shouted at my Jewish brethren. "Go to Israel, before it's too late!"

I saw lines of Jews streaming from various parts of the U.S. over the Atlantic Ocean and into Israel. Masses of them, carrying as many of their belongings as they could, crowded the airports and docks, desperate to escape and make it to the Promised Land. Others stayed put, reluctant to leave their homes, their comfortable lives.

"Oh, Lord!" I exclaimed, turning to Yeshua in great agitation. "Why won't the rest leave? Why do they stay and wait for destruction to overtake them?"

"Because they refuse to see," he replied sadly. "I have made opportunity for those who will leave to leave, but I cannot force them to go against their will."

I turned back to watch the happenings on the earth, and saw that those Jews who insisted on remaining had burst into flame. Sickened, I closed my eyes.

"What about my family?" I asked Yeshua, my eyes still closed.

"What happened to us?"

"Open your eyes," he said, "and I will show you."

I looked, and saw below me a small town on the outskirts of Jerusalem. Inside a large apartment complex, sitting at a kitchen table and speaking earnestly with a family of new immigrants from America, sat Dave and me. "We already had moved to Israel?" I asked incredulously.

"Yes, my daughter. When the time is right, I will bring you to my land. You will not stay in America once things turn."

"But what of other believers? And Jewish believers? Will we all be rescued?"

Yeshua shook his head. "Not everyone's story is your story. But this I will show you." He pointed to the lines of refugees heading across the Atlantic and I saw in the midst of them my parents and my brothers with their wives and families.

"Oh!" I gasped, heavy with relief. "So they make it out!"

"Yes. It would have been easier for them if they had heeded the call earlier but they do get out."

"And do they..." I hesitated. "Do they came to salvation?"

"That I cannot show you," said Yeshua. "You must be faithful to keep praying for them. This is when God's people need to be diligent."

Slowly, I nodded. Again, I looked down at the earth and saw wars and great turmoil. Terrorism grew worse and worse until all the peoples of the earth could stand no more. A man arose from the Arab nations, and he seized control of all the differing factions. With hypnotic power and words of persuasion, he subdued the terrorists. In gratitude, the nations bestowed on him leadership and authority such as one man had never had in the history of the known world. Even Nebuchadnezzar, even the caesars, even Napolean, had not held sway over the nations like this man.

I saw him establish his rule over the earth, and then he went to Jerusalem and set up his throne on the Temple Mount. I shuddered as I saw this Abomination that causes Desolation. This man then proclaimed himself a god and battled the horrified ones who would not accept him as such. Much blood was shed and the true believers in the land fled to the desert. I saw the red rocks of Petra, and the caves which became home to the refugees.

Then followed three years of privation and great difficulty but they were also years of miracles and gladness. We, the believers, knew that the time was short and that soon Yeshua would be returning to earth to set things right and take his throne.

"How long, Lord?" I asked him. "How long until you return to rescue your people?"

"I cannot give you the exact days and time," answered Yeshua. "But know this: the days will be cut short for the sake of the elect, lest all perish!"

As soon as he said this, I saw the sun darken, the moon turn blood-red, and the sky between heaven and earth roll up like a scroll. Yeshua, in great magnificence, sat mounted on a noble white horse, while the armies of heaven followed him, dressed in white and likewise mounted on white horses. He raised a great shofar to his lips and blew a blast the likes of which had never been heard before or since. The piercing sound reverberated from one side of heaven to the other and even the great mountains of heaven trembled. Then I saw those on the earth who had held fast to their love for him, and who had not worshiped the anti-messiah, and they rose up in the air to meet Yeshua.

He descended to earth, and entered the City of Jerusalem through the East Gate. I saw my brothers and sisters, my fellow Jews, the ones who had survived the great calamities of the last seven years, and they rose up as one man and proclaimed loudly, *"Baruch Haba B'Shem Adonai!"* (Blessed is He who comes in the Name of the Lord!) Tears streamed down faces and people tore their garments as they mourned for him whom they had not recognized as one mourns for a firstborn son.

Then the Lord destroyed his enemies and cast the man who claimed to be messiah but was not into the lake of burning fire. After that, a mighty angel came down out of heaven, seized the dragon (that ancient serpent, HaSatan), bound him with a great chain, and threw him into the Abyss. He locked and sealed it over him, keeping him hostage for a thousand years. And peace, true peace, descended on the smoldering earth. I looked toward Petra and saw the believers walking toward Jerusalem. Many were old and sick and exhausted from years of privation. They came slowly, but with gladness of spirit.

A river flowed out of the City, and the believers stumbled toward it. When they waded into it, health and healing overtook them, and all emerged shining and rejuvenated. Dressed in white, they proceeded into Jerusalem, a great army: a people prepared to meet their king.

I saw myself in the midst of that exalted throng and avidly watched as I approached the King of kings and the Lord of lords. I knelt before him and he placed his hand on my shoulder. "Well done, good and faithful servant," reached my ears just as the vision before me swirled and faded. I realized that I was still kneeling, and the hand of the Lord *was* upon my shoulder. But I was in heaven and not on the earth.

Tears filled my eyes then, and I sobbed copiously, with great emotion. "Who am I? And who is my family, that you should bless us so?"

And my king bid me rise and held me close to him, so close that I could see the nail prints in his hands and catch sight of the wounds on his feet. "It is my will to bless you," he said, his voice the sound of rushing waters and the sensation not unlike the thunderous thrill of a crashing waterfall. "You did not earn it; it is a gift."

He kissed me, and as his lips touched my forehead, I swirled at tremendous speed down, down, down to the earth. I slipped through the partition that separated heaven from space and plunged into my body, still kneeling in prayer. The sensation of extreme lightness ended abruptly and I could feel again the mild strain in my neck, the itch from a mosquito bite, the fatigue from lack of sleep. The vision had ended.

Glancing over at the digital light-up alarm clock, I saw that it was 3:04 a.m. No time at all had passed, though it seemed to me that I had been gone months, even years.

I knew I would spend all day writing down every detail I could remember. I knew that the Lord had just added a dimension to my ministry for him the likes of which could not even begin to be calculated. I knew that I had many years in front of me: years of heartache and privation but also years of astonishing joy. And I knew that when all was said and done, at The End of the Age waited the ultimate Paradise: my Lord, Yeshua. But before all these things would happen, before the first word was written, there was something I had to do.

I climbed back onto my bed and shook Dave's solidly sleeping form. "Dave," I whispered loudly, excitement making my voice vibrate. "Wake up! I have the most amazing thing to tell you...!"

Epilogue

And so the story continues. That night at the campgrounds in Palm Springs, California, when the Lord opened my eyes to the vision of what will be, my perspective changed forever. For I know that someday the floodgates of heaven will swing open, and all Israel will be saved!

What started out as so beautiful in The Garden—the intimate companionship between Adam and Eve and the Lord and their ability to commune face-to-face—will become a reality once more in heaven. How I long for that day!

Yet in the meanwhile, I know he has called me, Rebecca Hermon, a daughter of Eve (who, because of my own sin and rebellious past, can understand so intensely how Eve could fall from grace—I, too, have experienced the healing mercies of the Lord's gracious forgiveness) to be faithful to pray for those who are yet outside the comfort and protection of the Lord's arms.

More than anything, I want to kneel someday before the Lord's presence, feel his hand on my shoulder, and hear the glorious words, "Well done, good and faithful servant."

Becky Hermon's Challah Recipe

Ingredients:

6 cups unbleached white flour
3 tablespoons sugar (or honey)
4 large eggs plus an extra egg
  for basting
water (at least 2 cups)
optional: sesame seeds, poppy seeds.

1 tablespoon salt
2 teaspoons instant
  dry active yeast
¼ cup oil (canola is best)

1. In a large bowl, measure and mix together flour, salt, sugar, and yeast.
2. Lightly beat eggs in a separate bowl. Add to flour mixture along with oil and 2 cups water.
3. Mix well. Scrape dough out of bowl onto tabletop. Start to knead, using the palms of your hands. Gradually add additional water until dough is "perfect" (pliable but not soggy).
4. Form into ball and place in clean bowl. Cover with a clean, dry towel and let rise in a warm place (around 80 degrees is best) for 1 ½ hours. A gas oven with the heat turned off works really well.
5. Push the dough down, reform into a ball, and let rise for another 45 minutes.
6. Push down, roll flat, and cut into three equal pieces. Form each piece into a ball. Cover with a damp towel (all excess water should be wrung out of it). Roll each ball into a snake shape, taking care to keep the dough you're not working with covered with the damp towel.
7. Grease a cookie sheet. Sprinkle seeds on it, if desired.
8. Braid the three snakes from the middle out on both ends, and then seal the ends with wet fingers.
9. Put braided dough on cookie sheet, cover with damp towel, and let rise in a warm place for 40 minutes.
10. Preheat oven to 350 degrees for 15 minutes. (If you have the dough rise in the oven, don't forget to take the dough out!)
11. Baste braided dough with beaten egg. Sprinkle seeds on it as desired.

12. Bake for 50-60 minutes. Challah is done when the bottom taps hollow and the top springs back when lightly pushed.
13. Cool on wire rack for at least 2 hours before sealing in plastic.
ENJOY!!

Yield: 1 large challah.

Hint: This is really good with butter and honey, and also makes great French toast when it's a couple of days old.

*I prefer to buy yeast at either health food stores or wholesale grocers, as supermarkets tend to vastly overcharge for this item. A good price for yeast is $3/lb. Pour it into a glass jar and keep it in the freezer. It'll last until Pesach, when you have to throw it out anyway!

Also by Deborah Galiley

Two gripping historical tales that transcend centuries and hearts
to show that every life...and every life circumstance...
has ultimate purpose.

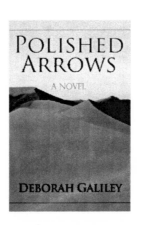

It was a time of great tumult...
and even greater evil.

When the Moavite King Eglon's reign of terror ends abruptly in the fourteenth century BC, the yoke of bondage is at last broken for the people of Israel. Now is their chance for a new start...but will it be enough to turn their hearts?

Devorah, the oldest child of doting parents, has grown up beloved by her entire community. Everyone senses something different about her—that God has specially placed His Hand on her—but for what purpose?

Yael, a purchased bride, is torn from her home and plunged into a life she never wanted. Can she learn to love this man she must now call husband...or is there too much of a chasm between them? And what of her dreams? Has God forgotten her?

Little could these two women guess that their lives would become polished arrows in God's quiver, targeting an entire nation.

He could have been any of the men
I saw every day on the streets of Jerusalem.
But when he looked straight at me,
I was overcome with an emotion I could not name…

In A.D. 25, living in close proximity to the tempestuous Herod Antipas meant continually skirting the edge of danger.

Rumors abounded of an uneducated carpenter's son from the Galil—Yeshua ben Yosef, of Natzeret—who supposedly healed the sick. Yohana had never put much stock in so-called miracle workers. So many charlatans plied their trade in and around Jerusalem, making fantastic sums off a gullible and desperate populace. Yohana was determined not to be one of those drawn in, yet there was something different about this new miracle worker….

For more information on Deborah Galiley and her books:
www.greatbiblefiction.com
www.oaktara.com

About the Author

DEBORAH GALILEY grew up in a Conservative Jewish home on Long Island. After coming to faith in Yeshua in Los Angeles as a young adult, she met and married Steve, moved to central New York, and has been rebbetzin to his rabbi ever since. She is also a mother of five, percussionist, bread baker, youth group leader, and author.

In addition to her three novels for OakTara—*Polished Arrows, Yohana,* and *Seeking Paradise*—Deborah has written numerous articles for publications in the Messianic Jewish Movement. Along with her husband and oldest son, Josh, she is currently translating the text for a Messianic Family Bible. The New Testament is due out by the summer of 2009. For more information about the Bible, see **www.messianicfamilybible.org.**

Deborah has also supported Steve (with love, food, and encouragement!) in his pioneering of a Messianic and Contemporary Jewish internet radio station, www.soundsofshalom.com.

For more information:
www.greatbiblefiction.com
www.oaktara.com

About the Illustrator

GAIL INGIS CLAUS, ASID, a native of Brooklyn, New York, early on had a love of both drawing and music. All of her available time went into creating and studying in these two areas.

After earning a degree in interior design, Gail continued with studies in architecture and design criticism and ultimately studied with many prominent artists. A popular award-winning designer and artist, she is internationally recognized.

For more than thirty-five years, Gail has been involved in design, architecture, teaching, and art. Her career has spanned all aspects of design and art with an emphasis in interior design. She is successful as an ASID (American Society of Interior Designers) certified and registered interior designer, home stager, professor of history of architecture & design, photographer, artist juror, writer, design critic, realtor®, and the founder of the nationally accredited Interior Design Institute. Besides teaching at her school, she has also taught at the New York School of Interior Design, Kean College in Union, New Jersey, the former King's College, Briarcliff Manor, Tarrytown, New York, and in Connecticut at the University of New Haven, University of Bridgeport, and Fairfield University.

As an interior designer with architectural training, Gail incorporates her drawing skills and painting into her art and illustrative work. Her sought-after award-winning work is represented in private collections, galleries, museums, and corporations both in the United States and abroad.

For more information:
www.gailingisclaus.com

Printed in the United States
211129BV00001B/6/P

9 781602 901698